AKASHA

AKASHA

The Book of Adjórde

A.J. ALFORD

© 2025 by A.J. Alford

Idiosyncrasy Publishing House LLC
www.ajalfordwrites.com

All Rights Reserved.

No part of this publication may be reproduced, distributed, or transmitted in any form or by any means, including photocopying, recording, or other electronic or mechanical methods, without the prior written permission of the publisher, except as permitted by U.S. copyright law. For permission requests, contact bookstuff@ajalfordwrites.com.

The story, all names, characters, and incidents portrayed in this production are fictitious. No identification with actual persons (living or deceased), places, buildings, and products are intended or should be inferred.

ISBN: (paperback) 979-8-218-75378-8, (eBook) 979-8-218-77188-1

Library of Congress Control Number: 2025914213

Book Cover and Graphic Design by Ralph Samson
Illustrations by Maylor Mummert
Edited by A.J. Alford
First Edition

For my mom, who gave me the freedom to dream.
My father, who pushed me to be the best version of myself.
Fritz, upon whose back I built my foundation.
And Tre, my very first little character.

The Five Elemental Primuses

Water

PRIMUS HARUD P. ENGHERS
Water Faction

His Elemental Potential revealed itself not through violence or accident, but through intuition, discipline, and faith. After hearing whispers from across the continent of people awakening elemental abilities within themselves, Harud sought to discover if such power could be cultivated through spiritual devotion.

He spent months in meditation at sea, observing the tides, studying breath, and engaging in daily prayer. The ritual of wudu, a symbolic purification through water, became central to his practice. In time, Harud awakened his ability to move water with intention alone.

Guided by humility rather than ambition, he became a founding member of the New-Earth Directorate and served as its first Advisor.

At the time of his portrait, he was 37 years old.

The Five Elemental Primuses

Earth

PRIMUS ABELIA M. JUSTICE
Earth Faction

Her Elemental Potential revealed itself not through force or ambition, but through sustenance and care.

In the early years of the global water crisis, when crops failed and soil turned to dust across the globe, Abelia's modest farm continued to flourish.

At first, she thought it was due to luck. As seasons passed with thriving harvests and no explanation, she came to understand: the earth responded to her presence.

Upon being invited to join the New-Earth Directorate, she declined kindly and firmly. Instead, she chose to remain on her land with her wife and the soil that sustained them. Her crops nourished the people for years to come.

At the time of her portrait, she was 46 years old.

The Five Elemental Primuses

Space

PRIMUS TAMRA V. ADJÓRDE
Space Faction

She was a theoretical physicist whose work reshaped the boundaries of known space. Her early research into portal theory formed the foundation for what would later be recognized as interdimensional transit.

She remains the only recorded individual capable of manipulating ether, the elusive medium once dismissed as theoretical. Her ability to perceive and fold dimensional planes elevated her beyond the limits of science into something still not fully understood.

Today, the Space Faction has no active representation, no council, and no command.

She never pursued family, politics, or position. Her life was her research. Her work, her legacy.

At the time of her portrait, she was 48 years old.

The Five Elemental Primuses

Air

PRIMUS SEBASTIAN J. FRAY, THE THIRD
Air Faction

His Elemental Potential revealed itself during a heated argument with his younger brother, which ended in tragedy when Sebastian unintentionally suffocated him without making contact.

The guilt of that moment stayed with him. Determined to prevent others from causing harm they could not control, he became a founding member of the New-Earth Directorate and served as its first Director.

He dedicated his life to promoting peace, restraint, and cooperation among all people. He married a woman from the Earth Faction, forming a powerful alliance that still exists today.

At the time of his portrait, he was 44 years old.

The Five Elemental Primuses

Fire

PRIMUS RAISA A. FOLD
Fire Faction

Her Elemental Potential revealed itself the night her childhood home caught fire. As she walked through the house, the flames subsided around her. She saved her family from peril. Her parents, shamed by her difference, turned away. When word spread, they disowned her.

Despite being cast out, she dedicated her life to protecting others. She walked toward every blaze, asking nothing in return. What she didn't realize was that each fire left something behind. Methane built up in her body faster than it could escape.

No one since has possessed this ability. No one understands why she was different.

At the time of her portrait, she was 26 years old. She died of methane poisoning three years later, at the age of 29.

The Five Elemental Primuses

HARUD P. ENGHERS

ABELIA M. JUSTICE

TAMRA V. ADJÓRDE

SEBASTIAN J. FRAY, III

RAISA A. FOLD

Akasha, I put the weight of the world on your shoulders because I knew you could carry it.

~ A.J. Alford

They were men before they were monsters, and as such,
they agreed to be civilized for the sake of humanity.

PROLOGUE

<u>*Seven Hundred Years Earlier: On Earth*</u>

EIGHT HAD BEEN INVITED. Nine arrived.

A large man with hands like sculpted clay sat at the head of an antique satinwood table in the hall of an abandoned Roman Catholic church.

He stood slowly, the weight of his arrogance grounding him as he glared across the room at Adjórde, whose equally smug and resolute disposition kept her rooted firmly to the spot.

"For *whom* do you advocate?" he said.

She raised her head, as if to look down at him. "I advocate for myself, Sir Jameson."

The other men at the table didn't dare to breathe between the two as they stared spears, daggers, and all manner of other sharp things into each other.

Each man, a prominent citizen of his respective colony, boasted remarkable control of his Elemental Potential. Each was to put forth suggestions and offer terms that would result in favorable outcomes for his people—outcomes that would end the war they'd been fighting against each other for control over what had become the planet's scarcest resource: water.

Jameson winced, then leaned forward and braced his hands upon the unfinished tropical hardwood. "It is because of *you* that we are here."

Several men shifted in their seats, readjusting the tattered cloth they'd strewn together and called clothing.

Adjórde grinned. "*We* are the reason we are here."

"Nonsense," someone coughed, covering his mouth and looking away before she could meet his eye.

Jameson lifted his palms from the ancient satinwood. Two tar-black stains had been seared into the surface beneath his flesh and sent smoke rising into the air, filling the room with gray fog thick enough to choke anyone in its vicinity.

The men masked themselves, pulling ragged scarves above their mouths and noses, yet none dared to speak nor complain.

"We see only power and greed," she began. "For thirteen years we've fought among ourselves, scorching the Earth, and destroying its natural resources along the way."

Jameson clenched his fists at his sides, and everyone turned to look at Adjórde.

"It *must* stop." Her words were sharp, echoing through the hall. "We've only ourselves to blame. If we intend to see humankind survive, we *must* unite."

She was a proud woman, and she wore it well.

Her long ash-white dreadlocks were meticulously woven together into a single braid that ran the length of her back, stopping just above her waist.

Unlike the others, she had somehow managed to fashion herself a set of robes in the rare colors of purple and gold. The eight men around her wore scraps of shabby gray and brown tweed, not quite as regal as hers. They secretly envied Adjórde for this but said nothing of it.

A royal sash of sorts was draped across her shoulder, embroidered with symbols none of the men there could understand. She wore the history of her ancestry, embracing the old ways of a people she had never truly known—spirits of the past she clung to in pursuit of a place to call... home.

"None of us is without fault," she continued, "and so we must all accept responsibility for the series of events that have led us here today."

"The sheer *audacity*," Jameson spat. His large face flushed red. "That you, of all people, should find your way here. "We have come to make peace and *you*—" he paused. He seethed and his lips trembled as he fought to formulate his next words.

Adjórde eyed him through slits, preparing herself for an attack. She considered a countermove, in case he, like others from his colony often did, lost his cool. The thought of it sent the all-too-familiar prickling sensation from her fingertips up her arms and into her shoulders.

She stretched her neck and flexed her hands to regain control over both the situation, and her feelings.

"I've come to make peace as well," she said, softening her tone with a half-smile.

"Can you even control it?" said a man she didn't recognize.

Jameson grunted in agreement and the others stirred anxiously as they awaited her response.

She kept her chin high, though her breathing faltered for a moment. "I cannot. I've not been fortunate enough to have a colony with which to share my Elemental Potential."

"She admits it," the man snapped, ignoring her veiled plea for sympathy. He pointed at Adjórde and searched the faces of the others. "She ripped a hole in the sky the size of a mountain and left it there. Now she's come to tell us there's nothing she can do about it." He threw his hands into the air in defeat.

The room burst into a collective fit of rage.

"What have you come here for?" someone yelled.

"You are not welcome!" another said.

They jeered and shouted, and it wasn't until Jameson slammed one of his fists onto the table that they quieted again.

A small chunk of wood had broken off and for a moment he stared at his hands. They were unrecognizable to him and had been for quite some time. They'd been burned, healed, and burned again, and all that remained was scar tissue so thick he no longer had feeling in either of them. He had long since lost control of the seven digits that remained.

Silence sat heavy in the hall as lesser men waited for one of the two most powerful Elementalists of their time to speak, and Jameson was no longer up for the challenge.

Adjórde strode the length of the great hall as though she owned it.

"It seems we've fooled ourselves," she said, eyeing the faces of the men as she paced, men who found no fault in themselves and presumed to be there solely because of what *she* had done. "To think we could ever possess control over the elements is... childish. Fire is wild and unpredictable, water volatile and unknowing, earth stubborn and relentless, and air light and whimsical yet capable of snatching the very essence of life from our bodies."

The unfamiliar man stiffened in his seat, a hint of unease in his eyes.

Adjórde raised her hand and waved it slowly in front of her face, running her fingers through what appeared to be nothing to the others in the room. But she saw what they could not—her gift, and her curse.

They watched intently as she spoke, hanging on her every word. "We do not control the elements. We are honored to wield." She traced the broken edge of the table as she came face to face with Jameson. "I cannot undo what I have done, for I do not know how. But I can try to fix the problem I've created."

"And how do you propose to do that?" Jameson said. He stepped back and glared down at her, no more than a foot taller as he peered over his wide nose at the small but stout woman.

"By finding another sustainable water source."

The hall filled with curious expressions, and the unfamiliar man who had spoken before spoke again.

"You intend to open another hole in our world?"

The men shifted in their seats, a great rustling of tweed muffled only by their heavy sighs and disconcerted snorts.

"I do not know you," she snapped.

A grin pulled at the corners of his mouth. "Sir Sebastian Fray the Third. Air Colony Primus."

Adjórde eyed him, then nodded, a gesture of respect for the first of each colony to access their potential.

Sebastian nodded back.

"I've already opened a second portal," she said, "a bridge, of sorts. Beyond it lies a planet buried in ice. More water than Earth could drink in a thousand lifetimes."

"Another portal?" Sebastian said. "How?"

"My team and I engineered a device. With it, we channeled my potential and safely opened a stable doorway. It has its limits, but it served its purpose."

Jameson cocked his head, regarding Adjórde with suspicion. "Then why not use it to close the first one?"

"We tried," she said. "The device channels energy outward, but it cannot draw it back." She began to pace again, along the opposite side of the table. "The planet isn't suitable for long-term habitation. At night, temperatures fall far below freezing, and I fear indefinite stay would have profound impacts on our... abilities." She stopped and turned back toward Jameson. "What I'm proposing is that we send Elementalists from the Water Colony, on a rotating basis, to harvest the ice and return it to Earth."

"And why should *we* suffer the brunt of the work to fix a problem *you* created?" This time, a short man wearing tiny oval eyeglasses spoke. He stood, interlocking his hands behind his back before continuing. "Not only did you, in an apparent fit of rage, tear apart the sky. But now you propose

sending my people to some unknown planet to collect ice like slaves?"

Jameson sneered at Adjórde, and she at the others.

"We must all do our part, Sir—" she paused, unsure of the man's name.

"Enghers," he said.

"Sir Enghers. We must all do our part, some here and some there. And Elementalists from your colony possess a skill the rest of us do not: the ability to stabilize and transport water in its frozen form. Besides, soon it'll be the only water your people have access to."

He contemplated the idea for a moment. "And what will you do then?"

Silence pressed into the hall.

"The planet I've found could quell our crisis," she projected to the others in the room. "A crisis that will come to a head in ten years' time. I'll inhabit this planet for one year and conduct research, and I strongly advise that in that time, Sir Enghers, you prepare to send a group of Elementalists from your colony to aid in the work that *must* be done." She let the weight of her words settle before continuing. "When I return, I will find a way to close the portal through which all of Earth's water is evaporating. It will be my life's mission, as a scientist, and as the cause."

They each looked to Jameson and he to Adjórde. He nodded at her, she to him, and the men to each other.

They then agreed that one representative from each elemental colony, along with one laic, or non-Elementalist, would form a governing body. They would call it the New-Earth Directorate.

And D.C. would become Directorate City.

They were to strive for peace amongst each other. Their colonies were to become factions whose sole purpose would be to stop the water crisis that was slowly wiping out everything and everyone on Earth.

Their agreement was **not** upheld.

1
RULES

Present Day: On Adjórde

Gardley once spent twelve days in isolation for having a crush on a girl named Tori. When he finally got back, he didn't speak for almost a month.

I can't blame him, though. We're almost never alone.

Rule number three of the Adjórdean Occupant Governing Decree explicitly states that *any Miner found to be infatuated with another shall be subject to a period of seclusion, the duration of which will be determined by the Chief Elder of the settlement.*

It happens, though. Most people are better at not getting caught, or in his case, reported.

Tori panicked when he tried to walk her to the Mess Hall after work and filed a formal complaint with our Circle Elder.

He didn't even deny it at the review. Instead, he said she was cute, and that he just wanted to walk with her. But on

Adjórde, crushes are counterproductive to the work and feelings only get in the way.

I imagine he'd just about lost his mind out there in the middle of nowhere, with no way to get back if he tried.

We spend all our time together in the caves, the barracks, and the Mess Hall. If we can manage to convince a Junior Elder to chaperone, we can visit the Old-Earth Archives, but that's easier said than done; once someone moves up in rank, they don't look back on the likes of *us*.

Rule number two states that *no Miner shall traverse the grounds unaccompanied after the Second Moon without explicit permission from an Elder or, in certain cases, a Junior Elder.*

If spending twelve days alone in the middle of nowhere for flirting seems bad, I can't imagine what'd happen if someone got caught roaming the grounds at night without cause.

There are one hundred twenty-seven rules that tell us what we can and can't do on Adjórde, and the first is the one that landed me here tonight: *No Miner shall travel beyond the borders of the compound under any circumstance, for any reason, without permission from the Chief Elder of the settlement and a chaperone.*

Granted, there are a few things just beyond the border that are worth traveling to. They were added after the boundaries had been set, so they're conveniently out of reach: the Nursing Hall, Water Tower, and the Archives Barrack, which is where I managed to find myself alone two nights ago.

Each structure is just beyond the fence, but going there without permission and an Elder is forbidden.

Shosk knows how much I hate attention, so he was beside himself when he'd heard what I'd done.

But it was the only way to see him.

***

I place the heel of my cleated boot onto the head of the saw and push down hard until it breaks through the surface, penetrating deep into the floor of the cave. When I pull it out, the light from the oil-lit lanterns dance across the wet metal.

"The borders keep us safe," Junior Elder Shosk says.

I ignore him.

I take a step back, angle the saw, and attempt to cut through again. *Doesn't work.*

"Borders and Barracks, Akasha!" His voice deepens and cracks a bit.

I say nothing, even though he's practically standing over me at this point.

Avoiding eye contact at all costs, I reposition the saw just above the first cut and press down.

Won't budge. *Stubborn planet.*

"Akasha," he says, lowering his voice to a near whisper, "I won't always be here to protect you." He glances toward the cave entrance. "I got you off easy. Next time, they won't be so forgiving."

Who does he think he is? I don't need protection. *He* can't protect me.

We lock eyes for a moment before I turn away and lean back into the saw.

Centering myself over the blade, I grab the handle with both hands and press down firmly, cutting cleanly into the ice, as I've done countless times before.

This is my punishment.

It usually takes three Miners to move one two-by-six block of frozen water from the caves to the Icehouse: one to grid, one to saw, and one to haul. Tonight, I am all three.

"Faeya said she saw you and Elder Joll having a disagreement in Barrack 10," I say, finally breaking my silence.

I look up at him before returning to my work.

This grid stands zero chance against my cold alloy of redemption. The grid of punishment for traveling just beyond the border of the camp... *and getting caught.*

"Faeya says too much," he says.

"*Hmph*," I chuckle. "That, she does."

There's an awkward pause before he speaks again.

"What did she say she saw *this* time?" He folds his arms across his chest and glares down at me and I somehow manage to stifle my laughter. He's almost too much for me right now.

"You and Elder Joll got into an altercation," I say. "He pushed you, and you didn't move. He just bounced off of you... I guess. It seemed a bit—"

He furrows the pale skin of his brow. "A bit what?"

"Perfectly easy to believe." I snort at how ridiculous it sounds.

"Faeya is a nice girl, Akasha, but she's going to get herself into trouble sneaking around the outer ring."

"Borders and Barracks," I say, mimicking his earlier sentiment, and voice. I smirk, and from the corner of my eye, Shosk does too, though I don't dare look up.

Ever since his promotion to Junior Elder, he's been trying to *act* the part, when just a few months ago, we were barrackmates. We lived together, ate together and were friends.

He used to tell me he dreamed of New-Earth and couldn't wait to go back when he turned eighteen. And when he had nightmares of falling through the ice or getting stuck while crossing the bridge that connects the two planets, he'd sneak into my bunk as I slept. Some of the other guys sometimes saw and didn't miss a chance to poke a little fun at us.

By the time I'd woken up he'd either be back in his bed or on his way to the outhouse to start the day like nothing had happened. But I always knew he'd been there because my pillow smelled like his hair.

"Exactly," he says. "Under no circumstance should a Miner travel beyond the confines of the camp unattended, for any reason."

He's even beginning to sound like them. We call it "Elder-Proper"—overpronouncing each and every word and acting all dignified. Fact is, we're all here for the same reason.

"Right," I say, rolling my eyes as I stand to face him.

I pull the saw from the ice and shift it into my right hand. Then I prop it against the floor to support my weight before relaxing my shoulders and giving him a casual wince.

He cuts his eyes in disapproval, and I smile.

"How much longer here?" a voice calls into the cave from behind.

I quickly hurl the saw into my left hand and drive it into the ice in no place in particular.

"We're just about done," Shosk says, peering in the direction of the sound.

I look over my shoulder, then back at the ice as Elder Joll saunters halfway into the cave.

He leans in to inspect my work, his extra-large lantern swinging lazily in his hand.

I carefully saw around the edges of the now free-floating block of ice. Last thing I want is for Shosk to get into trouble.

"Kerr wants you both back at the barracks," he says. "Now."

I fight the urge to look up but settle for a peek through the heavily matted hair swinging in my face.

Shosk has shifted into his traditional stance—upright and circumspect, both hands interlocked neatly behind his back as he contemplates the directive from the settlement's superior, Chief Elder Kerr.

He's insufferable. Pure walking misery.

Everyone knows he doesn't wanna be here and despises every minute of every day.

Word is, he was sent on forced assignment. For what? Who knows? But he's as much an occupant as we are, overseeing the Elders who oversee us Miners. A total of two hundred and twenty people on Adjórde. Ice Harvesters. Sent to save the world... or something like that.

We just do as we're told. Work five days straight, then rest one. Hands calloused and worn from never-ending gridding, sawing, and hauling.

We've adapted to survive this place. A planet with no sun, two moons, and nearly twice New-Earth's gravity.

One moon comes, then the other. One moon sets, then the next. And for a while each night, there's nothing. Just darkness. Pitch black.

We harvest ice like they did over a thousand years ago and live like the ancient Inuit. Same food, clothes, and all.

Then, once a year, in quite the grand fashion, Foremen transport vessels arrive by the dozen through a bridge opened more than seven hundred years ago—a bridge located far beyond the borders of the compound that connects us to them. Or them to us. Depends on how you look at it.

That's all I know. It's all Shosk told me during his training. When I pressed for details, he simply said, "It's science" and that, "I wouldn't understand."

As for me, I keep my head down, work, and wait for my eighteenth year. The year of return, when I finally go back to New-Earth.

But we all have a part to play, and everyone must make a sacrifice—*some here, and some there*, as the Elders say.

Shosk nods at Joll.

He gestures to me, then at the pike pole propped against the cave wall. I swap it for the saw and use it to float the block down the channel toward the entrance.

The two exchange whispers as I guide the ice to the small sled parked just outside the cave and check its lantern. I swing the pole over my shoulder and tuck it into the folds on the back of my vest.

Their voices echo from within, low and tense. Joll's tone is stern but quiet, and Shosk responds with the occasional "Yes, sir."

It's weird to see him like this. He usually speaks his mind. But now, there's something different. Like he's lost a part of himself in Joll's presence.

I try not to think too much about it and shift my attention back to the sled. There's just enough oil in the lantern to get us to the Icehouse and back to the barracks, but only if we leave now. Oil is tightly rationed, and Kerr allowed just enough for tonight's mission.

Otherwise, Shosk will have to guide us blind, in complete darkness, while I depend on him to get us there safely. Assuming he knows the field well enough by now.

2

THE BLUE PLANET

I once saw an old photo in the Archives of a horse pulling a big metal wagon filled with scraps salvaged from the Thirteen Year War of the Colonies.

Its harness, ragged and worn, was strapped to its chest and wrapped around its large body. Even though it looked like it could snap at any moment, sending the weight of the horse flying in one direction and the wagon the other, it never failed.

That's me right now.

After barely managing to mount the block of ice onto the sled, I've secured the harness to my chest, fastening the twenty tiny metal clasps to my weighted vest. Then I wait patiently for Shosk and Joll to finish their conversation.

Joll exits the cave first. He passes me without so much as a glance.

When I hear Shosk coming, I press the toe of my cleat into the ice hard enough to break through the surface, then drive myself forward.

The weight of the 250-pound sled resists, but like the horse and its harness, I don't fail.

"Akasha, wait."

It's Shosk.

I stop, lift the lantern from the sled, and raise it to his height, which is just a few inches above me. But I can still barely see his face. "Yeah?"

"You have to do another block after Off-Day," he says. "...With Joll."

"What? Why?"

"For good reason." He turns to walk away before I can respond.

I set the lantern back on the sled, press the ball of my foot into the ice, and follow.

I scrunch up my nose and shake my head. The thought of spending hours under his watch sends a chill up my spine. He probably thinks Shosk's taking it easy on me.

As Second in Command, Joll's got a knack for being particularly critical and I'd rather not have the extra attention on me. Not after tonight... at least.

Despite the lantern hanging just behind me, I can't see a thing. Not Shosk. Not the sled. *Nothing.*

I stretch both arms out in front of me, searching for him and still... nothing. The darkness of Adjórde is absolute and all-consuming.

I put it out of my mind and focus on staying the course, walking in the same direction we started, one foot in front of the other as I count each step and trust the pull of the sled to keep me heading straight.

I have no idea how he's moving so fast on the ice. He's not even wearing cleats. Just those fancy new mukluks he got when he passed his Junior Elder Finals.

One of the tests is to walk the grounds after the Second Moon, without a lantern. You don't make Elder unless you can handle the darkness of Adjórde—a darkness that stretches on forever, empty and alive, swallowing everything until the entire planet disappears. And Shosk clearly can.

When I finally catch up to the sounds of his footsteps, my breathing is shallow; a faint whistle escapes my mouth with each exhale.

"Akasha, cover your face."

The tattered gray scarf around my neck has sunken deep into the front of my parka.

I stop and turn toward the lantern for light then fidget with it, trying to pull the fabric up above my mouth, but my gloves are so thick I can't feel a thing, and part of it's stuck on one of the clasps at the back of my vest.

Out of frustration, I tug so hard it tears. Now I'm fumbling around in the dark, trying to fix a scarf I can't see or feel and I'm just about over it.

Stupid Shosk. I mean scarf! *Stupid scarf.*

I reach down to take off my glove to get a better grasp when I feel something graze the back of my neck.

Sheesh! I jump.

"Be still," Shosk says from behind me, his voice low as he takes the scarf from my hands.

I didn't even hear him come over.

"There," he says, lifting it above my head.

I pull the front over my nose, then wrap each end around my neck and back again before tucking it into my coat. Then I put on my oversized hood.

The only visible part of my face are my eyes. It's the Adjórdean way to be covered like this outside any of the living or common areas of the compound. Otherwise, you risk freezing to death... or at least the early stages of frostbite. But I don't wear it when I'm working the caves. Makes it hard to breathe.

Shosk starts walking again.

I quickly reach for the harness, taking either side of the slack in my hands, and continue behind him. He maintains a consistent distance from me, and I follow, just like I always have.

I'm one of few people he's ever let get close. He mostly keeps to himself. He's always been somewhat of a loner, avoiding activities with the others because, as he once said, "Everyone's time here is limited, and I have no desire to build what I can't bring when I return."

I guess that makes sense, in some ways. But I don't know what that means for me, and I've never asked what'll happen when he leaves next year, when he turns eighteen.

The thought of it forms a knot in my throat almost too big to swallow.

***

I pull the sled into the Icehouse while Shosk waits outside. It's a massive wooden fortress, easily a hundred yards wide, held together by thick planks, metal bands, and a roof that looks like it could collapse at any moment.

Tons of ice blocks span the width of the shelter, extending out, back, and up like giant steps leading to the sky. Almost a year's worth of work.

There are no doors or systems in place to keep it cool, just Adjórde's below-zero temperatures acting as a natural freezer. At this point in the year, it's nearly full, so I don't have to travel far to unload my single, measly block.

"Let's go," he says as I step back out and lean the pike pole against the wall. *His tone's changed.* It's flatter than before. "How much oil do you have left in your lantern?"

"Not enough," I say, holding it up for his inspection.

"Blow it out and leave it with the sled. We'll use mine." He holds up a lantern he took from the Icehouse, its flame so weak it looks like it could go out at any moment.

My eyes widen at his request, which is less a request than a command.

Hesitantly, I lower my scarf and spare a puff of air to kill the flame. Then I set the lantern back on its pole.

Shosk grabs my hand, places it on his shoulder, and starts walking.

It's my first time touching him since his promotion. Not that we touched a lot before, but touching the Elders just isn't something Miners do.

It takes twenty minutes to reach my barrack from the Icehouse, and for the first ten, we walk in silence.

Shosk's breathing is rhythmic, methodical. And I've synced my steps with his to avoid kicking the backs of his heels.

Surrounded by nothing but the glow of the lamp, a tiny bouncing flicker that's barely producing enough light for me

to see the hand holding it, we push forward through darkness so thick it's hard to move.

Then the flame goes out.

Shosk keeps walking, and I tighten my grip. I've never been this far from the barracks without light.

I look left, then right—nothing. I can't even see Shosk in front of me.

The black presses against my eyes until I can't tell if they're open or closed. My chest tightens. I feel a surge of panic and inhale sharply before my hands go numb.

A tingling sensation creeps up my arms unlike anything I've felt before and spreads into my shoulders. Then my breathing quickens, and I feel lightheaded. I blink hard, and for a second, it's like the world shifts. Everything turns shades of red and green. I squeeze my eyes shut, and just when I'm sure I'm either about to crush Shosk's shoulder or pass out, he speaks, bringing me back to the moment.

"Have I ever told you about my journal?"

The question comes out of nowhere, catching me off guard completely.

"Huh?" I say.

"My journal, Akasha." A hint of frustration has seeped into his tone.

"Er... no."

"I found this really interesting journal about a year ago when I started my training. I took it, figured someone would notice it missing and trace it back to me—but they didn't."

"Oh," I say.

"I couldn't tell anyone about it," he continues. "Not even you. So, I tucked it away in my barrack, for safekeeping."

What is he talking about? Why would I care about some journal he found? And why wouldn't he have told me before? I'm not really sure what to say, so I just repeat, "Oh."

"I won't be able to take it with me... when I *do* go. It's too risky."

"What kind of journal?" I ask.

"I'll leave it where it is," he says, completely ignoring my question. "No one will ever find it there... and no one must, Akasha."

He stops walking so abruptly I slam into him from behind. My knees buckle slightly, and I grab his other shoulder to keep myself upright.

"Evan!" I say. "What the—"

"It's Shosk to you, Akasha!" he snaps.

My heart sinks. I bite my tongue, holding back my reply because what's the point? It's starting to feel like we were never even friends.

He grabs my hand and lifts it from his shoulder as I feel him turn to face me. Then he places the other on my lower back and guides me forward until I feel the first step of my barrack at my feet.

"We're here," he says.

"Shosk, I—"

"Stay out of trouble, Akasha."

"I'll see you at the bell tomorrow," I say.

He grunts, then walks away.

I step into my barrack and navigate to my bed. Seventeen and a half steps forward from the door, and I'm by the foot of my bunk. Four more to the right, and there's my dresser.

I climb under the covers fully clothed, scarf, boots, and all.

"Was it worth it?" Gardley whispers from above.

"No," I say, pulling the tweed covers over my head.

I grin sheepishly, replaying parts of our interactions over to myself, then fall into a deep, cold sleep.

***

Several hours later, the Moon-Cycle bell rings.

First Moon Rising.

Most of us are already up.

Elders and Miners prepare to gather at the center of the three-ring, sixteen-barrack circle for the daily headcount and ice-related updates.

We file into the middle, around the tall metal pole and its rusty bronze pull-string bell and watch as the Elders enter in their usual order.

Kerr comes first, followed by Joll, Arrell, and the twelve other Senior Elders.

Then, as expected, the five Junior Elders: Chambers, Byrd, Stokes, Fellows, and... Fo'Kahra?

Shosk is missing.

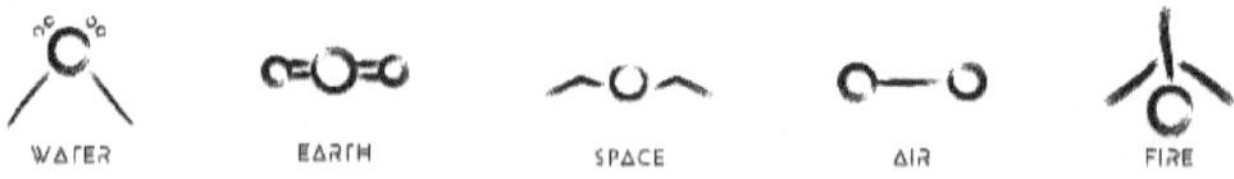

3

BORDERS & BARRACKS

The Moon-Cycle bell chimes gently as Miners brush past, its sound thin and hollow over the packed ice.

"He's gone," a voice says.

I look back so fast I nearly give myself whiplash.

It's Faeya, the camp sleuth and resident gossip, standing behind me, bouncing on the balls of her feet. Her piercing gray eyes are wide with excitement. If Adjórde had a newspaper, no doubt she'd be editor-in-chief.

She pulls her scarf down, exposing her chapped red lips and leans in close.

"Shosk is gone."

"What? Gone where?" I shake my head in disbelief. What does "gone" even mean on Adjórde?

No one disappears here, not before their eighteenth year, at least. The Elders don't even leave without cause. They either die... or retire.

"*Shhh,*" someone from the crowd hisses.

I turn back and spot Fo'Kahra. She's standing where Shosk should be. Same posture. Same blank face. Like nothing ever happened. Like no one's even missing.

I don't even know her Junior Elder name. She's just... Fo'Kahra. A pretentious know-it-all. Or... maybe not. I don't know. What I *do* know is she's in Shosk's spot. And no one goes missing on Adjórde.

"Two hundred nineteen." That's the headcount. Elder Arrell announces it like nothing's changed from the day before. She supervises all the Junior Elders and Trainees, so if anyone knows where he is, it's her.

"Grand rising," Kerr begins, speaking into an old battery-powered megaphone, his voice as dull and flat as his personality. He steps forward, positioning himself just above the other Elders. "We are days away from the transport and the Icehouse is nearly full. To ensure this year's harvest meets expectations, we will work at double speed from now, until the Foremen arrive."

"Greeeaat," Faeya says. "By *we* he means *us*."

A few people turn toward her. Someone tells her to be quiet, but she clicks her tongue and squints back.

"In that spirit," Kerr continues, "I am authorizing an extra half-ration of oil for all lanterns in the barracks."

Several Miners beam at the thought of how they'll use the extra hours of light. But my mind's still on Shosk. On where he could possibly be.

"There's hot tea and warm bread in the Mess Hall today," he adds. "Thirty minutes, then to the caves."

Kerr exits the circle. The Elders follow in the order they came, and everyone else begins to disperse.

Fo'Kahra catches my eye as she leaves, her gaze as void and emotionless as ever. I can't say the same for mine.

I hang back, just in case Shosk shows up late.

He doesn't.

"Come on," Faeya says, tugging at my arm. "Let's go."

The Mess Hall is big enough to fit every occupant on the compound. Four oversized barracks, welded together and packed with rows of tables whose chairs are bolted in place, buzz with excitement as Miners press in for breakfast.

Lanterns fueled by whale oil line the walls, their light casting everything in a soft, uneven glow. The air is thick with steam, sweat, and the sour tang of pickled whale blubber. The curtains are pulled back so the planet's blue hue can fill the dimly lit room.

Circle Elders Rask and Dansch are on watch while the others eat in a separate section at the back of the hall.

Hot tea's a rarity on Adjórde, something that only shows up when the transport is near, when we trade our year's worth of ice for new supplies. But they could be serving a New-Earth style holiday dinner with all the trimmings and I wouldn't blink twice right now. *I can't even think straight.*

I scan the hall for signs of Shosk. *Nothing.*

During my search, I spot Faeya already in the meal line talking to a group of Miners, no doubt telling some elaborate tale about her latest Adjórdean conspiracy theory.

"Come here," she mouths, motioning to me.

I take a deep, exasperated breath, catching myself halfway through, hoping she didn't notice. I don't wanna be mean, but if it's not about Shosk, I really don't care.

I cross the large hall, weaving between the long, rectangular tables spread across the floor. It's slightly warmer in here than outside. *Slightly.* Warm enough that no one's got their face covered.

Faeya's mimicking someone pushing her. She takes two steps back, stumbles a bit, and flails her arms like she's trying to catch her balance.

Her long, auburn hair is a stark contrast to her beige skin as it swings from side to side while she executes her theatrics. The dimness of the hall isn't enough to hide the orange freckles that dance across her face as she moves.

I glance over at Elder Rask standing on the stage at the narrow end of the hall, to see if she's noticed Faeya's antics. Fortunately, she hasn't.

"Are you talking about Joll and Shosk's fight again?" I ask.

She continues, "I swear, guys—he didn't move! He pushed him with everything he had, and he didn't budge!"

She looks around at each of us, scanning our faces for signs of belief. Her hands are outstretched in front of her, like we could just hand her our assurance.

"Yeah, right!" a kid in blue-rimmed glasses says. "What do you think happened?"

"His feet were glued to the ground and his whole body went stiff," says the only other girl in the group, adding to the now-building laughter.

"Better yet, Joll suddenly lost all his strength and bounced off Shosk," says Blue-Rimmed Glasses.

Faeya rolls her eyes and smirks. "Fine. Laugh all you want, Dmitry. Doesn't change what I saw."

By now, everyone's having a great time at Faeya's expense, and I feel bad.

She told me the story in private, and I kept it to myself for this exact reason. I wanna help but she digs her own graves. Besides, talking about Shosk like he's not missing feels weird to me, but I'm not about to be the first to bring it up, especially if it means getting looked at the way they're looking at Faeya right now.

She's always telling stories about strange things happening around the compound. We're all used to it.

Once, she told a group of us she saw a stream of water coming from beneath a Senior Elder's barrack.

We might've believed it if the ground wasn't frozen solid, nothing but old ice stretching across the planet's entire surface.

The caves are the only place you can find water that flows beneath us, and that's only because the walls act as an insulator. Shosk taught me that. He's really into science and understanding how things work.

The only time we get water on the compound is during meals and in the outhouses and barracks for washing, and even then it's almost never more than an occupant's share. But you can always count on a good story from Faeya. It helps pass the time.

"Faeya," I ask gently, "where did you see this happen again?"

She turns to me, hands still outstretched, a look of desperation on her face.

"It was inside Barrack 10."

"You were *in* there?" I say.

"No, Akasha. Of course not. I was watching," her eyes dart from me to the others, "through the window."

"Sheesh, Faeya," Dmitry, with the blue-rimmed glasses says. "You were looking through the windows of the Elders' barracks? If they catch you creeping around the outer ring..." he drops his head and continues down the breakfast line.

One by one, we follow, grabbing metal trays as we go.

Faeya enters last, just behind me. "Akasha," she whispers, so close I can feel her breath on my ear.

"Hmm?" I reply, hoping to sound only slightly disinterested.

"I know what I saw. Joll pushed Shosk, and Shosk didn't move an inch. It was like he was a statue. Joll gave it everything he had, too!"

I stop and turn to her. "I want you to be careful, Faeya. You don't wanna draw the wrong kind of attention to yourself." I turn back and keep moving down the line, grabbing what scraps of bread and tea are left.

"You're right, Akasha. I'll be more mindful, but I'm not making this up. When I find real proof, everyone will see."

Faeya hadn't heard a word I've said.

But I can't help wondering if Shosk and Joll's fight has anything to do with his disappearance. I have more questions, but I can't ask with everyone around.

"I'll see you later, Faeya."

I find a seat in a corner, away from the crowds, and quickly eat my bread and drink my tea before heading down to the caves.

Still... what journal?

4

COLLATERAL DAMAGE

They rearrange our work groups at the last minute, putting me with Faeya and Gardley.

I'm the fastest cutter, Faeya's got the steadiest hands for gridding, and Gardley, the biggest and strongest of us, does the hauling.

I usually work the caves next door, but this one's a mess. The younger Miners must've been here, since the ice looks nearly untouched.

By now, the floor should be so thin we'd have to hug the edges just to make it to the back and harvest what's left. But I can walk right down the middle without worrying about falling through.

Faeya fell through once. It was years ago, but the others won't let her live it down.

Took her a whole day to recover, just to get her temperature back up. But I think she also needed time to get over the embarrassment of it all.

She snoops so much that people said she got what was coming to her. Personally, I don't see what one has to do with the other.

Gardley heads to the Icehouse to get the sled, leaving Faeya and me alone.

She grids one block at a time. It slows us down, but keeps the ice clean, and with so many advanced Miners here, we're still working faster than most.

The cave is narrow but deep, dropping in layers, one sheet of ice stacked on top of another. The farther in we go, the thinner it becomes, and the more careful we have to be.

The walls and floor are a dark blue, slick in some places but rough and uneven in others.

Lanterns hang from hooks and rest on the ground and ledges where the Elders placed them. Their glow flickers across the ice, giving us just enough light to see. The water that runs beneath freezes over every couple of days, always leaving fresh ice for us to cut.

Faeya hasn't said a word since we got here, but after what happened in the Mess Hall, I'm not surprised.

"I believe you," I say, though I probably shouldn't admit it. I dig my teeth into my bottom lip and wait for her reply.

"Really?" She adjusts her grip on the single-blade plow and starts marking a second grid. "About what?" Her eyes shoot my way, then back at the floor.

She knows exactly what I mean, but I say it anyway. "About Shosk, and what you saw with Joll. That they had an argument."

"Why? Did Shosk say something to you?"

"No." I tuck my hands into the front of my parka and shift, thinking about the journal and the tension between them last night.

"I can't say, Faeya. Even if I wanted to, half the compound would know by dinner."

She stops and looks at me, her eyes sharper now. Not defensive. Just... disappointed.

"I *can* keep a secret, Akasha."

I snort before I can stop myself, a smile tugging at my mouth. "You told everyone what you saw in 10."

"*That* wasn't a secret," she says.

I pause, watching her work. Part of me wants to explain, but I don't know how to talk about something I barely understand myself. "It's not important. He didn't say much of anything." *Nothing that made sense, anyway.*

"Do I need to remind you what double-speed means?" Arrell's voice cuts in as she passes.

Faeya quickens her pace, pushing the plow with sharp, deliberate movements. I grab my saw and start cutting into the ice along the lines she's marked.

"Do you know why they were arguing?" I ask, keeping my voice low as Arrell moves down the cave, pointing out mistakes to the other Miners.

"Nope. All I heard was Shosk say something about Kahra. That she wasn't ready."

"Fo'Kahra?" I whisper. "Ready for what?"

"I wish I knew. I really do. I get that you want answers, Akasha, but I don't have them."

I nod and go back to cutting, though my grip on the saw tightens as I picture her standing in Shosk's Junior Elder spot earlier.

"Maybe you should ask Arrell," she says.

"Right." I roll my eyes. "I'm sure she'd be happy to explain it to me."

But... something about earlier doesn't make sense. "Faeya," I turn toward her, "how'd you know he'd be gone?"

She shrugs. "Someone told me. They said he probably wouldn't be here much longer."

"Who?" I ask.

She rolls her eyes. "I can't give my source away, Akasha. Like I said, I can keep a secret."

I decide to let it go.

"If I hear anything else," she says, "I'll let you know."

"Okay. But can you do me a favor, though?"

"What kind of favor?"

"If you do hear anything, can you tell me first?" I try to keep my voice steady, but her expression shifts.

She sets the plow aside and steps up to me, resting a hand on my shoulder. "Fine. But only because you two were friends *before* he got promoted."

"Thanks, Faeya." Her mistrust of the Elders is obvious but I don't think she'd break her word.

I'm still on the second block when Gardley and the other haulers return.

"What's taking so long?" he says, eyeing the grid.

I glance at the other stations. Most groups are already halfway through their third or fourth block.

"Akasha, if you don't pick it up, we'll be here past the Second Moon."

I can feel his nervousness—like heat rising beneath my own skin. I try to shake it off, but Gardley's stare only makes it worse. And without Shosk, everything feels wrong. I saw faster.

When the second block's free, I guide them both to the sled for him to load.

Before heading back to the Icehouse, he turns to me. "When I get back, there better be more." He points toward the untouched grid, then at me.

He's right. If we fall behind, they'll keep us out here through dinner.

Faeya and I pick up our pace. No talking. Just gridding and cutting at two-times our normal speed.

"He mentioned a journal," I say. The words come out so dry I almost choke.

She blinks, then leans into me. "A journal? What kind of journal?"

"I don't know." I try to remember what Shosk said but I can't focus. I'm working fast and thinking faster.

"Why would he mention a journal?" she asks.

"Do you think he wanted me to have it?"

"How should I know? You haven't even told me what it is," she snaps.

I fidget with the saw for a moment, pulling it from the ice and resting its teeth against the surface.

"He didn't say much. Just that he found it when he was training and couldn't take it with him."

"Take it with him?" she says. "You think he *actually* went somewhere?"

I shrug and keep my head down, then force the blade through five feet of dense, frozen weight. The teeth catch with each stroke, tearing at the ice like the confusion tearing through my chest.

What if Shosk was trying to tell me something, and I missed it?

I was so focused on the journal I didn't realize he might've been saying goodbye. But he's only seventeen. The Foremen haven't even arrived yet. Where would he go?

"Sounds like he wanted you to know about it," she says. "Did he tell you where it was?"

"In his barrack."

"The Elders' Barracks?" Faeya snorts. "Good luck with that."

Her doubt catches me off guard, especially since she's the one known for sneaking around that area.

"If he wants me to have it, I have to try, though... right?"

"I don't know, Akasha." She goes back to gridding without looking at me.

I don't even realize I've stopped working until she turns around again, eyes wide with revelation. *"The oil!"*

I blink, confused.

"Use the extra oil and sneak out. Say you're going to the Archives Barrack again. The others will definitely believe that."

Of course she knows I snuck out a few nights ago. She knows everything... and apparently, so does everyone else. But breaking into the Elders' barracks isn't like slipping past

the border. There's not even an official rule against it. It's just understood—you don't do it.

"I can't," I say. "Someone might report me again." And this time, it'd be real—not like the other night when I made sure a younger Miner from the middle ring saw me passing through.

"Well then, that's that." She starts gridding again.

I keep cutting, but my mind won't stop racing.

Gardley returns and sees the new blocks.

"We'll have two more when you come back," I say.

He smiles, then heads off again.

Arrell passes us a second time. Once she's out of earshot, I lower my voice. "Unless..."

Faeya grins up at me, her scarf pressing into the corners of her mouth.

"Unless I go on my way back here."

"Back here?" she says. "Don't tell me you got into trouble again, Akasha?"

"No." I hold up a hand to stop her before she spirals. "Joll popped in last night. He wants me to do another block with him past the Second Moon... after Off-Day."

Her brow creases, like she's working out the measurements for her next grid. "It's a Junior Elder barrack," she says. "They'll all be at dinner. If you skip, you'll have time." She glances over her shoulder, checking that no one's close enough to hear, then leans in a little. "The extra oil from Kerr, plus whatever you get for Joll, should be enough to get you there and back before it runs out."

I think through Faeya's plan in my head. It could work, especially since I always eat alone, so no one would be

looking for me. But it'd be the craziest thing I've ever done. And without Shosk to bail me out, my punishment would make Gardley's twelve days in isolation look like a night in the caves.

"Would you come with me?" I ask, realizing just how risky this is. "To keep watch?"

"Akasha," she says. "They'd notice me gone in an instant."

I give her a look. "Really, Faeya. You can't come up with something?"

She exhales sharply, the blade of her plow tapping against the ice. "You don't get it. If they catch me, it won't be a slap on the wrist like with you."

I meet her eyes, holding her gaze until she looks away.

She pauses, one last sharp tap ringing out, then shakes her head. "Still... maybe I could say I'm sick. But I can't stay long."

"Thanks." I chuckle. She'd never pass up a chance to do some sleuthing on the Elders. "I'll meet you at the bell the day after tomorrow... right before dinner."

"I can bring you something since you won't be eating... if you want."

"I'll be fine." We both laugh a little, quiet enough that Arrell doesn't hear. "Going a night without eating pickled trout will be easy."

Sneaking into the Elders' barracks... that's a different story.

5
DOUBLE TROUBLE

We arrive at the Mess Hall after our shift.

I head for my usual spot near the back, just out of sight of Rask and Dansch, who are still on supervision from this morning.

The clang of trays and steady murmur of voices fills the space, the smell of boiled fish hangs thick in the air.

Faeya follows with her tray and sits across from me. Since we won't see each other on Off-Day tomorrow, we decide to go over the plan again tonight.

"You need to make the most of the oil on your way back," she says. "Crossing the compound from Shosk's barrack is farther than you think."

I nod. Even with the extra ration, I could still run out halfway to the caves. The thought makes my stomach clench.

I picture myself stranded between barracks, lantern sputtering out, the black swallowing me whole. I'll wait until it's almost completely dark to light it. Otherwise, I'll be stuck until First Moon and definitely get caught.

I pick up the roll from my tray and split it into two, tearing it down the middle. Then I press a small piece of salted fish into the center before taking a bite.

Dansch once said the food here doesn't taste like anything. But it's the only food I've ever had, so I wouldn't know.

The bread is dense and dry enough to scrape against the roof of my mouth, but it fills the emptiness in my stomach.

Faeya pinches her fish between two fingers, holding it up and rotating it slightly as liquid drips onto the table and slides across its surface.

"You think this'll burn?" she asks.

I snort, and she chuckles.

"Whale oil and fish oil can't be too different," I say.

I notice a few people staring at us. They don't look for long, but there's suspicion in their eyes. One boy lowers his gaze, whispers to the person beside him, then quickly turns away when he sees me watching.

I straighten up, shifting slightly in my seat. *I don't usually sit or talk with Faeya like this.*

I glance down at the roll in my hands, now half-eaten, still dry in my mouth. Then I look up at Faeya, who's still playing with her food.

What's the point of all this?

Even if I find the journal, then what? Maybe Shosk meant for it to stay hidden. Maybe it's nothing. Just thoughts he needed to get out of his head onto paper.

And even if it isn't, if there's something in there worth knowing, what am I supposed to do with it?

I shouldn't even be thinking like this. I'm supposed to keep my head down, work, and make it to eighteen. That's the plan.

I shift in my seat again, suddenly it feels colder. The back of my neck prickles like I've drawn attention just by thinking too loudly.

This isn't me. I don't take risks like this. Risks that could get me into actual trouble. *So what am I doing?*

Besides, it's not uncommon for an Elder to miss a Morning Meeting every now and then. Sometimes they're sick, or pulled away, assigned to do something else.

But... there's always a reason when they're gone. And something about this feels different.

Kahra was standing where Shosk should've been. Right in his place. Not nearby, not filling in from a distance. Right there, like it had already been decided. That's what makes it feel wrong.

Faeya catches the stray looks too. She shifts slightly and lowers her voice. "Make sure you take the oil from your barrack and add it to what they give you for Joll," she says.

I nod.

"You know who's gonna bring it?"

"No." I shrug. "Maybe Byrd?"

"Or Chambers," she adds. "She's always with Joll."

We give each other a look, then go back to eating. I try not to get into the gossip. It doesn't serve a purpose.

Faeya finishes the drink in her cup and sets it on top of her tray next to her uneaten piece of fish.

"I'll see you at Morning Meeting," she says, shooting me a reassuring look. "Day after tomorrow."

We come to a silent agreement. I'm still not as sure about any of this as she is. This feels more like her thing than mine.

She gets up, carries her tray to the empty cart near the door, and walks out. A few people watch her leave, then glance back at me. When I raise my head, they pretend they weren't looking.

I wait a little before heading out, then walk back alone to get ready for bed.

By the time I'm in, just a few people have returned. Of the twenty-six Miners who live in Barrack 3, nine of us are back. The rest are still finishing up dinner in the Mess Hall.

I turn sideways, shifting down the middle walkway between the bunks pressed against both sides of the walls, my heavy parka catching on the frames as I pass. After a while, you get used to brushing against things in here.

Between every pair of bunks is a small metal dresser, shared by two people. Usually with the person in the bunk above or below you. The tops of each are cluttered with scraps: thread, buttons, dented cups, whatever anyone wants close by.

Everything's metal. The walls, the furniture and even the floors. The bedding is old and torn, and they'd probably be rotted through if the planet wasn't so cold. We all learn how to sew, at least well enough to patch holes when our sheets or clothes fall apart.

At the back is a basin that gets filled daily, when the Junior Elders drop off water from the Tower during their First Moon rounds, just before Morning Meetings. Mostly we just use it to splash our faces with.

The bathrooms are outside. Outhouses, set up between every two barracks. The flimsy doors rattle when locked. Even the slightest pull from someone trying to get in is a reminder of how thin the walls are between privacy and exposure.

I settle in, kicking off my mukluks and sliding them under the edge of my bunk. They're cold but never damp. Nothing on the compound melts, and any water that gets kicked up in the caves freezes on contact.

My thick wool socks are wrapped in a heavy cloth I made from old tweed shirts I'd cut and stitched together for extra warmth. I never sleep without them.

I take off my parka and hang it on the hook above my dresser. Then I open the drawer and pull out a ragged long-sleeved shirt and a heavy sweater with holes I should've stitched up long ago, spreading them across my bed before sitting down to put them on.

I grab a piece of string from my drawer and tie it loosely around my neck, knotting it at the back. Then I lift the front up over my brow and roll it back above my forehead, pulling the hair away from my face and holding it in place. The thick, dense strands that locked years ago are easier to keep. A look I've grown to like, and the only one of its kind on the compound.

The door swings open a second later. Gardley comes in first, followed by Tibbs, Abhishek, and the rest of the Miners who live here. The room fills fast with voices, the sharp clatter of boots on the floor, laughter, and half-finished jokes about something that must've happened earlier.

The sound bounces off the metal walls, a low roar that makes the barrack feel even smaller. A few of them throw glances my way, same as before. Like they're still trying to figure out what's going on between me and Faeya.

Tibbs breaks away and comes up to my bunk.

"Byrd's looking for you," he says. "She's outside."

Since she's a girl, she can't come in.

I wait until the others make it to their bunks, clearing the walkway enough for me to pass. Then I step out in just my socks.

The floor is freezing beneath my feet, and I immediately regret not putting my boots back on. My toes curl inside the wool, defenseless against the cold sting.

By the time I reach the door, Byrd is already turned towards me. She holds out a lantern, half full of oil. Just enough to get me from the Mess Hall to the caves for what Joll has planned for after Off-Day, and back to my barrack. She doesn't say anything. Just hands it off and walks away.

Faeya was wrong. She guessed it would be Junior Elder Chambers who came. But it wasn't.

I squeeze my way back down to my bunk, the lantern in my hand.

"Again, Akasha?" someone says.

Everyone knows what it means when a lantern shows up with just a thin line of oil resting at the bottom of the reservoir.

Someone snickers. Another coughs into his sleeve, the sound sharp in the quiet.

It's like a walk of shame.

I chuckle nervously and keep pushing through until I reach my bunk again. I slide the lantern under it, next to my boots, and sit back down.

I'll have to carry it with me when I leave for Morning Meeting after Off-Day. There's no time in the schedule to come back for anything. It's always the same: Morning Meeting, then straight to the Mess Hall for breakfast, then to the caves for work and lunch, then back to the Mess Hall for dinner, then back to our barracks. That's the entire day.

The only time we're allowed to stray from the routine is for bathroom breaks.

Someone should be coming by with the extra oil from Kerr. It won't be much, but more than we usually get. Perfect timing too since no one has to get up early tomorrow, so they'll burn through most of it tonight goofing off.

The rest of us will sleep through the noise.

Gardley walks over and reaches onto the bunk above mine, fishing around for something. I can't see what, but I feel the bed shift as he digs through it, flipping the sheets to the side and stretching over me.

"Sorry, Akasha," he says.

"No worries," I say, moving over to give him more space.

"Got it," Gardley says, pulling something out that's wrapped in a small cloth.

I don't know what it is, but he brings it over to Abhishek.

Tibbs joins them as they crowd around and examine whatever he has.

Abhishek double-checks to make sure no one sees. A couple people are watching, but nobody's going to question them. Not with Gardley at the head of whatever's going on.

I watch as they each take something from him and eat it. Then Gardley wraps it up and walks back over by me. When he gets to the bed, he looks around again and holds it out close, unfolding a flap.

"You want?" he says.

I lean in to get a better look. "What is it?"

"Candy," he says. "From New-Earth. They call it licorice."

I squint at it. "Why's it that color?"

He laughs. "It's *black* licorice."

"Oh," I say. I reach for a small piece and examine it closely. Gardley steps in front of me so the others don't see.

I take a bite, tearing it into two. It tastes like something I can't explain. Not good or bad, but it's the sweetest thing I've ever eaten in my life.

The sugar stings my teeth, coats my tongue, and makes my eyes water. I almost choke on the unfamiliar flavor. My face screws up and Gardley folds over from laughter.

In the background, Abhishek and Tibbs are laughing too, black pieces of candy rolling in their mouths.

"Where'd you get it?" I say, still trying to pull my expression back to normal. I place the other half into his cloth.

"I have my ways," he says, smirking as he reaches over me, tucking it back into whatever spot he took it from.

I'd stay away from those ways if I were him.

He rejoins Tibbs and Abhishek, and I force myself to swallow. Now I need something to drink, but the only water in here is face water from the basin. I'll have to wait until First Moon.

There's a knock at the door and it swings open. Stokes walks in, carrying a medium-sized bottle, dark brown with a cork in the top.

Someone closest hops off their bunk and takes off toward him, snatching the bottle and turning to run back. The others start shuffling about, grabbing half-empty lanterns, unscrewing the bottoms, and gathering around.

I scan the area, searching for one to use for the extra oil I'll need. I stand and use my foot to slide my own farther under the bed so no one sees it and asks me any more questions.

When I spot an empty lantern near the basin on the floor, I grab it and remove the reservoir. I walk back toward my bunk, place the top half underneath, then slip into the crowd with the rest.

I press my arm into the circle, waiting for my turn.

When I feel the container get heavier, I squeeze my other hand in and place it on top, capping it shut, then pull away.

I rush back before anyone sees, then add the oil to the lantern Byrd gave me. Then I screw the empty one on and return it before I'm noticed.

I haven't even fully convinced myself that I'll go through with it, but at least this way, when Faeya asks, I can say I'm ready.

Tibbs steps forward into the walkway and raises his hands. "Alright, alright," he says, almost yelling so we can all hear.

People turn towards him. He looks around, waiting for things to calm down. He's got this really relaxed energy that

settles the room when he talks. He doesn't say much, so when he does, everyone listens.

Gardley's more the talker. Abhishek's like Gardley's second in command... in a way.

"Let's be reasonable about how we do this," Tibbs says. "We don't all want to light our lanterns at the same time."

I watch as Gardley scans the barrack from behind him, checking for who's got oil and who doesn't. His eyes linger on each face like he's tallying loyalty, like he owns this room more than the Elders ever could.

Tibbs continues. "If you've filled a lantern, raise your hand."

A few people do. And in this moment, I realize I have to lie.

Abhishek looks over at me. "I thought I saw you getting oil, Akasha."

I shake my head. "There was none left by the time I got there." I nod in the direction of the empty one. "I put the lantern back over by the basin."

He doesn't push the issue.

I'm sitting at the edge of the bed, thinking about the double ration of oil beneath it, when my heel starts tapping. *A dead giveaway I'm up to something I shouldn't be.*

When Tibbs starts speaking again, the pressure lifts. "So, we'll light Foldley's and my lantern tonight." He scans the walls, peering up at the ones hanging from hooks high above, strung along the sides of the barrack. "These'll go out soon," he says, pointing to them. "If you plan to stay up, come to the front."

That's the only part of the barrack with a little open space. No beds or dressers. Just enough room to fit about twelve if they sit on the floor and squeeze in close.

That's about how many people jump up and head over, ready to hang out, talk, and sneak pieces of black licorice.

I decide to lay down. I slide the boots and the extra-heavy lantern from beneath my bed closer to the head of it, tucking them in for safer keeping.

It takes a while for me to fall asleep with all the noise but eventually, I do.

6
OFF-DAY

My body wakes me in place of the bell. Even when I try to sleep in, routine gets to me first.

There's no clang ringing out from the pole at the center of the circle letting me know it's time to get up.

No announcements from Kerr. No fighting to get to an outhouse before the crowds.

It's Off-Day.

Half the barrack is still asleep, buried in blankets. The room is quiet and dark, filled with soft snoring and the faint creak of beds shifting. The air feels lighter without the rush of orders, just the muffled sound of breath rising and falling in the cold.

Hints of the First Moon are just beginning to slip through the windows, casting a pale blue glow across the floor.

The ones who want breakfast are already gearing up, pulling on coats and boots without much talk.

A buckle snaps shut, a boot thuds against the metal as someone forces their heel in.

I do the same, falling in with the slow-moving stragglers, mukluks scraping the floor as we file out one by one.

No rush. No line. Just cold air, silence, and the promise of food and hopefully, hot tea.

I've always liked Off-Days. Not just because I don't spend them cutting ice in the caves, but because of the peace it brings to the compound.

The noise is gone. The urgency. The pressure to move fast and stay in step.

It's the only time the place feels quiet enough to breathe.

There's still routine, just... softer. There's an expectation that if you're not in the Mess Hall for meals, you're in your barrack. No wandering. No lingering anywhere else unless you've got permission.

We can visit the Archives, with supervision, and sometimes the Miners within our circle. *The part about boys and girls in each other's barracks stands, of course.*

But even with the rules in place, it feels like a break. A slight one. But... still.

I let my shoulders drop as I walk, realizing how rarely I do. I head down, cutting between my barrack and Barrack 2, crossing into the middle ring where the Mess Hall sits. The ground is packed flat from years of footsteps, but the ice beneath still shines through.

Every step crunches faintly, a sound I know by heart. This planet never warms. The sky is always dark, and the cold never lets up.

Even on Off-Day, everything looks the same.

I move slow, pulling my scarf up over my face and hold-ing it there with one hand. I didn't bother securing it before I left, so the air's cutting straight through.

Tibbs past me and nods. He moves much more confi-dently on the ice than I do. His balance almost looks prac-ticed, like he was born on this frozen ground. I feel like I might fall if I tried to match his pace.

I yawn as I step through the doorway into the half-empty hall.

Near the back, Senior Elder Voiyt is on watch alone. No need for two of them today.

Most people grab and go, taking whatever they can carry back to eat. I decide to do the same.

When I pass through the circle again, I glance over at Barrack 1, where Faeya lives. It looks quiet, like no one's been in or out this morning.

Back inside, I crawl into bed and sit up, eating the bread and berries I took.

Tibbs has a few cups laid out and the bottle from last night, cleaned and filled with water now.

He hands me one and pours.

I drink it, but it still tastes like the smell of oil. The tang clings to the back of my throat, impossible to ignore.

When I'm finished, I lay down again, curling my legs up beneath the cover, and fall back asleep.

I wake to a bang at the door.

Almost everyone's up, but most are still in bed, flipping through Old-Earth magazines from the Archives, eating left-overs from breakfast, or stitching up holes in sheets and

clothes. The sharp tug of thread, the rustle of pages, tiny noises filling the space.

Foldley makes it to the door first since his bed's one of the closest to it. He's a lot bigger than most of us and never complains about the cold.

When he opens it, it's lunch, which the Junior Elders bring here instead of the caves, like usual.

I turn over slowly, roll out of bed, and grab a tray.

Over the heads and hands of the others, I can't see who brought the cart and don't really care.

I go back to my bed, put the tray on the dresser, and sink beneath the covers.

Gardley wakes me, asking if I want my lunch. I tell him yes and sit up to eat it before someone else does. Then I head to the outhouse.

On the way, I stop and glance over at Faeya's barrack again. It still looks quiet.

I kind of want to talk to her, to go over the plan again and let her know I got the oil. But I can't go over there, with the rules and all. But if I happen to catch her on the way out, that's different.

I take my time leaving the outhouse and heading back to my barrack.

I circle around a bit, looking to make sure there are no Junior or Senior Elders nearby.

My stomach knots when a door swings open some-where, but it is only another Miner slipping out, half-asleep.

A moment later, Faeya's door creaks and she steps into the cold.

I guess she must've spotted me through the window.

She walks up with her arms wrapped across her chest, rubbing them like she's freezing, as if it's her first time coming out today.

"You got the oil?" she says. "For tomorrow."

I nod.

"Good. We'll meet back here, after we leave the caves."

"At the bell," I add, just to be clear. *I don't want anything to go wrong.*

"Yeah." She nods back. "See you at First Moon." Then she walks off fast, heading toward a nearby outhouse like she really has to go.

Later, I'm back at the Mess Hall for dinner, and it's fuller than it was earlier—more crowded now than at breakfast. It's the only place most of us actually see each other on Off-Days.

We're not supposed to spend too much time with anyone outside our own barracks, but some of us are still friendly enough to want to see each other's faces. So we linger. Move slower. Pretend we're still finishing our food just to stretch the moments out. Even when no one says much, it's nice to be together.

Across the room, I spot Kahra at a table with the Junior Elder's, eating quietly.

At one point, she glances over and looks right at me. Her expression is hard to read. Not quite curious, not quite disapproving. Just strange. The look makes my chest tighten, like she knows something I don't. Then she shifts her gaze away and stands.

Without a word to anyone, she walks toward the back of the room and slips through the door that separates the Senior Elders' section from ours.

Not long after, Faeya walks in. I didn't expect to see her again today. *Guess she had to come out to eat at some point.*

We catch eyes for a second, then she turns and joins a few girls from her barrack at a table. Eventually, one of them whispers something, and they both glance over. From the look on her face, I can tell it has to do with me. They giggle a little, and she shakes her head.

From where I'm sitting, today looks like any other Off-Day. Quiet, calm, and mostly boring. But underneath, it couldn't be further from that.

Every moment feels like waiting, like the entire compound is holding its breath.

This time tomorrow, I'll be sneaking into Barrack 10, hoping whatever Shosk was talking about is really there.

If it isn't, then this will all be for nothing.

7
THE WEIGHT OF IT ALL

There's something weird about Abhishek. The way he follows Gardley around, doing whatever he says and trying to act like him.

Even this morning, across the circle before the meeting, I catch myself staring. He tries too hard to be something he's not. He's a good guy, but he's not Gardley. And by trying to be, it's like this odd version of him comes out, some made-up act he's trying to copy. It doesn't quite fit.

I shift my weight, boot crunching softly on the ice. My eyes drift across the circle again, catching Abhishek's laugh as it trails behind Gardley's louder one. It looks forced, like he's trying to wear someone else's skin.

Tibbs is different. Everyone likes Tibbs. He's mellow and stays out of the way. He's funny and always knows just what to say. People respect that.

A couple of Miners call his name. Tibbs raises his hand in reply, grinning, scarf slipping just enough to show the crooked line of his teeth.

It used to be Dmitry and Gardley who stuck together, but that didn't last. They bumped heads too much. For power... maybe.

Truth is, I don't really know Dmitry. I've only ever seen him around and heard his name in passing, but I never put the two together until the other day in the Mess Hall with Faeya. *The kid with the blue-rimmed glasses.*

You'd think with only two hundred Miners on this planet, we'd all know each other by now. But the routine doesn't give us much time to talk. Friendships form early and stick. The older we get, the harder it is to make new ones.

Both of them stand out, though. Dmitry's a Cutter, like me, but he's better. A lot better. And I'm not bad.

He ended up getting close with Foldley, Kasahn and another Miner I don't really know or talk to. But they all still get along, more or less.

I picture Dmitry's saw carving through the ice, smoother and quicker than mine ever does, the sound ringing sharp in my head. He makes it look easy, like it obeys him far more than it does me. I haven't worked the caves with him in years, so he's probably much better now than he was then.

I'm waiting for Morning Meeting to start. My parka's on, hood up, and my pants are tucked deep into my mukluks. I've got my scarf wrapped tight around my face. A few of my locks have slipped free and rest against my forehead.

The cold seeps through the layers anyway, needling into my legs, crawling under my scarf until my breath warms against the cloth.

I shift my weight onto my other leg and fold my arms. No matter how many of these I've stood through, keeping still hasn't gotten easier. At least in the caves I'm moving more than I'm not.

There's chatter all around me, nothing I can make out or care to.

I think about breakfast, then work, and then what follows: sneaking across the compound with Faeya.

The thought drops into me heavy, heavier than the cold. I clench my fists inside my mittens and the rough fabric scratches against my palms.

The Elders walk in and Kerr starts the meeting. He tells us we're welcome for the extra ration of oil, though I'm not exactly sure who said thank you. We work hard for this. What he gave felt earned, not gifted.

The circle hushes as his voice carries across the still air. Even the shuffling dies down, boots grinding softer against the ground.

Joll stands beside him, scanning the crowd. He's a lot taller than Kerr, and doesn't need to lift his head to see clear across the circle.

He's got pale skin and dark brown hair, slicked straight back the few times I've seen him without his hood. And a beard that almost touches his chest. He reminds me of the mountain men I've seen in those old magazines my barrack-mates swiped from the Archives, the ones with guys in checkered shirts holding axes, chopping down trees.

His gaze sweeps the line. I tense up when it slides past me, like he might stop and pin me there. Nobody breathes

too loud when Joll's looking, and somehow his search cuts deeper than Kerr's.

No mention of the Foremen this time or more rations of oil. And when he's done, we all head for the Mess Hall.

I reach down and grab the lantern I put on the ice near my feet when I first got here. Figured if I wasn't holding it, people wouldn't notice right away. But it'll be with me all day, so someone's bound to see.

I glance around before lifting it, heart beating faster, but no one's watching. Not yet.

The reservoir is clear, so if anyone looks too hard, they might see there's way more oil in it than any lantern on Adjórde's should have at one time.

An old gritty strip runs along the bottom, wrapping around its entire base. It's what we use to strike the matches to light the wicks. The metal's pitted and scarred with edges rough like teeth. I run my glove over it before slipping the lantern close against my side, keeping it there as I head down to breakfast.

I have to force myself to eat today. My stomach twists into knots and my throat dries up. All I can manage is a cup of water and a tiny piece of bread. The walk from the caves to the bell, then across to the opposite side of the compound, isn't short. And there's so much that could go wrong along the way.

What if an Elder is out for some reason, late to dinner? We could run into a Junior Elder. Or maybe even a younger Miner. They'd tell in a heartbeat which is something I once counted on. But not now.

The bread tastes like dust in my mouth, the water somehow warmer than it should be. I chew slow, but it doesn't help.

A group of Miners from Barrack 5 invite me to sit with them. Probably feeling bad for me since I always eat alone. I tell them I'm okay though, and they give me a weird look. They probably think I'm being mean, but I just wouldn't know what to say to them. I'd be there, awkward, with nothing to add to the conversation.

One of them waves me over again, but I shake my head. His scarf muffles whatever he says after, and I stare down at my tray like I didn't notice.

Now that I think about it, it'd probably be less weird for me to actually be with other people than to keep eating alone—or eating with Faeya, who's sitting with the same girls from her barrack as yesterday.

Her laugh fills the hall, warm in a way I don't get to hear when it's just the two of us planning. I look away before she sees me staring.

I notice Kerr, Joll, and Arrell head through the door at the back, into the private Elder section. A minute later, Joll comes back out and calls Voiyt over. He follows him in without saying anything. A few moments later, all four come out and leave the Mess Hall. The metal doors bang closed behind them so loud the sound cuts through all the noise.

I glance around, expecting someone else to have noticed, but no one seems to care. Everyone's eating like nothing happened.

The chatter picks right back up, louder than before, like no one wants to admit the Elders act differently.

I look again, slower this time, scanning each table, and realize I don't see Fo'Kahra. She might be in the back, but the other Junior Elders are out here, with us.

My stomach knots again. The lantern feels heavier against my leg beneath the table.

On the way to the caves, I think about walking with Dmitry or even Gardley's group, just to take my mind off things, but decide it's better to stay to myself and think it all through.

I follow the frozen path, the line of Miners ahead moving like shadows in the dim light, hunched against the cold.

Faeya's here already, and she's got the first grid done.

"When did you leave?" I ask.

"Was one of the first to go," she says, marking points for a second grid.

Her voice echoes faintly off the cave wall, soft over the scrape of her plow. For the first time I notice her eyes, with lashes as red as her hair.

I walk to the wall and grab a saw. The handle bites cold into my palm, even through my gloves, the blade squeals as I drag it free.

Gardley shows up after me and pops in. Says he's going to get the sled. Part of me knows he's checking in to make sure we're working and not risking falling behind again.

He has to pass by the caves to get to the Icehouse anyway, so it's not like it's extra work for him to stop by.

His voice is loud in the narrow space, bouncing off the walls until it fades. Then he's gone, leaving us in silence.

Faeya and I are alone again, and this time under less suspicious circumstances. I start working on the first block,

pausing every now and then to talk to her about our plan for tonight.

"I have to stop by dinner first," she says. "If nobody sees me, they'll send someone looking."

"But won't that just make it more obvious?" I ask. "You showing up then disappearing again?"

She shakes her head. "Not really. With me, they're more likely to notice I'm missing than care that I'm there, if that makes sense."

I shrug.

"Once they see me, they won't keep looking for me," she adds.

"You know what's best," I say, then turn back to the ice and start cutting again.

The saw screeches as it catches on the seam. My shoulders burn with the effort. My grip tightens and the blade jerks as it bites, fighting against ice that doesn't want to give.

I press harder, trying to stay steady. But my mind drifts and goes straight to the worst-case scenario. *Getting stuck.*

I imagine the lantern running out of oil again. Or the match being a dud. Any of it would mean no light. No way to see my way to the caves. No way to make it back to my barrack before First Moon.

My hair slips into my face, blocking my view as I lean into the saw, driving it back and forth through the ice.

I keep cutting, but the chill feels sharper now.

I also feel like Elder Arrell is watching me while I work. She's walked by so many times Faeya and I can't get more than two words in.

Gardley's already come to collect the ice twice, and Arrell has lingered just out of reach the whole time. Her boots don't crunch like ours. They slide, measured, stopping too close every time. My back prickles with heat that doesn't belong in the cave.

Faeya tries to give me a look, confused why Arrell won't move, but I shake my head a little so she doesn't notice. Faeya understands: *no clue.*

When she finally walks away, Faeya widens her eyes at me. I can't see her mouth under the scarf, but I can tell it's open, shocked at how long Arrell stood there, just watching. Only then do I notice my shoulders loosening and the air around me becoming easier to breathe.

I flex my numb fingers around the saw, trying to shake the stiffness out. My shoulders ache from cutting, and being hunched low over the ice.

When it's time for lunch, the meal cart arrives with a Junior Elder, and we each grab a tray, find a spot, and eat. My stomach still twists and turns. When I'm working and talking to Faeya, I'm fine. But the moment it gets quiet and I have to sit with my thoughts, I feel sick.

Again, I'm questioning the point of it all. What difference any of this might make. But then I think, why would Shosk mention it? And where has he gone?

I force a bite down, but it sticks halfway. The question presses harder than hunger.

Soon enough, we're working again, the rhythm of the saw dulling everything else. And other than Arrell being weird for most of the shift, it goes by without incident.

The sled creaks under the weight as Gardley hauls off the last of the day's ice.

The saw's teeth still buzz in my hands long after I set it down.

8
THE BOOK OF ADJÓRDE

Despite spending fifteen of my sixteen years of life on Adjórde, I've never been this close to the bell before.

The rust is worse than I thought, peeling down the length of the frame, splitting and breaking like cracks in the ice. One sharp flick and it might shatter completely.

Faeya should be here by now, unless she changed her mind, or couldn't get away.

Everyone's at dinner—Miners, Elders, and Junior Elders alike. The circle is quiet. Dead silent.

The four inner barracks stare back at me, each marked by a number carved deep into the wooden plank beside its door: One. Two. Three. Four.

My lantern's still heavier than usual with twice its normal amount of oil. Gardley might've been all over me about it any other time, but my punishment with Joll gives me an out. So he hasn't paid it much attention.

"Akasha. Let's go." Faeya approaches from behind, dressed for the Second Moon, when temperatures drop from below freezing to near-death.

Her scarf is pulled above her head, covering her hair. The front is wrapped tightly around her face, all held in place by the hood of her parka. If it weren't for her eyes, I might not have known it was her.

Her breath leaks through the scarf in sharp bursts, puffing outward with each exhale before vanishing into the cold.

"Okay, Faeya," I say. The words pinch as they leave my throat.

She blows past me. With no lantern of her own, she'll have to head back well before it gets dark.

"Everyone's at the hall," she says, taking big but deliberate steps across the ice. Neither of us is wearing cleats, and even though we're used to walking in our pleated boots, we usually don't move this fast.

I take wide, clunky steps behind her as we cross from the inner to the middle ring.

This side of the compound is less familiar to me. The borders of the camp stretch in every direction and the only people who go where we're headed are the Elders.

The barracks are laid out in three rings: Elders and Junior Elders on the outside, advanced Miners in the middle, and Trainees and the rest of us packed into the center. The whole place was designed so they could keep watch.

It takes us fifteen minutes to reach the edge of the middle barracks, fifteen more to get to the outer ring. Faeya navigates the route like she's done it a hundred times before.

"Faeya."

"What?"

"How many times have you done this?"

She stops and holds up a hand, and I stop behind her.

"We're going the wrong way."

I look around. I know there are eight barracks on the outside, but from here, everything seems the same. I squint, trying to make out the number on one, but can't quite see it.

"This way," she says, pointing to the left of us.

The abrupt change in direction sends her feet sliding out from under her, and she slams onto the ice. Her mitten skids across the slick surface as she tries to catch herself, but she still falls hard. I snort, but she shoots me a deadly look, and my smile falls flat.

"I'm risking a lot to help you right now, Akasha," she says.

"You're right. I'm sorry," I say, extending a hand to lift her to her feet. The truth is, I can't pull this off alone. So I have to trust her and hope for the best.

I look up at the moon. I maybe have an hour to complete my mission. Faeya has even less. No lantern means no light.

Soon after, a barrack comes into view.

"There," she says, pointing at one of the Old-Earth military-style housing units in the near distance. The number **10** looms overhead.

My heart starts pounding. I'm about to sneak into Shosk's barrack. What if I find something I don't want to see? What if the journal's not even there?

I clench my fist so hard the lantern's handle bends. The frame creaks in my grip, metal pressing into my glove like it might tear through it. As I stare into the distance, my mind starts spinning out of control.

"Akasha. Akasha!"

It's not until I hear Faeya's voice that I loosen my grip. A prickling sensation ripples through my fingers, like static snapping in them. My heartbeat roars in my ears. I flex my hands, one at a time, shifting the lantern between them as the feeling fades.

Faeya stands at the barrack door, her mittened hand on the knob. "Come on," she says, pushing it open. She waves me in. "I don't have a lot of time."

I look around once then head for the opening.

"It's warm," I say as I push past Faeya.

"Very," she replies, sounding unimpressed.

It's not at all what I expected. It looks almost identical to ours, except for one noticeable difference: rugs. Dozens of them, in varying patterns, designs, and colors, cover the entire floor. Some are burgundy with gold stitching; others are made of animal fur. Not a single patch of the cold, gray metal I'm used to is visible.

Even with the extra padding, the ground feels different, less firm than usual and certainly not cold. I stomp my foot a few times, but the floor doesn't move like it does in my barrack.

There are no bunks—just beds, all lined up against one side of the room. Across from them are lockers, much larger than any I've seen before. Each one is labeled with a set of initials I don't quite understand at first: J.E.B., J.E.S., J.E.F., J.E.C., J.E.V.

It isn't until I see J.E.S. that it hits me—they're labeled for each of the Junior Elders who live here. *Together?* Boys and girls in the same barrack?

In the corner, I spot a board pinned to the wall with writing on it. I approach slowly and can make out some of it, but most is written in code, or shorthand, like Shosk used during his training, back when we still lived together.

I study it for a moment, but the only thing I can read is something about "not enough ice." Enough for what, I wonder?

I glance out the back window and see nothing. No movement, no lights. Nothing at all.

From my barrack I can see almost everything: the Mess Hall, the bell, people crossing to the outhouses. Shosk went from living in the middle of all that to being out here, away from everything. A few beds, even fewer barrackmates, and the closest neighbors are beyond reach. I can't imagine why he'd want this.

Out of nowhere, three sharp bangs crash against the door. The barrack shakes violently, sending vibrations running through my chest and gut. My heart sinks to my feet.

I don't give myself time to think. I drop to the floor and crawl toward the nearest bed, pressing myself between its base and the olive-drab metal dresser beside it.

My breathing becomes so shallow, it stops. I lean back against the wall and pull my knees to my chest, frozen with fear.

"Akasha."

No one travels to the outer ring without reason. No one. I'm caught. I must be. And this time, there's no Shosk to bail me out.

My head feels like it's about to explode. I still haven't taken a breath. The room starts spinning and I feel faint.

I need to breathe. *Breathe, Akasha.* I squeeze my eyes shut. When I open them again, the room is filled with color—reds, greens, yellows, orange—all dancing in waves like the aurora borealis reflecting off the Adjórdean moonlit sky.

"Akasha!"

I close my eyes again, and for a moment, everything sits still. The room is gone. No one's calling my name. And I'm no longer on Adjórde.

I embrace the peace, the calm and the quiet, and I'm okay with it until I realize this might be death.

Pffffffff... I exhale hard, and the room slams back into focus. I'm disoriented. I look down at my hands. They're shaking so badly I have to sit on them to keep them still. I've never felt anything like this before.

I lean forward and peer over the bed to see who's there. I notice metal hooks protruding from the wall, three of them holding parkas.

Breathe, Akasha, I tell myself, more calmly this time.

Covers, sheets, and pillows, all folded neatly and placed at the foot of each bed. *Breathe.*

Then, J.E.S. again, on the locker.

I scramble to my feet and catch myself before I fall into the dresser, then head for the latch.

Without thinking, I pull it open. It's empty, except for a pair of boots. Shosk's Junior Elder mukluks resting at the base of the iron container.

I reach down and grab one. It's huge. Much bigger than mine, and definitely a lot nicer. And it's heavy. Almost twice what I expected.

I reach for the other, which is somehow even heavier. I lift it over my head and examine the sole. It's worn, but surprisingly thin for how much the boot weighs.

Then I shake it, and something inside shifts. I set the first one down and pull off my glove before reaching inside.

Something hard. It's lodged in tight, so I wedge my fingers between it and the boot and slowly peel it out.

The journal.

It's surprisingly small, leather-bound, with no visible markings on either side.

I flip it over a couple of times, then slip it into the front pocket of my parka and place the boot next to the other.

"AKASHA!"

This time, Faeya's voice is unmistakable. She's straining so hard the words scratch and claw their way out.

"Where were you?" She approaches me, seething. I've never actually seen her upset before. She yanks the front of her scarf down and asks again.

"Where. Were. You?"

I look up slightly to meet her eye. "What do you mean?"

"Akasha, I came in here looking for you and you weren't here. I walked all the way to the end and back. I almost left!"

"I was in here, Faeya. The whole time. I... I panicked and froze."

She shakes her head in confusion, looking at me like I've got two heads or something. "No one was here, Akasha."

I don't know what to say. If she walked to the back of the barrack, she definitely would've seen me crouched in the corner between the furniture. I just stare at her, then shrug and shake my head.

"I gotta go," she snaps. "I can't risk any more light." She turns on her heels and heads for the door. "You should leave too. I don't think you're cut out for this kind of thing."

I don't think I am either.

Right before crossing the threshold, she looks back and says, "Don't forget to close the door. And put everything back exactly the way it was." She shoots me a stern look, and I nod.

I plan to travel along the outer edge of the barracks to avoid running into anyone on my way to the caves to meet Joll. The trip will be longer, but safer. And if I cut in around Barrack 13, it's a straight shot from there.

9
JUNIOR ELDER VAI

I leave the barrack exactly as it was when I got here and pull the door shut behind me. The faint click echoes louder than it should, like the sound could carry all the way to the caves.

From the look of the moon, it'll be dark soon so I'll need to light my lantern to make it to Joll. That means all the Miners are in their barracks, and the Elders are doing bunk checks on their way to the outer ring. The stillness here feels brittle, like it could snap if I breathe too loud.

I managed to sneak an extra match from our supply chest, just in case the first doesn't catch, but we're really only allowed one per lantern. They keep strict count, but no one's likely to say anything. Reporting it would put everyone under suspicion.

The sky shifts from dark blue to deep purple, and just before it goes completely black, I slip off my glove and reach into the front of my parka. My fingers brush against the journal tucked within. Its weight makes every step feel heavier, like the journal wants to drag me down.

I pull out a match, remove the lid, strike it against the gritty base, then carefully light the wick. The flare bites at my eyes, too bright after the dark, then shrinks back down to a weak glow.

For twenty minutes, the only thing guiding my way is the lantern, which I keep low to the ground to track my steps. The ice stretches on forever. Every step snaps too loud, then the dark eats it up.

I've traveled to the caves past the Second Moon before, but never from this direction. Faeya told me where to go and what to look out for on the way: checking for grooves that extend from beneath the Icehouse and pass between specific Elder barracks, letting me know I'm on the right path.

Just as I think I'm lost, I spot two lights in the distance, and the caves come into view. My breath grows sharp inside the scarf, hot against the cold fabric. *Joll's waiting for me.*

I quicken my pace, stepping lightly but carefully toward the dancing flames. But... that can't be him. The shadow standing in the opening is too small.

"Akasha. You're late."

"Fo'Kahra?" I scan the area. "Where's Joll?"

When she speaks, it's like she's looking through me, not at me. "Joll is not here." Her tone doesn't change from one word to the next. "And it's Junior Elder Vai."

I furrow my brow in confusion. "But—"

"We should begin," she cuts me off. "We must preserve the oil."

I flinch a little. We haven't talked much before, just a few words here and there and mostly in passing. But she

always speaks this way. Every word is chosen with precision and care. Even more so now that she's a Junior Elder.

I step fully into the cave, suddenly aware of how awkward I feel under her gaze. The cold seems sharper inside, the air heavier with her silence. The journal presses against the inside of my parka, and I subtly press it flatter.

She watches me closely. Her whole body shifts when mine does, her feet pivoting against the ice but never quite leaving its surface.

I set my lantern down, pick up the plow, and begin plotting points.

"You'll be doing two tonight." She holds up two gloved fingers before interlocking her hands behind her back.

I can't get a read on her. Her expression never shifts.

I mark out the second block, connect the grid lines, then reach for the saw. She watches in silence. She doesn't move, doesn't blink, and barely breathes.

But it's not me she's looking at, it's the saw.

She tracks it as it enters and exits the ice, calculating every move. The sound of metal grinding against the ice scrapes up my spine.

"Fo'Kahra... er, Junior Elder Vai," I say.

I hate the words as soon as they leave my lips. Joll should be here. Even another Senior Elder would make sense. What has she done to take his place?

"It's best to not speak, Akasha. It's counterproductive to the work."

I look down at her and blink. Again, it's like she's looking at something behind me instead of at me.

I peer over my shoulder, but there's nothing there—just the cave wall and two lanterns.

When I look back, I see Shosk.

I mean, he's not here, but something about Kahra reminds me of him. The image cuts through me, sharp and uninvited.

They both have slanted eyes and ear-length dark hair. But Kahra's much shorter, one of the smallest Miners on the compound, even at fifteen. Her skin is a warm brown that stands out against the black of her parka. Shosk is the opposite—tall, with skin so pale it almost glowed under the moons.

"Your grid is slightly off," she says.

"Where?" I lift the saw and shift to get a better look. "No, it's not." I lower myself to the floor and extend the end, lining it up with the grid. I know I'm better with the pike pole and the saw, but nothing about my grid looks off.

"Here," she says, snatching the plow from the wall as I stand. She draws a line so identical to the first I can barely tell the difference.

"Really?" I say, inspecting it. I hold out my free hand, using my arm as a guide to check the spacing.

"For storage purposes, all blocks of ice must be cut as close to two by six feet as possible." She swings her arms behind her back and interlocks her hands again before continuing. "In this case, it should have been better."

At this point, I've had enough.

"Junior Elder Vai. Where's Shosk?"

She blinks but doesn't respond. After an awkward stretch of silence, I go back to work.

Almost an hour passes before she finally decides to say something. "Evan is no longer in this post."

I look up, then stand. Both arms are at her sides now. Her head is tilted slightly upward, but she's somehow looking down at me from below. The angle makes me feel small, like I've stepped into someone else's place.

If it were anyone else, I might take offense to the glare, but with her, I don't think she means anything by it.

"What do you mean 'no longer in this post'? Where is he?" *And why is she calling him by his first name?*

There's another long pause before she responds, but this time I wait. I watch as she carefully calculates her words before speaking.

"His whereabouts are of no concern to me," she says.

What is she talking about? I'm not asking for her. I'm asking for me. *His whereabouts are of concern to me.*

"They are to me," I say, shifting the saw into my other hand.

"They shouldn't be." She shifts back into her previous stance.

The back of my neck prickles. I fight not to shiver.

She's right, and I'm coming dangerously close to violating one of the Big-Three. If my interest in Shosk seems like anything more than platonic, she'll have grounds to report me.

She looks at me from the corner of her eye, tilts her head slightly away, then shifts her weight so she's no longer facing me.

I lean back into the saw and decide not to push the issue any further

The silence as I work gives me too much time to wonder why I even care so much. If Shosk wanted me to know, if it mattered to him at all, he would've told me. But he didn't.

And we're just friends. *We were friends.* I guess.

"I'd like to be finished here within the next thirty minutes. Are you capable of that?" she says.

Of course I'm capable. I'm the second-fastest cutter on the compound.

She talked in circles then backed me into a corner. She was the only person I could ask about Shosk, and I know no more now than when I first brought it up. She said a bunch of nothing.

I continue to work in silence and don't respond.

When I'm done, I swing the pike pole over my shoulder, leave the plow behind, and haul both blocks across the field to the Icehouse, fighting the weight with every step. My shoulders burn, but I keep my pace steady. No way I'm slowing down with her watching.

On the way back, we cross through the middle ring, and I remind myself that Barrack 13 is a straight shot from the caves.

At the edge of the inner circle, she tells me to go the rest of the way alone. But just before we part, she catches me by surprise.

"Are you and Evan friends?" She brings her lantern to her face, so I can see.

I don't know what to say. Now I'm the one calculating my response. I follow suit and raise mine. "We were."

"Friends would want you to be careful, Akasha." Her eyes catch the lanternlight, searching for something I don't want to show.

She nods at me, her expression a little less flat than usual. Without another word, she turns and disappears into the dark.

For the rest of the walk back, images from the day replay in my mind.

Shosk is gone, it seems. And for good. I had a panic attack in the Elder barrack and must have blacked out at some point. Oh, and I have the journal, which I'll keep hidden in the same place Shosk did: my boot.

I'll find time to read it tomorrow. There's no way I can risk it tonight.

I need to get back, and there isn't enough oil—which, thankfully, lasted me through the entire ordeal. Plus, my barrackmates will ask questions.

Guess I'll be skipping dinner again.

10
A DIFFERENT TYPE OF 'R'

Faeya finds me the moment I step into the circle, like she's been tracking my scent since First Moon.

Her eyes are wide, lit with anticipation.

Around us, Miners shift in slow clusters, shadows stretching long beneath the early cold.

"What happened last night?" she whispers, glancing over her shoulder. Her voice is low, but the urgency in it is sharp.

She scans the circle like she half-expects Kerr himself to be lurking just out of sight.

I hesitate, the words catching somewhere between my throat and chest. She already thinks something's wrong with me, and maybe she's right. But the last thing I want is to confirm it.

My tongue feels heavy. Like if I speak, the words won't come out right.

"Grand Rising." Kerr begins his morning spiel.

I'm saved.

I shift my attention to the Elders at the front. Faeya's still watching me, waiting for an answer, but I keep my eyes forward and pretend to care more than I do about whatever he's saying.

"It has come to my attention that talk is spreading throughout the compound." His voice is low, but it carries over the megaphone.

The crowd stills.

He steps forward, readjusting the dark glasses he always wears. The lenses are round and flat, dark with curved sides that shield his eyes completely. You can never tell where he's looking, but maybe that's the point. It's like standing in front of a wall. You know it's there, solid and unmovable, but you can't see through it.

"Before we begin, I will be addressing a few misconceptions."

It's as quiet as Adjórde past the Second Moon. Almost like everyone forgot how to breathe at the same time. Miners stand frozen in place, eyes locked forward, shoulders stiff. Even the usual whispers between friends have disappeared, swallowed by the weight of Kerr's words.

He never comments on things like "misconceptions."

His daily address is always about production, cave logistics, and ice. Nothing more. So when he changes the script, you know it matters.

I glance at Faeya. Even she looks surprised, her brows drawn tight above the scarf covering her face.

I scan the rest of the circle and catch Dmitry's gaze. He's standing beside that girl from breakfast the other day. His

blue eyes, as bright as the rims of his glasses, flash toward me. He shrugs, then shifts his attention back to Kerr.

"Junior Elder Shosk has returned to New-Earth on re-assignment."

I shoot Faeya a look sharp enough to cut. She gasps softly and places a hand over her chest. The sound scrapes against me, too sharp in the silence.

She tugs her scarf down just enough for me to see. "I didn't say anything," she mouths, then shakes her head.

She seems genuinely surprised.

"Additionally," he continues, "there are reports of Miners congregating in various areas of the compound past the Second Moon."

This time I'm careful not to look at Faeya. I swallow hard, and she stays completely still beside me.

Kerr steps closer to the cluster of Miners standing at the front of the crowd. Three young Trainees glare up at him. Around me, several people rise onto their toes to get a better view as he looms over them.

They look pinned in place, like the ice itself has them trapped. Kerr doesn't move.

"Traversing the grounds for any reason other than going to the caves, Mess Hall, or an outhouse located in your own circle," he says, his voice rising, "is strictly prohibited unless cleared by an Elder."

I survey the crowd and catch several others doing the same. When my eyes meet Faeya's again, neither of us says a word.

"Any Miner caught breaking this rule will have two years of service added to their term."

A ripple of sound moves through the circle, and boots shift on the ice as people look to the reactions of the others around them.

My stomach drops. Two years feels heavier than any block of ice I've ever hauled.

I scan the faces of the Elders, all of them wearing vacant expressions, staring off into the distance above our heads—all except for Elder Nurse Batkins, whose bright eyes and friendly nature have always made her the most welcoming.

I've never heard of the punishment actually being enforced like this before. But why now?

A block of ice or two, sure. Maybe even a few nights in isolation. But two years of service added to our time? Can he even do that? Wouldn't they be expecting us back on New-Earth at eighteen?

"In a few days' time, the Foremen will arrive. Everyone must focus on the task at hand."

At one point, Kerr looks my way and I almost swear he grimaces.

The look twists through me, sharp and private, like he knows something I don't.

I grind my front teeth together and feel my hand twitch. Guilt rises in my stomach and I shove it deep into the front of my parka.

As I adjust my stance, the journal presses against the bottom of my foot, reminding me it's still there. Hot, hidden, and dangerous. Like pressure sealed inside the ice, waiting to crack.

"If I receive word of any further talk, speculation, or unauthorized movement, every Miner and Trainee on this compound will cut five blocks each at the Second Moon."

Kerr and the Elders have always been strict, but never like this.

"Something must've happened." Two Miners nearby trade a few quiet words.

"Probably Faeya," one says.

"It wasn't," Faeya snaps, spinning toward them. "Try again."

One of them shrugs. "Okay then."

"Sheesh," the other mutters.

She turns to me. "Akasha, do you think—"

"Shhh." I cut her off before she can finish.

Her voice cuts through me anyway. I don't want to think. Thinking means trouble.

I envy her—always bold enough to say exactly what she feels, and willing to take whatever consequences that come with it.

Me, I've learned to say only what's necessary. I pick and choose my battles, my consequences more calculated. But calculated doesn't always mean safe. Just survivable.

Arrell calls the headcount, and Kerr finishes his morning announcements. The crowd begins to scatter, heading toward the Mess Hall for breakfast.

I don't follow.

I glance over at Nurse Batkins then turn toward Faeya. "I'll meet you there."

She nods, gives me a look, then joins the others. Her hood bobs as she slips into the stream of bodies, and suddenly I feel smaller without her next to me.

The circle feels wider, emptier. Like space has opened between me and everyone else. I take a breath and make my way across to where Elder Nurse Batkins is standing. She's easy to spot, taller than most, and dressed head to toe in white.

Her parka, pants, boots, and even her scarf are all the same pale shade.

I have no idea how she got that past Kerr. But she's always worn it. She's the only patch of light in a crowd built from shadows.

Her eyes shine, even in the dim, and her scarf is lowered just enough to show the gentle curve of a smile as she chats with Kerr.

I hang back, waiting for them to finish their conversation before stepping closer.

He says something I can't quite make out, and oddly enough, Elder Nurse Batkins inspects her reflection in his glasses, smoothing out the folds in her scarf and fluffing the fur around her hood.

When he finally leaves, I approach her, cautiously.

"Elder Nurse Batkins," I say. "Can I speak with you for a moment?"

She turns toward me and places a warm hand on my back. "Of course, Akasha. Is everything okay?"

I pause. "I wasn't feeling well yesterday, er—, right before dinner."

Her expression softens. "What sort of not well?"

I hesitate. "I wanted to ask you about panic attacks."

"Panic attacks?" she repeats gently, raising a brow.

"Yeah. I read about them in the Archives. People on Old-Earth used to have them when they were under pressure or feeling stress. That kind of thing."

Her voice is kind, but she's watching me closely now. "And what kind of pressure are you feeling?"

I look away, then back at her. "Shosk," I say. "I didn't know what happened at first. Not really. Not until today."

She nods once, as if she already knew that would be my answer. "I have something in my hall that might help. To calm your nerves a bit, while you process."

She raises her hand and waves someone over.

Junior Elder Stokes approaches from the edge of the circle.

"I'll need you to accompany Akasha to the Nursing Hall," she says in a clear and easy tone. "Inform Chief Elder Kerr before you do."

Stokes frowns slightly, almost too quick to catch, but I notice it. Batkins does too.

"It's outside the boundary, technically," she says, still looking at me. "The rule's the rule. You understand?"

I nod. Of course I understand.

The words settle heavy. Rules always win here. Even when they don't make sense.

And just like that, I'm walking away from the circle with Stokes at my side, the ice crackling under our boots and the weight of Shosk, the journal, and everything I still don't understand pressing down all at once.

Stokes mumbles something about missing breakfast and mint tea. But I ignore him.

His voice buzzes like static against my ear, but none of it reaches me.

We wait outside until Batkins arrives. When she does, she tells me to come in but makes Stokes stay put, which he clearly isn't thrilled about. Instead of tea at breakfast, he's stuck with nothing in the cold.

The Nursing Hall is immaculate, made up of three connected barracks shaped like a boxy 'U.'

We pass through each section to get to the last, where Nurse Batkins keeps her natural medicines and remedies.

The first barrack is where the Helmsmen, the ones who drive the ships, stay during the few days it takes the Foremen to retrieve and load the ice. It reminds me of Barrack 10 with no bunks, and a carpeted floor. But instead of colorful throws and animal skins, a plain gray rug covers the entire room.

There's a basin in the corner, like in my barrack, with a small burner underneath that runs on whale oil to heat the water.

Aside from a few dressers, beds, and wall hooks for coats, it's empty.

The air smells faintly of oil and damp cloth. A lived-in nothingness.

The next barrack is the most important. It houses the new arrivals: one- and two-year-olds brought from New-Earth to replace the eighteen-year-olds scheduled to leave.

They live here until they turn seven, then move into the inner ring. There are usually no more than four or five

at a time, and while they're here, different Elders from the compound take turns staying.

Cribs line one corner, tiny beds the other, each one holding a sleeping child. The room is so still it feels wrong to breathe too loud, like even that might wake them. We pass through quietly.

Voiyt is here, settled into a chair between the two rows, a book open in his hands. He seems to spend more time here than anywhere else. He glances up at me once, then drops his eyes back to the pages, like whatever he's reading matters more than I do.

I can still remember my own years in this room. Scratching letters onto slates until they made sense, stitching clumsily until the thread finally held, learning to dress, survive, and endure.

Then I moved into the center ring—first the trainee barrack, and when I was old enough, the one I'm in now.

Finally, we reach Nurse Batkins' personal space, the most unusual barrack on Adjórde.

What makes it so different are the plants. There are dozens of them.

Potted greenery grows in real soil, actual dirt brought from New-Earth. Each year, the Foremen bring her fresh ground, and sometimes even new plants. They're everywhere, filling corners, lining shelves, reaching for the low ceiling like they've never known darkness.

I have no idea how they survive in these conditions, but you won't hear me complaining. She's the only reason we ever see mint and herbs in the Mess Hall. Sometimes even berries. The sight always knocks the air out of me. Green

doesn't belong here, not in this place. But Batkins makes it belong anyway.

She tells me to take a seat, pointing to a chair beside a table cluttered with tiny clear bottles, seeds, leaves, and other things she's grown. Then she sits across from me and folds her hands.

"So, tell me what happened, Akasha."

I freeze, not expecting to have to explain how I felt. My brain scrambles, trying to find words without revealing what actually happened.

"Er..." I stall. "My chest felt tight and I couldn't breathe. And my head started hurting. I closed my eyes to calm down, but when I opened them, I saw... a bunch of colors, and felt faint."

"Colors?" she repeats, leaning back in her chair. "What do you mean by that?"

I search for the right words again, careful not to say too much. "Just... colors," I mutter, already regretting bringing it up.

Her silence stretches, heavy, like she's weighing the word against something she already knows.

Batkins stands, pulls back her hood, and removes her scarf. She walks to another table, nearly as full as the first, and scans the rows before selecting a small bottle. Then she returns to her seat.

"Where were you when this happened?" she asks.

"In an outhouse," I lie. "I skipped dinner and stayed there because I wasn't feeling well." I surprise myself at how fast I come up with it.

The lie slides out too easily. That scares me more than the truth would.

She pauses. "Hmm. Were you by chance with Faeya?"

"Faeya?" I repeat, my heart starting to pound.

"You and Faeya were both noticed missing at dinner yesterday."

"Oh. No, I wasn't with Faeya."

In the back of my mind, I make a mental note to warn her.

"Hmm," she says again. Her tone isn't cold. Just more serious than usual. That one sound feels sharper than a whole lecture. "Why does Shosk's absence make you feel stressed?"

"I'm... I'm not sure," I say. "He's a friend, and he just... vanished."

She pulls open a drawer beside her, takes out an empty bottle, and carefully selects a few herbs from the table. After sealing them inside, she hands it to me.

"Take one with each meal," she says, breakfast, lunch, and dinner. Swallow it whole, if you can."

I hold the bottle up to the nearest lantern and shake it. "What is it?"

"It's called ashwagandha," she says. "It'll help ease your nerves."

"This can grow here? On Adjórde?"

She smirks. "I have what they call a *green thumb*."

I can't tell if she's joking or if that's her way of saying don't ask questions. Or is her thumb actually green?

She leans forward, resting her elbows on her knees.

"Akasha," she begins, "you need to know that..."

There's a rap at the door and Elder Arrell steps inside, cutting her off.

Batkins holds up a finger, signaling me to wait, then steps through the doorway into the adjoining barrack with her.

They don't go far, just past the threshold, and the door clicks shut behind them.

I can still hear their voices, echoing off the walls, but I can't make out what they're saying. Because... I don't think they're speaking English.

Batkins has an accent from New-Earth. Everyone knows she came over older than most and somehow survived. The reason they bring us young is so we can adapt. Not everyone does. It's not uncommon to lose a baby or two during the transition.

According to the rumors, Batkins was almost nine when she arrived. Her "r"s roll like they're dancing off her tongue. It's subtle, but different. Something she brought over with her.

Now, for the first time, I hear that same thing in Arrell's voice, but only when she's speaking to Batkins. Only in this other language.

I lean forward slightly, trying to catch a word or two, but it doesn't sound familiar.

The sounds twist and fold, sharp then smooth, nothing I can place. The only thing I can make out is "Vai," which has been said at least three times now.

They're talking about Kahra.

There's a loud tap on the window behind me.

I turn and find Stokes staring back through the glass. He scowls at me and shakes his head, clearly aware I've been listening to something I probably shouldn't. Then he disappears down the side of the barrack.

A few seconds later, his face passes the next window. Another loud tap follows.

The voices behind the door go quiet.

Batkins steps back into the room, smiling like nothing happened.

"You and Stokes are free to go, Akasha," she says gently. She reaches for a small tweed bag sitting on the table, something round inside, and hands it to me. "Take this, since you've probably missed breakfast."

"Thanks," I reply, accepting the bag.

"Remember to eat the herbs I gave you. Everything will be fine."

She smiles again and gestures toward the door.

I tuck the bottle into the front of my parka and step out, rejoining Stokes. We walk back in silence.

Stokes takes the bag and eats whatever it is Batkins gave me. I let him.

I wouldn't be able to keep anything down right now anyway. My thoughts are spinning again.

By the time we reach the Mess Hall, breakfast *is* over. So I make the rest of the way to the caves alone.

When I arrive, the first thing I do is find Faeya.

I need to tell her what I've learned.

11
MOMENT OF TRUTH

Faeya's a great gridder. Kahra would probably approve.

Gardley would have had a much easier time hauling two blocks across the field than I did. I'm strong, but he has years of practice, and he's learned how to move across the field with the full weight of the sled behind him.

Cutting takes real skill. Staying on-grid, keeping your depth consistent. Those things matter. That's Dmitry's specialty, more than anyone's. He's one of the best on the compound, probably in line to become a Junior Elder someday.

I like to think I contribute something to the dynamic too. But the truth is, if I wasn't here, Gardley could grid, and Faeya could probably saw. *They'd manage just fine.*

The pike pole is where I stand out. Most people think it doesn't take much effort, but it does.

I prefer the pickaxe head, which was designed specifically for work on Adjórde. It gives me better leverage and grip, and I can break up tougher ice when I need to.

Guiding the block down the channel takes precision. You have to feel it before it moves, control the weight as it shifts. And it takes time. Patience. Something most of us don't have, especially when we're being pushed to produce.

Patience feels like its own kind of rebellion here.

"Where'd you go?" Faeya asks as I join our work group. "You said you'd see me at breakfast."

"I was at the Nursing Hall," I reply, keeping my eyes on the rack of tools. "Where's Gardley?"

"Gone to get the sled." She folds her arms, pressing the handle of her plow into her shoulder. "Why were you at the Nursing Hall?"

I pull the saw from its hook. "I was freaked out after yesterday."

Without thinking, she stomps a foot hard onto the ice in frustration, then looks around to make sure no one noticed. Fortunately, the sound is muffled by nearby chatter and the clink of tools and saws against the ice. "Seriously, Akasha! You went to the nurse?"

I shrug, then kneel beside the block we're working on and line up the edge of the blade.

Her voice nags, but my hands keep moving. That's the only way to keep her from breaking me open.

Faeya huffs, clearly not satisfied, but joins me on the other side.

"I need to tell you something," I say quietly, rising to my feet again, "but you have to promise not to react. Not until I explain why I'm telling you."

She narrows her eyes at me, suspicious. "Fine."

"The Elders know we were both missing from dinner."

She freezes, then lets out a long breath. Her grip tightens on the handle of her plow.

"You promised," I remind her.

She nods again and forces her shoulders to relax.

"Nurse Batkins told me. She said we were noticed. I told her I was sick. That I'd skipped dinner and stayed in the outhouse. I said I didn't know where you were."

Faeya shifts anxiously and glances toward the opening of the cave, like someone might be listening. Her nerves spread to me like cold through a crack in the ice.

"They might ask you. If they do, you can't say you were with me."

She gives another short nod, but it's clear the tension hasn't left her body.

"You have to start laying low, Faeya," I continue. "We both do. I think we're being watched. I can't explain it exactly, but something feels... off. And if we want to find out what's really going on around here, we need to stop drawing attention to ourselves."

Her mouth opens like she's about to argue, but I shake my head.

"That means no more stories. No more snooping. And no more talking to people about weird stuff."

She exhales through her nose and agrees, reluctantly. The weight of it presses between us.

"Also, I found the journal," I finally say.

"I wanna know what's in that book, Akasha." She points at me, her eyes narrowing into slits as her tension turns to demand.

Elder Arrell walks by, as expected, and we both make ourselves look extra busy until she's gone.

"I deserve to know. I took the risk with you."

I guess she's right. I can feel her stare burning into the side of my face.

"Fine, Faeya. But where? How?" I glance around. "There's nowhere we can go without someone noticing us missing."

She goes back to gridding, but I can tell she's thinking. Her silence is louder than words, grinding steady with every push of her plow.

I cut into the first block of ice, and it takes me the entire time to free it before Faeya finally responds. "Meet me in the outhouse after dinner. The one between 3 and 4."

I make a skeptical face, and she continues.

"It'll be tight, Akasha, I know. But there's nowhere else we can go. We'll each use the trip we're allowed after dinner, before bed. Just wait until everyone in your barrack's settled. I'll do the same."

I think it over, and agree.

Gardley returns, and I guide the block to the sled.

He doesn't say much, which is unusual for him, but I don't push. Gardley quiet is worse than Gardley loud. It means something's chewing at him.

"We'll need a lantern," I say when I get back to Faeya. "No way we'll be able to see in there. Not that close to the Second Moon's setting."

"I can take one from my bunk," she says. "No one will care. They'll just think I'm up to something again."

"Yeah, but we don't want to draw attention to ourselves," I remind her.

"It's okay," she says with a shrug. "It's just a lantern. They won't even notice."

I hesitate, then give in with a skeptical nod.

We cut almost three times as much ice as yesterday since we're still expected to work double speed or better.

It takes a toll. My back aches and my arms feel so weak I can barely lift the saw onto the rack when I'm done.

Pain hums through my muscles like it's set up camp there, and no amount of stretching shakes it loose.

I press down hard on my left foot as we leave the cave, trying to hide the slight limp the journal in my boot creates.

If even one person notices something's off, I'll be sent back to the Nursing Hall. Twice in one day and Batkins will investigate. We can't afford injured Miners, especially this close to the transport.

***

It's loud in the Mess Hall, even from the isolated spot I found in the back when I came in.

I stare down at my tray—one section of fruit, another with a hard lump of brown bread, and a piece of dried fish in the last. All of it accompanied by a lukewarm cup of mint tea. *Unsweetened.*

For the first time, I look up at the meal line and wonder where it all comes from. Who makes it?

The bread is always the same shape, the same weight, like it's been copied over and over again. Never thought to ask who copies it.

As long as I'm fed, it doesn't matter.

I look back at the wall that separates our section of the dining area from where the Elders eat. I assume that's where they prep the meals. Nobody goes back there but them, the Junior Elders, and the Foremen... when they're here.

These are things I should know from being on Adjórde my whole life. But nobody questions it. Nobody questions anything. Except for Faeya. She questions everything.

The door in the divider swings open and Joll steps through, followed by Fo'Kahra. He leads and she trails after him.

Neither one notices me, but I see them.

She keeps her head down, hurrying after Joll as they cross the hall and exit through the front door into the cold.

She always looks so sad and disconnected from everything around her.

I wonder if that's how people see me.

Maybe I wear the same look without realizing it. Maybe that's why no one ever asks me anything real. Maybe I'm more like her than I think. Keeping to myself, eating alone, doing what I'm told without question.

Faeya and I notice each other during dinner but don't speak. We agreed it's best if no one sees us talking.

When I make it back to my barrack, everyone's getting ready for bed.

Fellows, one of the Junior Elders, is here doing bunk checks. He's chatting with Gardley, who still seems off from his usual self.

Tibbs and Abhishek are on a bed, playing a game they made up a few years back. They take turns stacking metal sticks on top of each other, and the first to make it fall, loses.

I'm rearranging the undershirts in my shared dresser, taking them out, folding each one, then putting it back, to distract from the fact that I haven't settled in yet.

Folding the same shirt twice feels safer than sitting still.

So far, no one's said anything, but Fellows still being here worries me.

A few moments pass and he finally leaves.

Tibbs follows behind, announcing that he's headed to the outhouse.

"Akasha. You okay?" Abhishek asks. He walks up to me, appearing genuinely concerned.

"I'm good," I say. "Gonna step out when Tibbs gets back. For the outhouse."

"Okay," he says. He returns to his bunk, which has been cleared of the game.

Gardley's in the bed above mine, his back turned, face buried beneath the covers.

When Tibbs returns, I leave to meet Faeya.

It's almost dark, with the Second Moon ready to set soon. I pull on the door of the outhouse and it rattles in place.

"Occupied," someone calls from inside. But it's not Faeya.

I step back and look around. She's standing on the stoop of Barrack 1, where she lives. She looks at me and shakes her head, clearly aware someone got there before us.

Without thinking, I turn and head across the circle to the outhouse between Barracks 1 and 2. *It's empty*.

I go in. A few moments later, Faeya joins me, carrying a lantern with barely a drop of oil left.

"Really," I say, pointing at it. I take it from her hand and tilt it slightly, then give it back.

"It's the only one I could get," she says.

"It'll have to do," I mutter, sitting on the edge of the toilet.

I reach down and take off my boot.

Faeya leans back against the edge of the basin.

"Don't sit there," I snap. "It's loose. It'll break."

She pops up and wedges herself between the basin and the wall while I pry the journal out and stand back up.

"Light it," I say, nodding toward the lantern.

Faeya gives me a look. "I don't have a match, Akasha."

"What?" I exclaim. "You brought a lantern and no match?"

"You said to lay low. Taking a match would be the opposite of that."

I run a hand across my face in frustration—then freeze, remembering the extra match in the fold of my coat from the night before.

I reach into my pocket and grab it. Faeya removes the lid, and I strike it and light the lantern. Its glow is weak, but when I hold the journal close, angled just right, I can make out the words engraved on the inside of the cover:

BELONGS TO DR. TAMRA V. ADJÓRDE

Faeya pulls her scarf down and scrunches her face up. "Adjórde's a person?"

I flip to the next page. The edge is torn, cutting off part of the writing.

She leans in closer with the lantern, peering over my shoulder.

"It's dated almost seven hundred years ago," she says.

I flip through the pages more carefully now.

It's in rough shape, but most of the writing is still legible—except for a few faded lines and scattered symbols here and there.

"Slow down," Faeya says. She points to a line in the middle of one of the pages. "Look."

She pulls off her glove and traces a sentence just beneath a row of strange symbols.

Five elements, four factions.

I shake my head. "This doesn't make sense."

Let me see," she says, trading the lantern for the journal in my hands.

She flips back to the beginning and starts reading aloud:

The conditions on Earth are as such: individuals have learned to manipulate the four natural elements (water, earth, air, and fire). Approx. 1.2 years post-breach, the manifestation of elemental abilities began, first appearing in the northern regions of the country and spreading west along the coast of what was once considered the state of Cal-if...

She squints at the word.
"Ca-lif-ona?"

"California," I say quietly. I shrug and shake my head, remembering seeing it before on an old map with Shosk once. Him saying he'd live there if we were alive during Old-Earth times.

She continues, flipping to a page somewhere midway through.

Frederick Jameson: Fire Colony. His uneven temperament appears to influence the manifestation of his Elemental Potential. When angered or aggravated, his hands would catch fire—

"Catch fire?" Faeya looks at me. "What does that mean?"

I point at the words below the ones she just read, not knowing how to answer her question.

Sebastian Fray: Air Colony Primus. The first of his kind to access his Elemental Potential. Fray could manipulate oxygen alone, wielding the energy around him to make air flow and move at his command.

And beneath that:

Dr. Tamra V. Adjórde: Space Primus. I am the first, and only known person to date, with the ability to manipulate ether—an element capable of folding and bending space. This allows me to become hidden in plain sight and to perceive energetic fields, or colorful auras around people and objects that emit them.

"Akasha, why does it sound like this is saying people can control the elements?" She looks up at me, and for the first time ever, there's fear in her eyes. "Like... magic."

The word rattles in my head, but it won't stick. Her fear just makes it worse.

"I don't know, Faeya," I say. "But I need to tell you something else while we're here."

She deflates, like she can't possibly handle anything more. Her breath trembles as it leaves her, and for a second, I think she might bolt on the spot.

"The other day, while I was in the Nursing Hall, Arrell came in. She and Batkins started talking in some weird language. Using words I've never heard before. A language from New-Earth."

"Akasha... what?" She sighs.

"And my punishment last night was with Kahra. Not Joll."

Faeya starts shaking. We're close enough that I can feel her knees buckle slightly. This might be more than she bargained for. It's like every suspicion she's ever had about this place is true, and stranger than she ever thought possible.

Me, I'm surprisingly calm. Maybe because the calm is fake, stretched tight over everything I don't want to feel.

"I don't know what's going on around here," I say. "But I think we've been kept in the dark about a lot."

Someone pulls at the door.

Faeya and I both freeze.

A few moments later, a knock, then another pull.

"Occupied," I say.

"Akasha?" a voice calls. "That you?"

Faeya mouths Tibbs, then covers her face with her glove and buries herself into my shoulder.

"Yeah. I'm in here," I say.

"Oh, okay. It's me, Tibbs. Not feeling well. Must've been something I ate at dinner."

"Yeah," I say. "Me too."

Faeya's shaking hard, pressing all of her weight into me. I place a hand on the basin to hold us both steady, hoping it doesn't give. Her whole body buzzes against mine, which makes it hard for me to keep us both upright.

"Alright. I'll use another one," he says.

I don't respond, but I hear the ice as he walks away.

Faeya stands up and looks at me, tears swelling in her eyes, her hands shaking almost violently in front of her face.

She flicks each one hard, then folds over, clutching them between her knees. "I'm hot!"

"What?" I say.

"I don't know what's happening, Akasha."

She swings the door open and bolts, heading for her barrack. Surprisingly, she never loses her footing.

I sit down again and slide the journal back into the bottom of my boot, then peek out carefully before stepping into the circle.

My barrack is farther from this outhouse than the one we originally planned to meet in.

I readjust my scarf, pulling it over my face, and squint through the moonlight. Then I tread lightly across the circle, careful not to step on any chunks that might make a sound.

I'm almost back, just passing the front of our original meeting point, when I hear voices, and the door of Barrack 2 swings open. Joll, Kahra, and Fellows step out.

I hurl myself behind the outhouse, press my back to the cold metal, and sink to the ground in fear before they can see me.

It's not unusual for Miners to be out this late to use the bathroom, but at this point, it'd be all they needed to question me. Especially if Faeya gets seen.

Every sound feels like it's hunting me. The scrape of boots, the drag of breath, even the ice shifting under the weight of the outhouse.

I close my eyes and tell myself to breathe, just like that night in 10.

I imagine Kerr would only give me an extra year if I say I was at the outhouse and he actually believed it. Between the whispers, spending time with Faeya and my visit to Nurse Batkins, I doubt he would.

My hands start to tingle again, like the feeling right before frostbite sets in. Warm at first, then sharp. It creeps up my arms, then settles back into my fingers.

I clasp them together and squeeze hard, trying to distract myself from the sensation.

When I'm calm, I peer around the edge and make out three figures. Three shadows where none should be. And all I can think is—I'm not supposed to be here.

What on Adjórde are they doing down here now?

12
CRACKED ICE

There's not a lantern between the three of them, even though the Second Moon is nearly set.

The light is almost gone, but they move like they couldn't care less.

I lean back again, my mind racing as I try to figure out how to get to my barrack without being seen.

What are the odds that Joll, Fellows, and Kahra are all here together, and at this exact moment?

It feels wrong, like they've stepped into place exactly when I happened to be looking.

These past few days have been a whirlwind.

I've stayed mostly off the radar. Now I'm living like each one might be my last on Adjórde.

Part of me wants to blame Faeya. The other half, Shosk.

But it's me, and my decisions, that have me crouched behind the back of an outhouse that, even in the cold, stinks of long days and even longer nights.

The smell burns in my nose. Proof I'm still here, even when everything else feels like it's slipping.

Out of nowhere, a weightless feeling comes over me, and the world shifts. The ground peels away beneath my body. It's quick, slight, but enough to throw me off balance. I fling my arms out, searching for something to steady myself, trying not to slide into view.

The ground shifts again, first a little, then all at once. I skid forward a few feet, stopping just before I break past the edge of the outhouse.

Instinctively, I push myself back, dragging against the ice, and wrap both arms around the sides of the structure from behind to keep myself still. My grip aches, fingers locked so tight my joints scream, but I don't dare loosen them.

My mind can't make sense of what's happening, and I can't fight the panic rising in my chest. A hundred possibilities race through my head, but there's no way to explain it.

I close my eyes again and feel the world spin out of view. When I open them, the colors are back... and this time, they stay.

I'm too scared to let go to get a look, but I hear footsteps approaching.

I press my back to the wall and exhale a quiet, shaky breath, then inhale deeply and hold it again.

When I finally lean forward and stretch around the side, it's not just Joll, Fellows, and Kahra anymore. It's three glowing figures trailing across the center circle, their outlines pulsing in the night.

It's like their bodies have been carved out of the dark itself, the edges glowing so I can't look away.

I shift back, then bend around the opposite side to keep them in view.

Fellows is red, gliding across the ice with Kahra—brown—in tow, her arm caught in his grip as he pulls her along. Joll, black, follows behind.

Kahra scurries to match Fellows' pace but stumbles, her feet catching as she trips over herself.

I exhale, and just as I do, she glances over at me.

We lock eyes for far too long, but she doesn't say anything. Her gaze cuts straight through me, like she knows I'm here and chooses to let me stay. They cross into the middle ring and disappear from sight.

I stand and press my hands to my eyes, rubbing so hard that tears start to form. Then I drop to my knees, struggling to hold back the scream rising in my throat. I fight so hard a sob escapes instead, and tears stream down my face, falling onto the ice.

The sound that slips out doesn't even feel like mine. My cries come muffled, my face buried deep in my gloves as I wipe at the tears. What's wrong with me? *I'm scared.*

I rise again and look around to make sure no one's there, then carefully walk toward Barrack 3, scanning the ground as I go. The closer I get, the more uneven it feels.

There's a crack. A crack in the ice? *It can't be.*

It stretches from where Kahra, Joll, and Fellows were standing, running across the circle and under the outhouse I hid behind.

It's deeper than any crack I've ever seen outside the caves, almost as if it splits the ice in two.

I kneel and press four mittened fingers deep into the divide, then look up to trace its path with my eyes. The cold bites hard at my glove, but I don't pull away. I need to know it's real.

The lantern in Barrack 4 goes out, pulling my attention back. There's no time to make sense of any of this. Not right now.

When I slip into my barrack, everyone's in bed.

I bury myself beneath two layers of tweed covers, still fully dressed.

My thoughts jump from one thing to the next. The journal. The ice. Tibbs almost catching us. Wondering if Faeya made it back without being seen.

I'm trying to piece it all together like a puzzle. But the pieces keep changing shape, no matter how I turn them.

Then I remember the lantern. The one I left sitting on the edge of the toilet when Tibbs first knocked.

I forgot to give it back to Faeya before she ran.

We left the lantern.

13
INSTANT REALIZATIONS

When I wake the next day, Tibbs is gone, which is early, even for him.

I'm still rattled from the night before and have to fight to keep my feet steady as I get ready for the morning meeting.

I head to the basin at the back of the barrack, which has already been filled, a burner lit underneath.

The water's barely warm, but better than freezing.

Abhishek blows past me and nearly knocks me down.

I look over at him but he just keeps going, steps into his boots, and heads out the door.

When I go outside, the crack is gone. Vanished. Like it was never there.

At the circle, Faeya is avoiding me.

She stands alone on the opposite side, arms crossed over her chest, staring straight ahead.

I try to catch her attention a few times, but she doesn't look my way.

Near the front, Dmitry and Gardley are whispering to each other. Gardley glances back, catches my eye, then returns to his conversation. He doesn't say a word to me. Not one.

I'm suddenly aware I'm being avoided, and I have no idea why.

From where I'm standing, I've got a clear view of Barrack 2.

No crack.

I exhale hard, pinching the fold at the front of my parka, unable to make sense of it. But my glove hits something hard. The medicine.

With everything that's been happening, I completely forgot about the ashwagandha Batkins gave me.

I remind myself to take one at breakfast. At this point, I'm willing to try anything.

Kerr and the Elders enter the circle, but I'm distracted, staring at the spot on the ground where the crack should be.

Elder Arrell announces the headcount. "Two hundred and seventeen."

That's two less than the day Shosk went missing.

Faeya and I make eye contact for the first time, but our expressions stay flat.

"Grand Rising," Kerr calls out before anyone has a chance to react.

His threat of five blocks per Miner for talk or speculation holds. No one moves. No one speaks. No one questions.

But who's missing?

I scan the crowd, but nothing seems out of place.

Then I look to the row of Elders behind Kerr—

Fo'Kahra...

I glance at Faeya again. She's staring at me.

She shrugs, then nods toward the front, prompting me to shift my focus back.

Beneath what I hope appears as calm, a frantic feeling builds inside me.

The image of Fo'Kahra being dragged into the dark by Fellows and Joll loops in my mind as I stare at the empty space where she should be standing.

The same spot Shosk once stood.

Shosk. I hadn't thought about him lately, not with everything else going on.

If he were here, I could tell him about last night. About the blackouts... which probably shouldn't be so colorful, if that's even what they are.

He wouldn't say much, but he'd listen. He'd tell me it's okay, and that I'm not losing my mind.

Somehow, he'd help me make sense of it.

Kerr's going on about rations, the arrival of the Foremen, and something about Adjórdean Steel, a metal made specifically to withstand the planet's cold.

It's in everything we touch—the cups and trays, the furniture, even the handles of our tools—thin veins of steel, almost invisible, but strong enough to keep the wood from splintering in the freeze.

It comes with the Foremen, and only every few years.

We must be getting new stuff.

Nothing's said about where Kahra is, or the other missing person.

When the meeting ends, a few Miners gather in small clusters, trading whispers with quick glances. No one lingers though. Staying too long might look like gossip, and gossip draws attention.

Faeya walks over, arms still folded. I join her, and we head to the Mess Hall.

"What happened with Tibbs?" she asks, keeping her voice low.

I shake my head. "What do you mean?"

She leans in, eyes on the path ahead. "Everyone's saying he got caught in the circle before First Moon... with a lantern."

"What?" I say. "What was he doing out with a lan—"

I shoot her a look. Her eyes go wide. She nods once, hard.

"Why would he take it?" I ask, panic rising.

"Abhishek's telling people Tibbs was trying to cover for you. That he wasn't feeling well and went back to the outhouse again last night, saw the lantern, remembered you were in there, and took it. Joll was out and caught him with it on his way back."

My eyes flick around as her words sink in.

What was Joll doing out again?

I'd planned to get the lantern myself before First Moon, knowing that if the wrong person found it, the whole circle would be questioned. But I forgot, distracted by the missing crack in the ice.

"Tibbs wasn't at the circle," I say, though I meant to only think it.

Suddenly it all makes sense. Abhishek blowing past me this morning, Gardley and Dmitry's whispers, even Faeya keeping her distance.

I see it clearly now. They're all pulling away from me, one by one. And Faeya—she's the only one still here. Barely.

I glance around again, and the weight of her risk catches in my throat. She's putting a lot on the line just by walking and talking with me right now.

"How does everyone know?" I ask.

"When he didn't come back, Abhishek went looking and ran into Joll interrogating him," she says. "Tibbs said he found it in the outhouse, but Joll didn't believe him. When he wouldn't say it was you, Joll sent Abhishek back and took Tibbs with him."

I clench my jaw, trying to steady the rush of panic climbing up my throat.

"Joll told Tibbs to give the lantern to Abhishek," she continues, "to take back to your barrack. That's when he was able to tell him it was you. During the handoff."

The image hits me hard. Tibbs, face pale, being pushed to hand over the lantern. Abhishek taking it back, hearing the truth in the moment no one else could see. That it was mine.

I let out a long, shaky breath.

"I know," Faeya whispers. "It's our fault."

Up until this very moment, I'd been blaming myself. But hearing her say "our" lets me know I'm not as alone as I've been feeling. It's still heavy—but somehow, it lightens the weight.

"It's my fault, Faeya. But it's weird."

I hesitate, deciding whether to tell her what I saw. I trust her now, but I don't want this to spiral into another wild plan.

Part of me wants to pretend it never happened. That I didn't see anything. Didn't feel anything.

No one else seems to care or even notice that something about Adjórde just doesn't seem right.

The image of Fellows dragging Kahra from the barrack is still stuck in my head. She didn't even fight back.

"Something strange is going on around here," Faeya says, interrupting my mental spiral.

Her words take some of the tension off. Make me feel a little less crazy, at least this time.

"You're not wrong," I add. "Something happened... after you left."

She scrunches her brow at me.

I take a deep breath before telling her what I saw. How the crack came and went, leaving no trace. How I hid behind the outhouse. And Fellows dragging Kahra away, with Joll in tow. I leave out the part about the colors around the figures in the dark.

When I finish, she's staring at me in disbelief.

"Are—are you sure you saw a crack in the ice?"

"I know how it sounds, Faeya. But not only did I see it... I felt it."

"You felt the ground move?"

"Yes. And I touched the crack with my hand. It wasn't big or deep, but it was long. It was there," I say.

"And now it's not?" She narrows her eyes slightly. "That doesn't make sense."

"How far-fetched could it be?" Frustration creeps into my voice. I feel the anger rising, but I direct it where it belongs... *at Joll.*

He's the reason Shosk is gone. And he's the reason Kahra isn't here.

"Remember what we read in the journal," I add.

She grabs my arm, bringing me to a stop beside her. I look around at the others. A few of them glance up as they pass, their stares lingering on us for too long.

I widen my eyes and tilt my head slightly. Faeya gets the point and keeps moving.

"Akasha," she says. "Magic?" She squints at me. "Really?"

I hesitate. This must be what it feels like to sound crazy. I reflect back to that morning in the Mess Hall, when she told a story in the breakfast line and everyone laughed it off. I know what I saw. I just don't know how to explain it.

"No. Not magic," I say. "Science."

Faeya huffs.

"Think about it." I cut her off before she can speak again. "The book talked about controlling the elements. People's hands catching on fire. Making air move around you at will. And even—"

A feeling crashes down on me like the world collapsing inward. It wraps around my throat. Fear, sharper than I've ever felt before. A hard realization, paired with a denial I thought I'd buried, breaks the surface.

I open my mouth to finish the sentence, but nothing comes out. My throat goes dry. I feel so sick I could vomit.

"Even..." I struggle, taking a deep breath. Forcing the next words out takes everything I have left. "Even someone who could see colors around people. And fold space, hiding in plain sight."

I look at Faeya. Her expression shifts from curious to concerned.

She looks away, and for whatever reason, we walk the rest of the way to breakfast in silence.

We eat apart. I take the ashwagandha, then head for the caves.

WATER EARTH SPACE AIR FIRE

14
THE UNWRITTEN RULE

"What's with you two?" Gardley's eyes bounce between me and Faeya. "You've been dead quiet since we got here."

Faeya and I glance at each other, then back at the ground.

I press the saw into the ice.

"Nothing," she says.

Gardley snorts, makes a face, and heads back to the sled.

The moment he's out of sight, she looks up at me.

"We need to read the book again."

Her comment stops me in my tracks.

I check her expression to see if she's serious, then go back to cutting.

"I'm for real, Akasha," she says. "There's something they're not telling us."

I look around before answering.

Arrell is outside the cave, talking to the Haulers. They're all standing around her, nodding in unison.

"You're kidding, right?" I ask, even though she's clearly not.

"No. I'm not." She sets the plow down and walks toward me.

I stand up and take a step back, almost stumbling.

At least three people nearby notice.

"What are you doing?" I snap.

She clasps her hands in front of her body. "Something's going on. Something they don't want us to know."

"Faeya," I try to cut her off before Arrell sees, but she keeps going.

"We need to know," she says, her voice urgent. "I need to know."

A sharp whistle cuts through the air from the back of the cave. She turns toward it, then to the front.

Someone's warning us. Arrell's coming.

And she doesn't look pleased.

Faeya grabs her plow and scrambles to get back to work, but Arrell pulls her aside for a talk.

I finish cutting well before she returns.

Every push of my saw feels heavier with her gone, like I'm working under a weight no one else can see. Eyes burn through me as I wait. Like everyone's blaming me for Tibbs, but no one wants to make it worse by saying so.

She's gone so long, I grid the next block, cut it, and Gardley comes back to haul them both off.

When she finally returns, her eyes are red, like she's been crying. I don't know what to say.

I've never actually seen Faeya cry before. So I wait to see if she speaks first. But she doesn't.

We near the end of our shift, and she still hasn't said anything. I want to reach for her, say something, anything, but the rules feel like walls closing me in.

Also, my mind's been stuck on something, and if I don't say it now, I might not get another chance. Not with people disappearing by the day.

"We need to talk to Fo'Kahra."

Faeya looks at me for the first time in what feels like hours.

"Have you lost your mind?" she says.

"The book can tell us about New-Earth," I say. "She can tell us about Adjórde."

One look at her face tells me she thinks I'm crazy.

"Kahra," she repeats. "Fo'Kahra? The Junior Elder who doesn't talk to anybody?" She shakes her head. "Ever?"

I reach for the saw and pull it from the ice. "I think she's in trouble."

"This is what she signed up for, Akasha. It's what she deserves."

I turn to her, my voice sharp. "You think she deserves to be taken in the middle of the night? To just disappear without a word?"

"Like Shosk?" she fires back.

Her comment sends the blood rushing to my face. My hands start to tingle.

I can feel the space around me tightening, pressing in from all sides. I take a deep breath, trying to steady myself.

"Akasha," she whispers. Her eyes go wide. Her expression shifts like she's seeing something I can't.

She places an unsteady hand on my arm and backs me toward the wall, guiding me into a corner where I'm hidden from sight.

"You need to calm down." Her voice is shaky, and paired with that look on her face, it scares me a little.

Slowly, I feel myself begin to settle.

The pressure around me eases, and the air feels lighter.

Faeya's hands are trembling again.

"They hurt," she says, clutching them together. "Burn," she adds, locking eyes with me.

She pulls off one glove. The hand underneath is red and blistering, the skin tight and glossy, as if seared by a flame.

Without thinking, I grab her wrist and press her hand to the cave wall. She resists at first, but then lets it happen as her hand cools.

A moment later, another whistle echoes. We exchange a quick glance and rush back to our station before Arrell notices we're gone.

She pulls her glove back on carefully, wincing a little as she does, her eyes scanning the area to make sure no one sees.

I half watch her, half work, not saying anything.

She struggles to maneuver the plow, adjusting her grip every few minutes. Each time her eyes meet mine, it's clear she's hurt.

Gardley comes back and sees we've only finished one new block. "What's going on with you two today?" he says, his words like daggers now.

As he approaches, I feel a strange surge of energy pulsing from him. Like invisible anger. Heavy, and dense. It's almost dizzying.

I raise a hand to stop him before he gets too close, pressing it against his weighted vest. Then I make a face I don't even recognize, and he backs down.

He glances at Faeya, then at me.

"Look," he says. "With everything that's been happening, and with the Foremen set to arrive in two days, we can't afford to be slacking."

Faeya shoots me a look, and I get it right away.

How does Gardley know when the Foremen will be here? We never know the exact day until they show up.

"They're doubling down on punishments right now," he adds, a hint of desperation rising in his voice.

I don't say anything. I simply nod, acknowledging his concerns.

He gives me a look, then Faeya again, and turns away, shaking his head as he goes.

I guide the block to the sled then make my way back.

I eye Faeya, then agree, "We need to read the book again."

"Mmhm," she says, continuing to grid.

I heed Gardley's concern and cut fast. He isn't happy with us, but I don't care how he feels.

Faeya and I eat lunch separately and don't speak for the rest of the shift.

"She's changing our group," she says as we walk toward the Mess Hall for dinner.

"Who?" I say, knowing exactly who she means.

Her tone is flat when she responds. "Arrell. When we talked, she said I have to do a block with her past Second Moon, and that she's taking me out of the group."

Out of the group? The first thing that comes to mind is who Arrell's going to replace Faeya with. This changes everything.

"Why, though?" I ask.

Faeya shrugs. "Because we were talking, I guess."

She's not telling the truth. I can tell by the way she's avoiding my gaze.

"Faeya," I say, nudging her arm with mine. "What happened?"

It takes her at least a minute to get the words out.

"They think we're... together."

At this point, it doesn't matter. I know what she means, but after I felt the ground literally move beneath me, nothing feels the same. Isolation would be just the push I'd need to push back.

"I don't care what people think, Faeya. We need to get to the bottom of what's going on around here."

Finally, she looks up at me, tears swelling, her eyes red again. "Honestly, I thought you'd be mad," she says, wiping them away with the back of her glove.

Other than the fact that I could get in trouble for breaking one of the Big Three, I don't know why she thinks that. They'd have to prove it, and neither of us would ever admit to something like that for it to even make it to review. And it's not likely anyone else would agree.

"Mad?" I say. "Why?"

It takes her even longer to get her next thought out, and I'm beginning to understand.

"Just that... being associated with me, in that way."

"No, Faeya," I say. "There's nothing wrong with you. And I really don't care what people think about me. Never really have." I rest a hand on her shoulder and lean in close, which forces her to finally look directly at me. "To be honest with you..." I hesitate. Now I'm the one struggling to get my words out. "I... I don't think I like girls. Not like that, at least." *Not like we're allowed to like anyone on Adjórde anyway.*

There's silence for a few moments before she responds.

"I kind of figured. Given your relationship with Shosk, and all."

"What do you mean?"

"Nothing," she says quickly. "Not like that. It's just—you two seemed really close. And with you doing all this to find him, I figured, well... you know."

I don't know. Not really, at least.

"It's not like that," I say. "We were close, but... not like that."

"Oh. Okay," she says, dropping the matter completely.

We're almost at the Mess Hall when I bring up the journal again. We both agree there's no way we can meet to read it together, so I'll have to do it alone and fill her in next time we talk. And since we're no longer in the same work group, and being watched, neither of us is sure when that will be.

The thought of being left alone with the journal makes my throat tighten, but it's the only option we have left.

I give her some of my ashwagandha and tell her it'll help calm her nerves. She promises to take it with dinner, though I'm not entirely sure it works.

We eat separately again, as part of our ongoing agreement to not be seen together outside of work, then I go back to my barrack where everyone's still avoiding me.

I guess I should at least be grateful someone warned us in the caves about Arrell. I really didn't mean to get Tibbs caught up in any of this.

As I lie in my bunk, I wonder where he and Fo'Kahra are, if they might be somewhere together.

I think about Shosk too, and what I told Faeya.

I've never actually thought about my feelings for him. I just knew I liked having him around.

The memories come in flashes, his voice, the way he moved, the rare moments he let himself laugh. I picture his face, pale and serious, and the way he would fight his smiles, though I always knew how to get in.

His dark brown curls, which I only ever saw in the barrack when we lived together, before he moved into the Junior Elder quarters. And the way he'd run his hands through them.

Had he ever thought about me like this? But what difference would it even make, now that he's gone?

Thoughts of him, Fo'Kahra, and Tibbs keep me up. The compound feels too quiet without them, like each missing person has carved out their own hollow in the dark.

I plan to head to the outhouse just before First Moon, to get another look at the book.

But right now, I need to get some rest.

After taking what's left of the ashwagandha, I drift off to sleep in what feels like a matter of seconds.

15

HIDDEN TRUTHS

The First Moon hangs high, spilling just enough light into the outhouse for me to see.

There's a map, a rough sketch of the compound. Three rings of barracks circle a central point, marked by what looks like a bell on a stick. The inner, middle, and outer rings are all labeled.

Just beyond the border are three structures: the Nursing Hall, Water Tower, and Archives Barrack.

Two clusters of caves are drawn between the middle and outer rings. To the right of them is a rectangular shape with the words Mess Hall written across it. The Icehouse is behind Barrack 6, closer to the border between Twelve and Thirteen. The only things missing from the map are the outhouses.

It all lines up. But when I turn to the next page, I spot something new. Something I haven't seen before.

Drawn in the distance, far beyond the border, is what looks like a tiny house, like the ones I've seen pictures of before. A triangle-shaped roof sits on top of a square, with lines down the sides like wooden slats. And just before that, a single unmarked box.

The house looks out of place, almost like it doesn't belong on the map. Like whoever drew it wanted to tuck it away but couldn't help themselves.

I rotate the book, trying to figure out which direction they are from the compound. Then I turn back to the previous page to compare. I flip ahead again, and the next page has a title across the top:

WATER FACTION ROTATION SCHEDULE

Halfway through scanning it, the Moon-Cycle Bell rings, letting everyone know it's time to get up. That means thirty minutes until Morning Meeting. I shift my focus back to the journal. The page outlines a plan for an ice-harvesting rotation.

Rotation?

Something about the Water Faction, whoever that is, coming here to harvest ice, then swapping out on a yearly basis. It says that's the only way they'd stay safe and be able to withstand the atmospheric difference.

Safe from what, though? The cold? The Foremen? Or something else we don't even have a word for yet.

I finally sit down after standing the whole time. The moon's higher now, so I can see much better than before.

The bottom of the page is torn, so I can only make out part of what it says. Something about "ships" and a "bridge," which must mean the Foremen and how they travel between Adjórde and New-Earth.

On the back of the page is another map with strange drawings that make no sense to me. Thin posts rise from the ice with stick-like shapes branching out from them. Kind of like... trees? But the only pictures of trees I've seen have leaves on them. These have none, just bare bones scratching at the sky.

Strokes that curve up, then down, one on top of the other, sit close to the edge of the page, and above them, a dark smudge. Like someone had drawn something and rubbed it with their finger to make it look like a black, circular blur. It makes my skin prickle, like the blur is moving even though it's not. I stare at it all until the pull of the outhouse door startles me.

"Occupied," I say, pressing the book against my chest in case I need to hide it quick.

I listen as whoever it was walks away. The sound of their steps fades too quick, like the ice swallowed them whole.

How am I supposed to explain any of this to Faeya without sounding like I've lost what little of my mind I have left?

I flip through the pages a few more times before heading to the circle early to meet her, like we'd planned on our way to the Mess Hall last night.

When I arrive, no one's there. I stand by the bell where she'll be able to see me from her barrack.

A few moments later, she steps out, checking the area before coming over. Neither of us assumes we can't be seen, but as long as it's not an Elder, we should be okay.

"This is only going to make the rumors worse," she says.

I snort, hoping to lighten the mood a bit. "Doesn't matter."

"I guess," she says. "What's new?"

"I don't even know where to start."

The sound of a door slamming makes both of us jump. One of the girls from Faeya's barrack is headed toward an outhouse.

"Just tell me what you saw," she says, pulling my attention back.

For the next five minutes, I do my best to explain what I learned. She doesn't say anything the whole time.

I watch her eyes and brow shift, her expression changing as I try to describe the tree-like things with no leaves and the black blur floating above the wavy strokes, then the two structures far off into the distance.

When I finish, we just look at each other.

"What do you think the house is?" she asks.

I shrug. "What's any of it, really?"

"Well," she says, adjusting her scarf so I can hear her better, "as for the square, I heard there's a place they send you to when you're isolated. No one ever talks about it when they get back, though."

"Because you're not allowed to," I add.

"Right," she says. "But Gardley told me that when he was gone... those twelve days, they took him far."

The way she says *far* twists in my head. Far here doesn't mean distance. It means unreachable. Somewhere you don't come back from the same.

Another door slams, distracting us again. Must be Faeya's barrackmate going back in.

"Gardley told you that?" I ask. "Since when does Gardley tell you stuff?"

Faeya doesn't answer. She goes on with her original thought. "But he wouldn't tell me how he got there. Said I'd think he was lying."

I shake my head, and she watches as I process this new information.

"You think that's the barrack?"

She nods. "What else would it be?"

"But it's square," I say. "Barracks are rectangles."

Faeya sighs. "Akasha, none of this makes any sense. So why should that?"

Before I can answer, the sound of boots approaching cuts me off.

A few Miners start trickling into the circle for the Morning Meeting. Faeya readjusts her scarf just as Kasahn strolls up beside us.

"You were missed," he says.

"What?" Faeya looks at me, then back at Kasahn.

"Not you," he says. "Akasha." He points straight at me. "Mann came to the barrack this morning looking for you. You weren't there."

The words hit me like ice water. Elder Mann doesn't look for people unless something's wrong. What could she possibly want with me? I wonder if Kahra said something about the night she saw me hiding behind the outhouse.

"What did she say?" Faeya asks.

"Nothing," Kasahn shrugs. "She wanted to know where Akasha was and when no one knew, she just left."

Faeya tilts her head, but I keep my eyes on the ground. A cold wave settles over me that has nothing to do with the

air. I shift my weight and glance toward the Mess Hall, already dreading what's coming. She'll be in there. Waiting.

"You two better stop spending so much time together." Kasahn eyes us. "People are starting to get suspicious." He turns to walk away.

Faeya and I look at each other.

"What does she want with you?" she asks.

"I don't know," I snap, sharper than I mean to. She takes a small step back, and I fix my tone. "I mean... I'll let you know what happens when I see her," I say. I swallow hard, forcing the knot in my throat back into my chest.

Kerr steps into the circle, the other Elders falling in behind him like usual. A ripple of quiet moves through the crowd.

Faeya shifts several steps away from me, just enough to make it look like we aren't together.

I scan the lineup of Elders, then the crowd of Miners. Kahra and Tibbs are still missing.

Their absence burns a hole straight through the compound. It feels wrong, like the circle itself is lopsided without them.

Kerr steps forward and begins. "The Foremen will be here soon." The usual murmur passes through the crowd. "They'll stay for two," he adds. "Then return to New-Earth."

Faeya and I keep our gazes straight ahead.

We all know the drill. The Foremen never stay long. They take two days to collect the ice, which they do after the Second Moon. Then they're gone.

Kerr continues, reminding us of the protocol. Helmsmen will stay in Batkins' Hall. The Senior Elders will share

their barracks with the regular Foremen who do the work of transporting the ice to the ships. They'll all eat in the closed-off section of the Mess Hall. And Miners are never allowed to interact with them, and they won't interact with us. It's a line that's never been crossed.

For the first time in my life, I wonder how Kerr and the others know when the Foremen are set to arrive. How they communicate with people on New-Earth. And more importantly, where exactly is the bridge located? I've never considered anything outside of the immediate area.

The thought makes me dizzy, like the compound is smaller than I ever imagined and the world outside is so much bigger. I can't wrap my mind around any of it. It's so confusing it's making my head hurt.

"Faeya," I say, waving her over.

She looks at the other Miners and brushes me off, shooting me a side eye that could cut.

I insist, waving her over again, and she approaches, reluctantly.

"What, Akasha?" she hisses, her words piercing like her plow.

"How do the Elders communicate with the Foremen?" I ask.

"Huh?"

I repeat the question. "How do Kerr and the Elders communicate with the Foremen? To know when they'll be coming."

Faeya's expression shifts, and she looks just as puzzled as I do. For once, even she doesn't have an answer.

The walk to the Mess Hall is longer than usual today.

I trail just behind Faeya as we move with the slow shuffle of Miners. Around us, the usual chatter rises, snippets of conversation about tools, ice, and the arrival of the Foremen—but we say nothing. Not a word.

Our silence is loud. Drowning out the noise around us.

She doesn't look back, and I don't expect her to.

We blend into the crowd pressing toward the Mess Hall doors. The cold sharpens everything. My breath. The ache in my legs, even Faeya's breathing, which is heavier than usual.

My thoughts shift to Elder Mann. What she'll say when she sees me, and what she wants.

I keep my eyes on the ground as I walk through the doorway.

My mind jumps from Mann, to Kahra, to Tibbs to Shosk. Then back to the questions that came to me in the circle. How have the Elders been communicating with New-Earth all this time? What are all of these things beyond the border drawn onto the map?

I've never dared to ask myself any of this. Never let questions like these take shape, even when things didn't quite make sense. I've never been bold enough to speak certain things out loud, not even to myself.

But Faeya has. She always has. She asks what no one else dares to. Not the Miners. Not the Trainees. Maybe not even the Junior Elders.

And now, my own thoughts suddenly feel dangerous.

I lift my gaze.

Faeya moves toward a group of girls huddled in the corner. She doesn't say anything to them. She just stands there, arms crossed, trying to blend in.

I scan the room for Mann, sure she's expecting me. She's probably already decided what she'll say the moment our eyes meet.

But then I spot Fo'Kahra, and my stomach drops.

I glance over at Faeya whose back is to me, then turn again and head in the opposite direction.

I make it halfway across the hall before I'm stopped.

"Akasha," a voice calls. Elder Mann's approaching me.

Her sharp green eyes lock onto mine—a serious gaze that doesn't blink. I look up, having to raise my head more than I do for any other female Elder on the compound... and most of the men too.

Her lips are drawn into a tight grimace. "Kerr wants to speak with you."

For a moment I consider questioning her, but instead, I turn on my heels and follow her lead, heading in the opposite direction of Fo'Kahra.

We approach the door of the divider that sections off the main part of the Mess Hall from where the Elders eat.

I glance around. Several eyes are on me, including Faeya and Fo'Kahra's.

Mann knocks twice, and someone opens it from the inside. Then she steps in without saying a word.

I stop and wait at the threshold before she turns back and nods for me to come in.

When I step through, all eyes shift to me. Almost every Elder on the compound is here. A few of them glance over at

Kerr who's sitting at a table by himself at the back. He waves for us to both come over.

As I cross the small room, I notice a long table set up on one side with rows of food spread out along its surface. Trays are stacked at one end, and forks, knives, and reusable napkins at the other.

In the corner rests a large metal container with a spout, a neat row of cups lined up beside it.

And on the opposite side, sitting next to Elder Joll almost like he belongs here, is Dmitry. His yellow hair is so long it brushes against his blue glasses, hiding as much of his eyes as his hood does when it's pulled on.

We lock eyes, each wondering why the other is here. And when I finally look away, I'm face to face with Kerr.

He motions for me to take a seat across the table from him, then thanks Elder Mann, who leaves the two of us alone.

I sit, pulling the seat forward until my knees hit the metal bar beneath, then I look up and wait for him to speak.

"I'd like to discuss an opportunity with you," he says.

I search his face, but he gives nothing away. "An opportunity?" I say, having no idea what he means.

The reflection of myself in his glasses looms back at me. The brown lenses, almost the color of his skin, hide his eyes completely. It's like I'm seeing myself from his point of view.

He tears off a piece of bread and dips it into his drink. The liquid in the cup is dark, and whatever's in it stings as it enters my nose.

"I'd like you to join the next Junior Elder class," he says, stuffing the piece of soaked bread into his mouth.

I imagine it burns as he chews, and even worse when he swallows. But I'm not sure I heard him right. I don't say anything, since I don't trust that my voice won't betray me.

"You and Evan were close, weren't you?"

My throat tightens, and the words squeak out when I finally speak them. "We were friends."

He leans back in his chair, resting his palms flat on the table in front of him.

I glance down at them. The sides look burned... or singed. Like old scabs that healed but never went away.

When I look up again, I examine him closely for the first time in my life. Just beneath the rims of his glasses, which are pressed so tightly to his face that they crease the skin around his eyes, I notice the same kind of scarring as on his hands. It's faint, and barely noticeable. And just as I realize I've never seen Kerr without his glasses, I remember—I've never seen him without gloves, either.

"I'm sure you're wondering why I'm offering this to you, given your recent issues with the rules."

I catch my reflection in his glasses again. It's one I don't see often since we don't have many mirrors here. My hair falls further below my ears than I'd like, almost touching my shoulder blades. In the front, at least two pieces have joined to become one, partially blocking my view. I'm past due for a trim.

"You're a leader," he says. "And people trust you."

I clear my throat before speaking again. "Thank you, Chief Elder Kerr. But I—"

"Akasha," he cuts me off, bringing a blistered hand to his face.

I watch as he fidgets with his glasses. They don't move an inch as he pretends to readjust them.

Dmitry comes out of nowhere and places a tray of food in front of me before walking away in silence. He rejoins Joll, who's looking over his shoulder, assessing the whole interaction.

"Eat," Kerr says, gesturing at the tray.

He lifts the cup with the strong-smelling liquid to his mouth and finishes it in one gulp. When he sets it back down, his next words shock me. "Shosk was a leader. The kind others followed without needing to be told. We could count on him." He doesn't pause long before adding, "Faeya's a troublemaker. Always has been. If you want to go anywhere here, you'll stay clear of her."

He lets the silence stretch until I feel pressed to fill it.

"He was a good friend," I say.

"You'd be wise to keep your distance from Faeya," he adds.

I can smell the stench of the burning liquid on his breath. Everything about this is wrong, and all I can think is how to get myself out of here.

"Do I have to decide now?" I ask, as if I have a choice in the matter to begin with.

He tilts his head, seemingly examining me from the corner of his eye.

"You have until the Foremen arrive," he says. "Give your answer to Dmitry. He'll bring it to me."

I look over at Dmitry again and wonder what he's doing here. Then again, I always figured he'd be a Junior Elder one day.

I nod again, and we sit in silence until he finally says I can leave.

When I step back through the dividing door, the Mess Hall is empty. I hadn't even realized how quiet it got.

I walk to the caves alone to join my work group, which no longer includes Faeya.

I wonder who's going to replace her.

16
QUIET AS KEPT

The cold settles into my coat like it's got claws. I step inside the cave, expecting the usual push-back from Gardley or a glimpse of Faeya's scarf in the dim light. But neither one's here.

Instead, the first person I spot is Fo'Kahra. She's hunched over near the far wall, gridding by herself. Just the steady scratch of her plow marking lines into the ice.

My boots crunch over frozen grit as I make my way to the rack for my tools. I keep my eyes on her, half expecting her to glance up or bark an order. *She doesn't.* She just keeps marking her grid, the same precise motions over and over.

It's much quieter than usual. Foldley looks up at me, then at Fo'Kahra, then back at the ice.

What's she even doing here? And why is she gridding?

I scan the cave until I spot Arrell near the back, her gaze moving across the stations and the Miners scattered throughout.

I make my way toward her. With Faeya gone and Gardley not here, I have no idea what I'm supposed to be doing.

When I reach her, she peers over my shoulder, like she's looking at something behind me. "You'll be working with Kahra today."

The words sink in, and I feel my shoulders tense against the cold.

I turn to find her again, still gridding near the far wall, never taking her eyes from the ice. When I look back, my face is twisted in confusion.

"You're to work with Kahra," Arrell repeats, catching my expression. "Begin cutting immediately. Gardley will be back soon to collect the ice."

Heat rises up my neck. Working with her is not something I expected.

A dozen questions race through my mind. Why is she gridding? Why is she even in this cave? And why is Arrell calling her Kahra instead of Junior Elder Vai?

I approach cautiously, studying the lines in the ice. They're perfect. Far better than any Faeya's ever done, which is saying something, considering Faeya's one of the best gridders on the compound.

After finding a good spot to begin, I place the saw at the edge of the line and glance up at her briefly before attempting to force the blade into the ice with my boot. But before I can, she stops me.

"Start here, Akasha," she says, pointing to a spot on the opposite side of where I'm at.

She never looks up at me, it's like she's talking to the ground and pointing away at the same time.

Her voice is flat, almost mechanical, and it sends a chill deeper than the cold air. But I don't question her.

I walk around to the other side, place the saw at the edge, and with the heel of my boot, press it into the ice.

She doesn't speak, and neither do I. We work in silence until Gardley comes to collect the two blocks we've finished. He doesn't say anything either. Like Foldley, he eyes Fo'Kahra, then me, before turning to head for the Icehouse again.

While cutting along the side of the grid, I accidentally back into her hard enough to knock her down. But she barely moves. "Sorry," I say quickly.

She looks up at me and our eyes meet for the first time today. "It's fine," she says, then continues to work.

Something about the way she dismisses it so easily leaves me unsettled.

A moment later, it hits me. I almost fell forward from the impact, but she didn't move at all. I think back to what Faeya said about Joll and Shosk, how Shosk didn't move when Joll pushed him.

This is actually the perfect time to ask her about Shosk. Who knows if we'll still be in the same group tomorrow. I think of Faeya, and what she'd do in this case.

When chatter starts to build between the work groups, I speak. "Fo'Kahra," I say, keeping my voice low. "Can I talk to you about something?"

She doesn't pause or look up. "There's nothing for us to talk about, Akasha."

The words are sharp, closing me off before I can push the matter further.

I scan her profile, trying to read anything in her expression, but she's all focus on the grid.

She also doesn't correct me like before, telling me to call her Junior Elder Vai.

I decide to press the issue anyway, refusing to back down this time despite her obvious attempts to brush me off.

"It's about Shosk," I say. "Why was he sent back to New-Earth early?"

What seems like frustration flickers in her, but her expression still won't change. I can feel it more than see it.

Each time I speak, she rotates the plow in her hand, once one way, then back again, like she's willing me to be quiet. The sound of metal scraping ice begins to feel like a warning in itself.

My mind flashes back to the night I saw her with Joll and Fellows, and the moment she saw me. She never said anything about it. If she had, Kerr would've made sure I knew.

"I'm not allowed to speak on such matters," she says.

"I don't care," I tell her. "What's going on around here?"

Kahra shifts her weight. She glances around, and when she spots Arrell heading our way, she leans in just enough to whisper, "She's coming."

We both busy ourselves with the ice.

"How's it going over here?" Arrell asks when she reaches us.

Fo'Kahra nods, and I say, "Good."

She chuckles under her breath and flashes us a look before moving on to check the next group. It's a look that lingers with me, like she knows more than she's letting on.

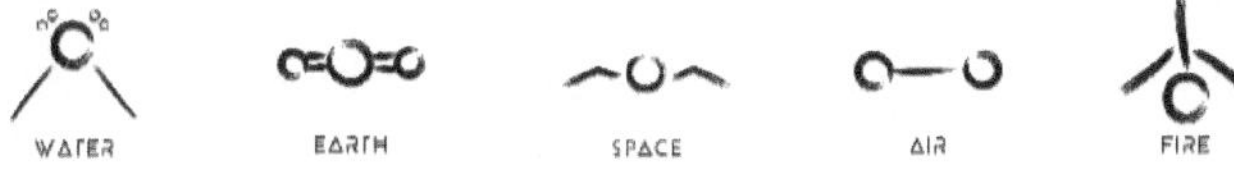

I guide the next two blocks of ice outside and wait for Gardley to return. I haven't let go of the issue and plan to keep pressing her once I get back inside.

Surprisingly, when he comes, he asks, "How's it going? Working with her?" He nods toward the cave, and I know who he means.

"Er—it's fine," I say. "Why?"

Gardley pauses, like he didn't expect me to question his curiosity.

"Because," he says, "she's been demoted. I wanna know how she's taking it."

I frown. "Demoted?" Then I tilt my head and squint at him.

"Never mind," he says, grabbing the sled. He makes a sharp tsk sound as he leaves with the ice, dismissing me as "acting dumb."

I know exactly what he's saying, which is why I'm playing like I don't.

Kahra's gridded more blocks than I can cut. When we break for lunch, I decide to join her, which she doesn't seem too pleased about. I find her in a corner, eating by herself.

It's strange how she holds one roll of bread with both hands, taking tiny bites as she looks around like someone might come out of nowhere and snatch it from her.

She lets out a deep sigh when I sit across from her on the blanket she's spread over the ice.

The sigh feels like a wall going up between us that I can't knock down. But I decide to try a different approach.

"Gardley asked about you," I say.

She pauses just long enough for me to notice.

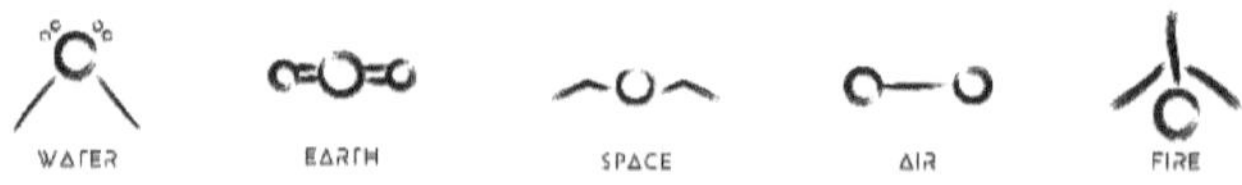

"He wanted to know how you were taking being demoted."

I'm a bit disgusted with myself almost instantly. But I have no idea how to get through to her. And she's the only chance I've got at figuring out what's going on around here. But she doesn't answer, which I can't say surprises me.

I finish my food fast without really noticing. I hadn't eaten breakfast because of Kerr. My eyes wander around the cave and catch a few people watching us. Heat prickles the back of my neck as I realize how visible we are.

I scoot forward, inching closer to her. She recoils, pulling her legs tight to her chest. Her eyes snap up and lock onto mine. She shoots me a look like I've never seen before and I inch back slightly, careful not to fully come back into view of the others.

"I don't care what Gardley thinks," she says, after what feels like forever.

I perk up a bit. *She's finally talking.*

"I don't care what anyone thinks," she adds. "He's asking questions he'll never have answers to."

Her words throw me for a loop.

"Gardley thinks he knows something because Dmitry tells him. What Gardley doesn't know is I know why he wasn't accepted to be a Junior Elder."

I'm shocked.

I watch as her eyes scan my expression, first my hair, and brow, then my mouth.

The air between us feels charged now, like something important just slipped.

Gardley was trying to become a Junior Elder, but wasn't accepted? That would explain his less than pleased attitude lately, and maybe even the whispers he shared with Fellows that night in our barrack. It's another thing to think about, but it's not what's important to me right now

"Why didn't you tell anyone you saw me that night? When I was hiding behind the outhouse?" I ask.

She looks uneasy, and considers her response very carefully before speaking. "I don't break the rules, Akasha... even the unwritten ones." She takes another bite of her bread.

There's only one rule that exists between Miners, and it's not written anywhere for eyes to see. *Never tell.*

Since Miners become Junior Elders who later become Elders, everyone knows it but no one says a thing about it— not unless it threatens to compromise the integrity of the system, like with Tibbs, who's still missing because of me.

Anyone would be well within their right to report me because I compromised Tibbs, and he's suffering a punishment in my place.

"Fo'Kahra," I say, now that I think about it. "Where's Tibbs?"

She shifts on her bottom, her knees still pulled to her chest.

"Tobias is in isolation, Akasha. As you should know."

Her words hit hard, like a blow. She never tries to soften the way she says things.

I feel a sense of guilt and anger twisting together in me.

I'm also starting to feel like I'm either the last to know what's going on around here, or I never find out at all. It's probably because the only person I ever talked to wouldn't

tell me anything. A feeling comes over me I'd been trying to deny since he first went missing—anger.

Shosk left me and did nothing to protect me from whatever it is that's really going on here.

I would ask him questions and bring things up but he'd always dismiss what I was saying or, after getting as much information out of me as he could, redirect the conversation to something else. I'm starting to hate him for keeping me in the dark all this time.

I hesitate, another question tugging at me about that night. "Why was Fellows pulling you by the arm like that?"

She goes silent. Doesn't even look at me. The quiet stretches... heavy.

"Are you okay?" I ask gently.

Her eyes flick to mine, then away. "I will be."

I hear her words, but I can't shake the worry in my gut. I don't even ask about the crack in the ice.

A sharp whistle from Arrell cuts through the air—the kind where she uses two fingers pressed to her mouth. The sound echoes off the icy walls, stirring everyone to their feet. Miners drop their lunch trays at the cart in the front, pick up their tools, and get back to work.

Fo'Kahra and I finish the shift in silence.

I decide not to bother her with any more questions today, even though I don't know if I'll have the chance to again.

When we're done, we head over to the Mess Hall, where I hope I'll be able to talk to Faeya about everything that's happened. But I probably won't get the chance to—not if I'm smart enough to listen to Kerr's warning.

By the time I get there, she's already sitting with the same girls from breakfast. Our eyes meet briefly from across the room. Fo'Kahra's here too, tucked away, alone. Just like me.

A few Senior Elders, including Kerr, linger in the main part of the hall, their presence somehow makes the air feel heavier.

The whole room is tighter with them here, every one of our movements feels watched.

I get in line, grab a tray, and slide into a corner seat where I can see without drawing attention to myself. Faeya mirrors my move, keeping close to her group, while Fo'Kahra sits silent and separate, never looking my way or anyone else's.

Talking to Faeya here feels too risky.

I eat slowly, waiting for the moment she stands to clear her tray.

When she does, I follow and catch her near the cart.

"Meet me at the outhouse between One and Four," I whisper, then turn away before she can answer. It's a shot in the dark, but I hope she takes the risk.

I head toward the door and catch Fo'Kahra's gaze. She's watching me now. Her stare lingers long enough that I have to look away first.

Back in my barrack, Gardley keeps glancing over at me but says nothing. By the third look, I decide to approach him.

"Everything okay, Gardley?" I ask.

"You tell me," he replies, his eyes narrowing.

"If you have something to say, say it," I add.

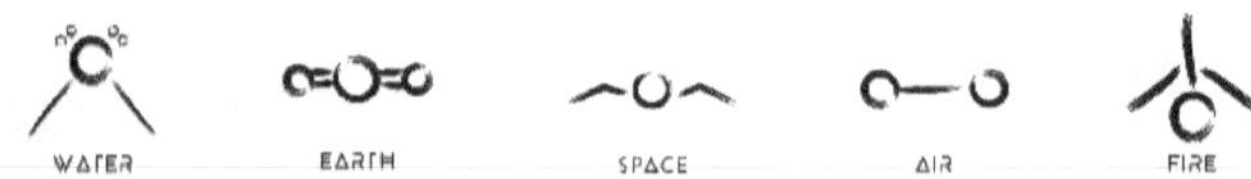

He shifts his weight and approaches like he's pulling a sled, all power and no stop, instantly putting me on the defensive.

My fingers twitch at my sides, the urge to brace myself rising. I feel tension creeping into my hands, arms, and neck. I still don't know what it is, but I know I can't let Gardley or anyone else see. So I force myself to relax, accepting the fate of whatever happens here.

I take a step back and smirk, which seems to make him mad.

"Tibbs," he says.

"Hmph," I respond, not knowing what else to say in this moment. I don't like his tone, his approach, or his body language. At this point, I feel the need to stand my ground. "What about him?"

Gardley looks around. Abhishek is folding his shirts on his bed, pretending not to see or hear us. Someone squeezes behind to get to the basin, apologizing as he brushes past.

I've never had any issues with Gardley before, or with anyone for that matter.

"What's your problem, Akasha? Ever since Shosk left, you've been trouble. Sneaking around with Faeya like no one notices, breaking rules others have to pay for, having secret meetings with Kerr."

This is the second time Gardley's mentioned knowing something he shouldn't, which means someone's definitely been feeding him information. The only person that comes to mind is Dmitry.

I'm tired and fed up with everything that's been going on around here. All the secrets and shady behavior, Kerr and

his weird proposition and Fo'Kahra, who obviously knows what's going on but refuses to share. Wanting to have conversations with Faeya but being unable to get close without everyone thinking the worst.

"Meetings with Kerr?" I say, tilting my head in suspicion. "What meetings with Kerr?"

Gardley steps back, acknowledging my challenge. He huffs, then pushes past me and storms out of the barrack.

I smash into the rail of the bunk and catch myself before I fall, deciding to let it go so things don't get worse.

When I turn back around, the whole room's staring at me.

I wrap my scarf around my face, throw my hood on, and storm out behind him, heading for the outhouse to hopefully meet Faeya.

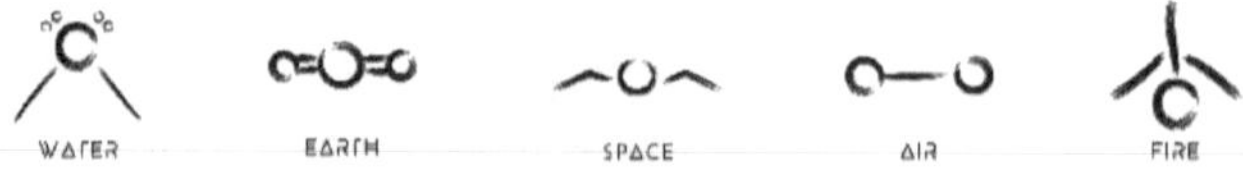

17
LEVERAGE

Once again, me and Faeya are squeezed into an outhouse, the one between Barracks 1 and 4.

Oddly enough, it was free this time.

It seems, whenever I find myself in one, someone else comes knocking. Then again, there are only four in our circle that are shared among about a hundred of us.

"When's Off-Day?" she asks me.

"Um…" I run the numbers in my head. Today makes four days straight, which means tomorrow's our last day in the caves. It went by faster than I realized. "Two days," I say.

It used to be called Free-Day, but since we're not actually free to do what we want, we call it Off-Day.

"You think we'll have it when the Foremen are here?" she asks, flipping through the pages of the journal as I hold the lantern high enough for her to see.

I shrug. "Not sure. Gardley did say they'd be here in two days, and that was yesterday. So it's possible."

"Interesting."

"Why's that interesting?" I ask.

She looks at me. "I don't remember ever being off during one of their visits."

She's right. I can't think of a single time where we weren't working while the Foremen were here.

"See anything new?" I ask.

She rotates the journal in her hands, kind of like how I did the last time I read it. "Not really… but, what do you think this means?" She points to a line of tiny words scribbled down the side of a page.

I step beside her and lean in closer with the lantern. Then I squint to try to make out the writing.

"It says conduction," I say. Next to the word there's a hand drawn picture of a long pole with etches drawn into it.

"What do you think it means?" she asks.

I take the book from her and rest the lantern I managed to take from my barrack on the edge of the basin. One I won't forget to bring back this time. Then I lean in to get a better look.

After inspecting it for a while I answer, "No clue." Then I give her the book back.

It gets quiet again. The journal felt heavier in my hands than it should've.

The only reason I'm here is because I wanted to fill her in on my meeting with Kerr, my conversation in the caves with Fo'Kahra earlier and what happened between me and Gardley in my barrack. But she wanted to see the journal again.

What surprised me was how unfazed she was about Kerr offering me a Junior Elder position—like it didn't even

matter. She said it'd be a chance to find out more about what's going on around here. But that's not what I want.

"There's really nothing else in here," she says, handing it back to me. "So, now what?"

"I still think we should talk to Fo'Kahra."

She throws her head back and rolls her eyes. "About what Akasha? You barely got anything out of her today." Her voice rises a little too sharp, echoing in the cramped space.

"But I did get something out of her," I add. "And I want to know more... about the Foremen. And the bridge."

Faeya looks at me, lowering her chin slightly because she's a bit taller than I am. "What about it?"

I sit and place the book back into the bottom of my boot. When I stand, I look her directly in the eye. "I want to know about the trip back to New-Earth."

"Akasha, what more do you want to know? In about two years, you'll find out everything when you're old enough to return."

Her words sting. Two years suddenly feels like a life-time. I shift my weight. The idea that's been on my mind all day is ringing at the front of my thoughts. So much has happened so quickly, it makes me question everything I've ever been told. Everything I thought to be true.

"What if I don't wanna wait two more years?" I say.

It goes silent. Faeya examines my expression. She reaches for her scarf and pulls it down beneath her chin.

"What do you mean?" she says, shaking her head.

I grab the lantern and raise it to my face so she can see me perfectly clear.

"What if I want to leave, when the Foremen do?"

Faeya brings her gloves to her face and rubs her forehead hard enough that it turns red. "I need you to say exactly what you mean, Akasha. Because I don't want to assume you're saying that you're thinking of sneaking back with the Foremen."

My throat tightens, but I don't back away.

"What if I am?" I say. "Or what if I want to find a way to leave... like Shosk?"

She leans back against the wall and the outhouse shakes a bit. Her shoulders drop, like the weight of the world is rolling off of them.

"And what is your plan?" she asks, doubt rising in her voice. "We don't even know why Shosk was sent back."

She's right. But the plan is the same plan I mentioned to her before, and I know she's tired of hearing about it.

"Fo'Kahra. She's the plan."

The silence between us is so thick it could crush.

"I'm going to give you the benefit of the doubt here," she says. "Why is it that you think Kahra would help you in any way?"

"Because she doesn't want to be here either."

"And she told you this?" she says.

"No, but I can sense it. And the way she's treated here, like she's less than everyone else... it doesn't sit right with her. It doesn't sit right with me, either."

Her eyes narrow, searching my face like she's trying to see if I actually believe what I'm saying.

She looks up at the openings in the roof, searching for signs of lingering light. "We have to go soon. Moon's setting."

"I'm going to talk to her," I say. "I'm going to be very direct and ask her exactly what I want to know and see what she says."

One thing I've learned about Fo'Kahra from interacting with her recently is that she is more likely to respond if I'm direct. The more exact I am with her, the more likely I am to get a reply.

"Leave me out of it, Akasha. If you choose to talk to her and expose yourself, don't mention my name," she snaps. Her tone is final, the kind that makes me swallow my protest.

"I won't mention you," I agree.

She gives me another look, and I reassure her that I won't say anything about her. *I don't need to.*

I don't expect her to go along with any plan I have to get off this planet early. I know how crazy I sound.

"You go first," I say, stepping aside so she can slide past me.

She pulls her scarf back up and fastens the top button of her parka, securing everything in place.

I open the lid of the lantern and blow it out. There's no reason for me to have it with me. Every Miner and most of the Trainees know how to get from their barrack to the nearest outhouse and back in the dark.

I hold it low, and slightly behind my leg so when I step out it's not visible. It's too big for me to tuck it anywhere.

"When are you gonna talk to her?" she asks, turning toward me, her hand placed at the center of the door, ready to push it open when we're done.

"Tomorrow," I say. "Whenever I see her."

She nods, shrugs, and rolls her eyes again. Then she turns and pushes the door open, and standing there, hand outstretched as though they were going to grab the handle to open it themselves, is Gardley, staring both of us back in our faces.

My stomach drops and the lantern follows.

18
AWAKENING

Faeya tried her best to reassure me that Gardley won't tell. But she doesn't know him like I do.

She gets a very different version of him than most.

If I'm right in my thinking, Dmitry's been feeding him information, which means he definitely knows I was offered the opportunity to become a Junior Elder. The same opportunity he wasn't. It also means he'll take any chance to knock me down a few pegs.

The only thing remotely keeping me safe is Faeya, who seems to have some weird relationship with him that I plan to never ask about. There's no way to tell on me without telling on her.

The walk down to the Mess Hall for breakfast today feels long.

Every step echoes in my chest, the weight of what I'm about to do pressing harder than the cold air.

I consider exactly what I'll say to Kahra when I ask for her help. It's not about choosing my words carefully. No. It's beyond that at this point. It's about choosing the *right* ones. Words she'll understand.

"Are you sure about this?" Faeya says, coming up beside me.

"Yeah. I have to be." I can't doubt myself now. Not this close and not after I've set my mind on doing it.

Faeya's eyes are blank and void of expression.

"Don't worry," I say. "I won't mention you at all, like I said."

"Alright, Akasha." She shrugs and nods.

I spot Gardley and Abhishek in the crowd, walking together. They both eye me, but don't say anything.

Faeya doesn't notice. I shake my head and keep going.

We are among the first to arrive.

The only other people here are Elders Mann, Kerr, and Voiyt, who I don't actually know much about since he spends most of his time in Nurse Batkins' Hall with the new arrivals.

"It's best if we split up," I say, stopping at the before we go in.

She nods and enters the hall while I wait outside and watch as the others go in.

There's no sight of Fo'Kahra.

My pulse kicks up. If she doesn't show, this plan dies before it begins.

I stare up at the blue night sky as the rest of the Miners go in. It isn't until I look back down that I see her approaching with Arrell by her side. As usual, she looks out of place and uncomfortable, especially with her former supervising Elder next to her. But I need to get her alone.

Before they see me, I turn to enter and quickly join the meal line. I might as well eat... since I'm here.

I find a corner and scarf down my food, realizing I haven't had a full meal in days. Something always happens where I end up talking, skipping, or sneaking around.

The taste barely registers. My stomach doesn't care, but my head feels clearer with something in it.

I imagine what the food is like on New-Earth. A lot has changed, I'm sure. Who's to say how accurate the magazines, books, and pictures in the Archives even are at this point?

The only reason they let us go there sometimes is to keep us working toward what we'll one day be returning to.

Fo'Kahra joins the meal line, grabs her food, and sits in a corner.

I don't take my eyes off of her. I study her movements, her eyes, and the way she eats. Anything that might help me understand how to get through to her.

My attention is broken when I notice Arrell walking toward me with a tray in her hand. What does she want? *I hope it's not to have me talk with Kerr again.*

"Akasha," she says.

"Yes?" I respond.

"I've been told to give you your Junior Elder Surname."

"Uh—"

"As I understand, you're to begin immediately after the Foremen return to New-Earth." She stares at me, like she's inspecting my reaction. "It's Kamari," she says.

"I—," I pause to consider my next words carefully. If she's been told, it means it was by Kerr. "I was under the

impression that I could give Chief Elder Kerr my answer through Dmitry when the Foremen get here."

Arrell cocks her head to the side, furrows her brow, and pokes her bottom lip out. "What gave you that impression?"

Her stare drills into me, daring me to slip.

Deciding it's best to play along for now to avoid any tension I say, "Kamari?" then nod. "Thank you."

"Good." She gives me an assured look before leaving to join the Elders in their section.

None of us Miners know our families on New-Earth. We're taught very early on that there's a mandate, in which each family is expected to send a child to serve for the cause. This has been the tradition for generations now. That it's custom to not know your family name. But it's seen as an honor to serve for all of humanity.

I've even heard rumors that Miners who turn eighteen and leave with the Foremen get some kind of sendoff—a small farewell with them and a few Elders who want to see them before they go. *I can hardly picture it.*

All I know is one day they're here, the next they're gone with the Foremen, and we never hear from them again.

I finish my food: a few berries, some tea, and dried caribou. Then I make my way to the caves with the others.

I'm about halfway there when Abhishek joins me, wrapping his arm around my shoulder.

In no way do I want to be touched right now, especially by him. I haven't forgotten the cold shoulder he was giving me the morning Tibbs went missing. Which at the time, I didn't even know about.

To keep the peace, especially when I know what he's gonna say, I just keep walking with his arm around me.

"I heard about last night," he says, grinning from ear to ear, which even through his scarf I can see.

"That so?" I look over at him. "What did you hear?"

"You and Faeya," he chuckles. "In the outhouse."

The words burn in my ears, louder than his voice.

I'd never taken Abhishek for a jerk before. Gardley, yes, he has those tendencies, but not Abhishek. It feels like he's letting the worst of Gardley rub off on him and using Tibbs as an excuse to try to push me around.

"I don't know what you think, but I wouldn't believe whatever you've heard."

"Oh, I believe it," he says. "Just like I believed Tibbs when he said that lantern was yours."

"That was an accident," I say. "How was I supposed to know he'd take it?"

Abhishek stops, which stops me with him. "Here's the thing, Akasha," he says, rotating me until we're facing each other, which immediately puts me off.

"Abhishek," I say, trying to stop him before he goes too far. I can already feel my heartbeat rising. My fingers curl into fists on instinct.

"No, no—you listen to me first."

I breathe out hard through my nose, hard enough for him to hear but he doesn't relent.

"You need to tell Kerr, Arrell, whoever, that it was your lantern that was left in the outhouse, and not Tibbs. I don't care how you explain it, but if you don't, I'll tell them about you and Faeya's late night meeting in the outhouse." He

takes a step back from me and smirks. Though I can't see his mouth, his eyes light up, sharp at the edges, locked on mine.

The threat settles like ice in my gut.

A sudden pressure shoots up my back. It starts at the base of my spine and despite how fast it comes, I feel it rise in steps. One section at a time.

I blink, not hard like before, just a regular blink, and Abhishek is glowing red. And for the first time since whatever this is that's been happening to me, I let it.

I take a step back as I watch the glowing aura around Abhishek change from red, to brown, to black.

Out of nowhere, he reaches across his chest and grabs his shoulder and when he does, I feel my own gaze intensify.

I watch as he stares back at me, his eyes far less menacing than before, clutching his shoulder which now looks like it's being pulled backward, as if something were trying to move him. The more he resists, the harder the pull becomes and the more intensified my focus gets.

My eyes flick, and I don't even realize but what looks like a small black cloud appears in thin air, just behind the shoulder that's being pulled.

I don't know what it is, but it feels... *it feels*. It has a feeling to it and everything about it feels like a place, or... an opening. If it feels like an opening, then something must be able to go through... I think.

The sensation is terrifying and freeing all at once, like standing at the edge of a cliff.

An awareness hits me and I let myself sit in this moment, which is an escape from everything around me. An

escape from Shosk, Faeya, the journal, Kerr, Fo'Kahra, Adjórde, and even myself.

For a time, whatever this is, feels like the release of something I've been holding onto for far too long.

I shift my weight, and rotate my body and as I do, his shoulder pulls back further.

Abhishek's eyes go wide. He looks over, then back up at me, then over again.

"Wha—," he stutters. "What's happening?"

From the corner of my eye, I notice a few Miners passing, making weird faces at us. I open my fists, which I hadn't even noticed were still clenched.

Then I blink a few times and shake my head. The aura disappears, along with the tiny black hole floating just behind his shoulder.

He looks at me one last time before taking off in the opposite direction, sliding in place for a moment before gaining enough traction to go.

What's crazy is I have no idea how long we've been standing here. Through it all, I feel like only one set of faces had passed, the two girls that were looking at us weird. But it felt like time had slowed down, yet so much had happened.

When I look back again, he's gone. Out of sight. The last of the Miners passing me pay me no mind.

I wonder if he'll tell Gardley, or maybe Kerr. But what would he even say? How would he even sound?

I guess my secret's safe with him after all.

19
AN UNLIKELY ALLY

Fo'Kahra's still in my work group today. Lucky break.

And this time, she actually seems like she wants to talk.

"They've got eyes on you," she says.

"I know."

"You don't understand, Akasha." She's so short she has to tilt her head to meet my eyes. "Things work a certain way here, and they have for a very long time. You're expected to play your part."

Her words feel like they're carved in ice, solid and un-movable. But the only part I need played right now is hers.

I let a beat hang between us, my pulse hammering in my ears. This is it. The thing I've been rehearsing in my head. The thing I can't afford to mess up.

"I need your help," I say.

The words sound too thin in the air, not nearly as strong as I meant them.

Again, it takes her a while to respond. So I wait. The silence stretches, filling the space between us.

I watch her plow shift in her hands, scraping against the ice, a sound that grates against my nerves.

Finally, she speaks. "What could I possibly help you with, Akasha?"

My throat closes. The courage I'd been building up feels like it leaks out through the cracks in the soles of my boots. I hesitate.

I swallow too hard, and a tiny piece of food I'd eaten earlier comes back up and sticks in my throat. I cough into my scarf, trying to force it down, my chest aching with the effort.

What if I can't trust her? What if Faeya was right?

The thought clouds my head, and suddenly even thinking about it feels like a risk.

"I— I" The piece of food halts my speech. I hold my breath and feel a sense of panic come over me. When I think about what happened with Abhishek earlier, I calm down.

My chest loosens. I force myself to breathe steady, matching the sound of her plow scraping ice.

She's staring at me like she actually sees me for the first time.

"What do you need help with?" she says, repeating her question.

"I... er. What do you know about the Foremen and the bridge?"

She tilts her head slightly, her face unreadable, eyes fixed on me without a flicker. "What are you planning?"

"To leave," I say, forcing the words out as I pull myself upright, trying to sound more certain than I feel.

"Where would you go?" No change in her tone. No shift in her expression. Just a simple question.

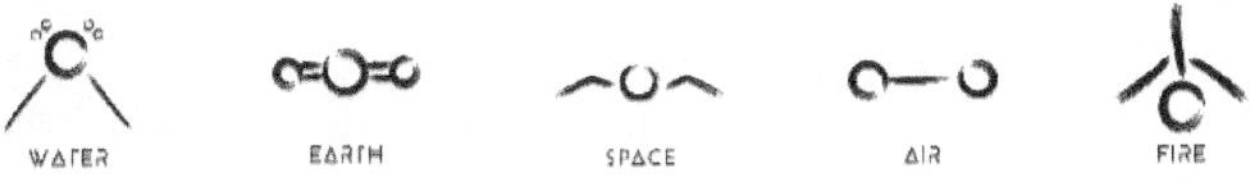

"Wherever the Foremen are going when they leave." My voice catches, and I tighten my jaw to steady it.

"It won't work," she states plainly, like she's describing the weather, her gaze still steady on mine.

"It has to," I say, sharper now. "I can't stay here."

She stares at me and above her head in the distance I see Voiyt heading in our direction. He's replaced Arrell today, it seems.

I get to work, to avoid Voiyt saying anything to me, but he still comes up to us.

"Kamari," he says, nodding as he passes by.

There's a stutter in Fo'Kahra's step, and her grid goes off a bit. Not much, but enough to catch Voiyt's eye.

"Mind your grid," he says, pointing down at the ice. Then he gives her a look that doesn't sit right with me. I don't know what it is, but there's something about him that makes Fo'Kahra act different, more different than usual.

Not to mention the fact that he talks funny. He's the only person on the compound who calls our tray carts "trolleys." He also once referred to the outhouse as a "loo." No one knows why but like Batkins, it seems like something from New-Earth.

When he walks away, I notice a pause in her work.

"What is it?" I ask, since she doesn't volunteer any information herself.

She doesn't respond, and I remember my new approach and try again. "Kerr offered me a Junior Elder position," I say. "I don't want it."

"You don't have a choice," she says.

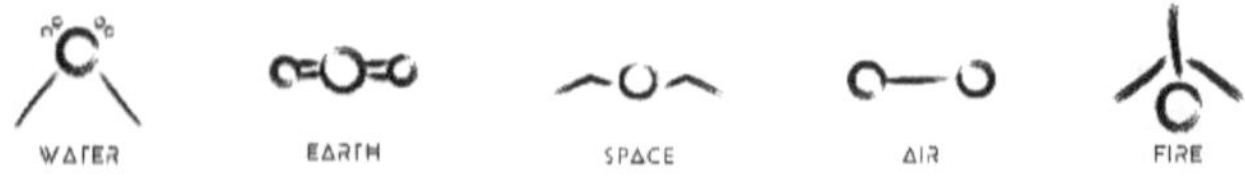

Her words hit hard. My saw bites shallow into the ice as my grip falters. I know I don't have a choice. Which is even more of a reason for me to leave.

"What aren't the Elders telling us?" I finally ask. "What is the big secret around here?"

Out of nowhere, she looks up at me, stopping her work completely for the first time in two days of being in a group with her.

"If I tell you what I know, Akasha, you have to take me with you."

I feel my mouth drop. "Really?" I say. "You want to leave?" I'm actually not surprised. It's more so that she's *telling me.*

The weight of her words drop heavy into my chest, confirming what I've always suspected.

I look around at the nearby groups, none are paying much attention to us but I realize we're falling behind. I shift my focus to the work, to avoid any issues with Gardley.

We don't speak again until Voiyt walks up and down the cave, shouting lunch.

Fellows arrives with lunch and Gardley meets him at the opening.

I walk up to get my food and Fo'Kahra stays behind, coming up only after everyone else has gone. I stand to the side, taking small bites of dried fish while I wait for her to find a spot. Then I join her.

"No blanket?" I ask, placing my tray on the ice.

Sitting directly on the cave floor, even with our thick pants on, will lead to a very cold bottom that might bruise later.

I watch her and wait for a response that doesn't come.

When I go to the back to grab one, the metal tin that usually holds them is empty, which is weird because there's always enough—one for each group.

I spin around, searching the ground to see who might have an extra blanket and find Gardley has taken the one for our group and joined another in the back.

I glance at Fo'Kahra, who's still sitting alone in a corner, on the ice, eating her roll with both hands like usual.

"Gardley," I say, walking up to him and the group of Miners he's decided to join. "We need our blanket."

He shifts on his butt, turning back to look up at me as I stand over him, closer than he'd probably like.

The rest of the group stops eating, one of them sits their cup down and Gardley rises to his feet.

When he stands, we're nose to nose, and I don't back down.

"Guys," someone hisses, but I don't move. "Guys," they repeat. "Voiyt's coming."

I stand my ground. To hell with it. If Voiyt sees, we'll both get in trouble.

Heat rushes through me, daring me to push further, but I stay locked in place.

Gardley sees I won't back down and snorts, steps aside and holds a hand out at the blanket.

I bend and scoop it up in one swift motion, then turn to rejoin Fo'Kahra.

When I do, I hear him say something under his breath which sends the weird sensation pulsing up my spine again, but I keep walking and push it out of my mind.

"Get up," I tell her.

She stands, quicker than I might've imagined, bringing her feet beneath her body and rising in one smooth motion, almost as if floating.

I furrow my brow in suspicion, and in the back of my mind, I add that to the list of strange things that have been going on around here.

After laying the blanket out, further back in the corner than she was originally seated, I kneel beside her and reach for my tray.

It must've been my fast motion, but she recoils again, pulling her knees to her chest like before.

"I'm just getting my food," I say, slowing my movements as I lean back into my spot.

"Where was the blanket?" she asks.

"Gardley had it," I say as I bring the cup of cold, bland tea to my mouth and drink it in one big sip. It's disgusting. It's always been. Somehow, it's even worse than usual and I'm sick of it.

People always say the closer you get to eighteen, the more difficult it is to push through because you start thinking about life on New-Earth in comparison.

That's not what this is, though.

I'm tired of being pushed around, told what to do and more importantly, feeling like I've been lied to my whole life.

"He gave it to you?" she says.

Her questions throw me for a loop. I'd been eating my food, replaying the scenario with Gardley over in my head and not really paying much attention to the fact that she's actually questioning me.

"No. I took it."

"Hmm," she says, like she's analyzing my words more than the actions that took place between me and him.

Now it's my turn to ask her a question. "Why do you want to leave?" I make sure to keep my voice low and check the area.

She looks down at her bread, tearing off tiny pieces and slipping them between her front teeth. Her lips move quickly, chewing bits so small they're gone almost as soon as they touch her mouth.

My question is a loaded one, and I hadn't realized it until now. She won't look up at me, which is not surprising, but when her legs come close to her chest again, I can tell she's uncomfortable.

Just as I decide to let it go, she starts to speak.

"Being a Junior Elder isn't what everyone thinks it is," she says. Her voice gets low when she adds the next part. "They expect you to do things, things I'm not willing to do."

I set my tray aside, taking it off my lap. "What kind of things?" I ask, thinking about Kerr's offer to me.

"I can't say."

She places the bread down, the majority of which she hasn't eaten, and wraps her arms around her knees, pulling them even tighter to her chest. Then she looks off into the distance.

I place a hand on her arm, to reassure her, and she jerks it back. "I don't like being touched."

She's louder than we both expected. I can tell when she covers her mouth with the back of her glove and looks up at me. It's innocent, almost like one of the younger Miners.

Her eyes are wide with something close to fear, and I make myself stay still, careful not to startle her.

Everything about her is different. The way she talks, looks at things, takes in information and makes sense of it.

"Sorry," I say, bringing my arm back into my own space. "But, if you need someone to talk to, I'm here."

"I didn't want to be a Junior Elder either, Akasha. I only wanted to stay hidden, turn eighteen and go back to New-Earth. Like everyone else. But..." she stops.

"But what?" I say.

"Everything's a lie."

I feel the weight of the world crash down on me. I lean back, to see if anyone is near before speaking my next words, which come out sharp. "What do you mean 'everything's a lie?' What is? What part?"

Three questions in a row is too much for her to handle. She picks up her tray, carries it to the cart, and exits the cave.

This isn't something I can let go. I do the same.

"Outhouse," I say, as I pass by Voiyt.

When I round the corner, she's there, her face buried into her gloves and her body pressed into the outer wall.

I check the area, to make sure no one sees. Then I approach her carefully, so I don't scare her again.

"Uh... Kahra," I say, gently, shortening her name for the first time.

I lean in, trying to get a look at her face. She's not crying, just... hiding.

"*Mrr you g'na take meh wif you*," is all I can make out as she tries to speak through her gloves.

I start to reach for her hands, to remove them from her face but stop, remembering what happened last time I touched her.

"I can't hear what you're saying."

She slides her hands up slightly, just above her mouth, then speaks again. "Are you going to take me with you?"

"Yeah," I say, nodding, even though she can't see me. "I am."

She nods back, still pressed against the cave.

"Go to the outhouse," I add. "Get yourself together, then come back."

She nods into the cave wall one more time before turning and walking away.

I wait a few minutes, to make it seem like I'd gone myself, then head back.

Our blanket's been folded and put away with the others and everyone's back to work.

I pick up my saw and start cutting again. When Kahra returns, she continues to grid.

We do enough blocks that Gardley doesn't say anything. Either that or he doesn't want to cause another scene.

At the end of our shift, I make the walk to the Mess Hall with Kahra beside me.

We're near the back of the crowd as they squeeze in through the double doors, whispers and snickers rippling from the front to the back.

Several Miners are standing on their toes, trying to get a look at something over the head of the others.

When the whispers make it to us, the word is clear.

The Foremen are here.

20
THE FOREMEN

"One lantern and two days of oil is all I can do."

Kahra and I whisper over breakfast the next morning. Faeya's watching me from across the hall at a table with the girls who seem to be her new best friends.

Even though it's Off-Day, the hall is more crowded than usual. Instead of sleeping in like they normally do, people have shown up early, drawn by the chance to see the Foremen up close.

Each time the door to the Elders' section opens, heads turn and eyes strain for a glimpse inside. The whole room feels restless with curiosity, like just being in the same space with them is something worth holding on to.

Kahra glances at me from the corner of her eye. "I'll leave them in the cave, near the back, under the slab of ice."

"They won't notice?" I ask.

She shakes her head, sipping from her cup with both hands wrapped around it.

I lean back and run my hands across my face. *This is crazy.* "Why are they still making you look after Tibbs?"

She'd confirmed mine and Faeya's suspicions about the square drawn on the map. It's a box for supplies, tools, parkas, blankets, and other things we'd need on the compound if something had to be replaced. But they'd added a bed and an outhouse so they could use it for isolation.

"It takes half a day to get there on foot," she says. "Even if you leave at First Moon, by the time you arrive with food and provisions, you can't make it back before Second Moon sets. You have to stay overnight and return the next day. No one wants to do it."

"It's a punishment," I say.

Kahra nods.

"But it gives you an out," I add.

She nods again.

"I need you to get a message to Faeya for me."

She doesn't answer. I watch her eyes shift, calculating.

"Tell her to make a trip to the outhouse five minutes into lunch."

She shakes her head. "I don't like Faeya."

"I get that," I say. "But I can't go near her. And I need to talk to her."

"I'd rather not," she says.

I keep my frustration in check. "We have to work together if we're going to pull this off. I can't just disappear without talking to Faeya first."

"You can't trust Faeya, Akasha."

I snort. "She said the same thing about you." I picture the two of them in a conversation, telling each other how they both can't be trusted.

"I'll tell her to meet you in the outhouse five minutes into lunch." Out of nowhere, she stands and crosses the Mess Hall, heading straight for Faeya.

Her eyes widen when Kahra approaches. Her gaze flicks to me, and mine widen too. I fully expected her to wait, or to be less obvious with it.

Half the hall watches as Kahra leans in, says something to Faeya, then steps to the side with her hands clasped behind her back.

Faeya stands, slowly, scanning the hall, then the two walk to the shelves bolted to the wall near the big metal water pitcher, stacked with napkins just out of Kahra's reach, but well within Faeya's.

I study them. Faeya reaches up, grabs one of the square gray cloths, then hands it over. Kahra says something, points at me, and my stomach drops.

Faeya frowns. Kahra speaks again and Faeya grabs another napkin and passes it to her.

Kahra turns back and heads toward me again. She sits, then slides one of the napkins across the table.

"She said okay."

"What just happened?" I say, genuinely curious how she pulled that off. Even though a lot of eyes were on them, no one questions the interaction.

"People are more likely to think we're both just being weird, instead of mischievous. Especially since we're never seen speaking."

I hear her, but I'm sure at least one or two people raised a brow, and I have a feeling she knows this too.

"Kamari. Kamari!"

Kahra looks over at me and I perk up, recognizing the name.

"Kerr wants you in the back," says Chambers. She's glaring down at me from beside Kahra.

What does he want this time?

"Now." She adds, thumbing over her shoulder in the direction of the Elders' section.

I get up and look at Kahra, who of course is not looking back at me but instead staring down at the tray in front of her.

As I trail behind Chambers, I catch several people watching me.

We pass through the familiar door and when I enter, it's packed. There's gotta be at least twice the normal amount of people in here.

The air thickens, pressing down on me harder than the cold ever has.

I freeze in place, scanning the room and feeling a bit overwhelmed. It's like Elder-Effect, doubled. Twice the amount of intense energy and every eye in the room is on me.

I look over to where Dmitry and Joll were sitting the other day and in their place are two Foremen.

I recognize neither of them.

In all my years of being here, I've never seen the Foremen up close before. They don't wear parkas like us or the Elders. Instead, they're wearing what looks like fitted black jackets made of a material I've never seen before. Every inch

of their bodies is covered, not unlike ours, but the texture seems different.

"This way," Chambers says, looking over her shoulder at me.

As I cross through the middle of the room, I pass more Foremen, getting a much closer look at their clothing.

Their long, heavy uniform jackets are cut from a stiff fabric, the hems brushing mid-thigh. A row of silver buttons climbs from the chest to a stiff, high collar that closes snug around the neck. The shoulders are structured and rein-forced, the sleeves fitted tight at the wrists.

Wide belts cinch the waist, carrying pouches and tools, while dark trousers tuck neatly into scuffed combat boots laced tight up the shin. The overall look is rigid, practical, and built for endurance, every line of the outfit speaking to discipline and order.

All of them are dressed the same, except one small de-tail, a tiny metal crest pinned to the chest, pressed flat against the fabric and embossed with a symbol.

Faeya and I have seen those symbols before in the book. I don't know what they mean, but they aren't all the same. Some Foremen wear matching crests, others bear different ones.

When Chambers and I reach Kerr, he rises to his feet. Beside him stands a woman dressed in the same style as the other Foremen, the silver crest on her chest catching my eye. I recognize it immediately. It was the last one drawn in the row in the book, a circle with a single line extending upward, two shorter lines branching out on either side.

On her head is a scarf. It's like the ones we wear to shield ourselves from the cold, but hers doesn't wrap across her mouth. Instead, it drapes over her head, covering her hair completely, then winds around her neck without ever crossing her face. The fabric is black, smooth, and gleaming, made from a material I've never seen in person.

On her right shoulder, a single strip of fabric runs down, sleek and deliberate, a deep red that stands apart from the rest of her clothing.

When her gaze lands on me, her eyes narrow to slits. She smiles, but it's not the kind of smile you return.

A cold knot twists in my stomach.

"This is Helmsman Iman," Kerr says, stepping aside so I can see her fully.

"Er—" I look to Kerr, then back at the woman.

"Iman is fine," she says, as if noticing I was searching for what to call her.

"Helmsman Iman," I reply, knowing Kerr would likely lose it if I called her by her first name.

She nods, her gaze fixed on me, studying me like I'm something rare and out of place.

Kerr turns to her and gestures toward me. "This is Akasha. Or—" he stops short, catching himself, "Junior Elder candidate Kamari."

"Interesting to meet you," she says, folding her arms across her chest as she continues to study me.

I stand there for what feels like forever before glancing around.

Everyone is watching.

In the corner, Chambers is whispering with Arrell. Only a few people act as if they don't see us.

"Thank you, Akasha," Kerr says. "You may go."

I'm not sure what that was supposed to be, but it leaves me wondering.

Chambers steps in beside me without a word, steering me out of the Elders' section and back to the main hall.

The moment I step in, heads turn. A few Miners watch openly before leaning toward each other, trading whispers. Kahra and Faeya are nowhere in sight, even though breakfast isn't over.

The space feels too small, eyes burning into my back with every step.

I keep walking, go to my seat, and eat in silence. I'm not skipping another meal. When I'm done, I head straight for my barrack.

Everyone's here except Tibbs, who's still in isolation. Thanks to Kahra, I know exactly where.

I realize Gardley's gone too, which is strange. He moves like clockwork, never missing a beat. He's not the type to break routine. He wasn't in the Mess Hall when I left either.

Things are still awkward between me and Abhishek, and by now, no one's talking to me at all.

I keep my head down at my bunk, flipping through the pages of a beat-up picture book I swiped from the Archives almost ten years ago. But really, I'm planning our escape.

I want to tell Faeya. It feels like the right thing after what we've been through. I also know if I turn up missing, she'll be the first one questioned, and I want her to have time to prepare.

Kahra might end up more of a burden than a help, but the knowledge she's got is invaluable. I wouldn't make it twenty feet past the border without her. As much as it scares me, leaving is starting to feel... real.

"You gonna take off those clothes?" Abhishek says from across the room. "*Kamari*," he adds.

The way he says it makes my chest tighten. He's heard the name passed around, knows what it means.

Heat flashes through me before I can stop it. *I lose it.*

"What's your problem?" I yell across the room. "You got something you want to say to me?"

"What's *your* problem?" he fires back, louder. "You planning on sneaking out again?"

The rest of the barrack goes quiet, all eyes on us. When Abhishek walks up on me, I swing before I can stop myself, my fist connecting with his face. Everything I'd been holding in comes to a head.

Shouts erupt as we crash into each other, falling into the narrow space between bunks. We knock into dressers, yank hoods over each other's heads, drive punches into ribs and sides. The others egg us on, voices blurring together in the heat of it.

No one steps in. We roll across the floor, shoving and swinging, boots scraping against the ground. Someone laughs, someone else shouts for him to hit me harder. A dresser tips just enough to slam back against the wall with a bang. The air is hot with sweat and noise, our grunts and shouts swallowed by the chorus of voices urging us on.

Every hit lands like fuel on fire.

It takes almost five minutes before someone comes, the door slamming open so hard the barrack shakes. *It's Joll.*

Abhishek and I shove each other a few more times before he reaches us.

Joll lifts a hand toward my chest that never touches me, yet somehow still drives me back, sending me stumbling into the wall.

"What's going on in here?" he yells.

No one responds.

His gaze sweeps the room, his face turning a shade of red I've never seen before.

He storms up to Abhishek, grabs him by the neck of his half-ripped shirt, and yells the words again, louder this time. "What's going on here?"

Then he turns to me. I keep my gaze steady and unflinching. Let him see it. I'm not the one to test right now. Besides, I don't know what would happen if he tried.

This is the same guy I blame for Shosk leaving, who sneaks around the grounds with Junior Elders, who let Kahra be dragged away by Fellows like it was nothing.

If he put his hands on me right now, I might just level this place and I wouldn't even know how it happened.

Suddenly, it's not my thoughts that feel dangerous anymore.

It's me.

21
ISOLATION

Being in isolation isn't so bad.

Tibbs is gone, which is good. In a way, it feels like it balances the scales. I'm serving the punishment I was supposed to in the first place, and he's back at the compound.

I get up from the bed and take a look around.

The room is square, just like the picture on the map, and definitely a supply space. Lanterns line the shelves along one wall, all of them new. I can tell because the wicks are still fresh and the metal bases aren't rusted.

On the other side, saws, pike poles, and single-blade plows hang in perfect rows—about ten of each.

The bed sits against the far side, away from the door. In the corner, a bit too close for comfort, is the outhouse. The same one Tibbs used before me. It being inside instead of out is crazy.

It hasn't been emptied so I covered the toilet with a metal board and an extra blanket I found. It helps with the smell. *Kind of.*

There are no windows, just tiny airholes that run along the top of the walls, and the door is locked from the outside, so I'm stuck here until Joll returns with provisions. He's put me on an oil schedule. I suppose I should be glad I'm allowed light at all, but if I let the few lanterns I've been allowed burn too long, I'll be without until he comes.

I can't tell night from Adjórdean day in here, and I don't know what time it is or which moon might be in the sky. I can see how this place could drive someone mad.

Still, it's quiet here. Peaceful, even.

No Gardley keeping a close eye or secret meetings with Kerr. No beds to make, routines to follow, or ice to harvest.

And for the first time since I was a young Adjórdean Miner, back when I'd only been on the planet a few years, I cried, freely and openly.

No strange introductions to Helmsmen or need to hide my friendship with Faeya from everyone. No Dmitry watching with suspicion, or Mann asking for anything.

I could stay here, forever.

I never got to talk to Faeya or finish the plan with Kahra. She knew there were lanterns in here and was going to take two without anyone noticing when she came to bring stuff to Tibbs. I'm still not sure where the oil was supposed to come from, though.

Today's Off-Day, and I'm in the isolation box.

The Foremen are probably out there right now, readying themselves for their second night of work, hauling ice to their ships while we sleep. I can see it in my head—Elders with lanterns, shuffling back and forth, guiding them across the compound. Load after load until the ships are full.

This time tomorrow, they'll be gone. And they'll be leaving without me.

Joll brought me here after my fight with Abhishek, before lunch. I was blindfolded and put into something that moved... something I know I've never seen before.

There's nothing on Adjórde, other than the sleds and food carts, that can move across the ice. But whatever it was, it felt massive with a deep, constant rumble that filled the air, so loud I could feel it in my chest.

It went on so long I started to feel sick. The blindfold didn't come off until I was in here, just me and Joll. When he left, he took Tibbs with him, and whatever food he had was gone too.

Joll said he'd be back at the Second Moon tonight with more so I could make it through the next few days. But I wouldn't be surprised if he left me here to starve. I don't think he likes me, for some reason.

What's most odd about this place, besides the lack of windows, no door handle, and a toilet inside instead of out, is that it's warm. Not hot, but warmer than anywhere back on the compound.

I had to take off my parka and my sweater because I almost started to sweat.

After trying the door again, I run my fingers along the frame, feeling for anything I might have missed. Then I grab a lit lantern from the shelf and take it back with me to the bed.

I sit on the floor beside it, leaning back against the metal frame, and set the lantern at my side. Then I reach for the journal again.

The Book of Adjórde. And all her secrets.

Faeya and I have looked through these pages so many times, and everything's still the same.

I flip through them again. Then again. And for a third time, slower. We've already gone over all of this.

Factions. My fingers trace the row of symbols printed in a neat line across the top.

I stop, staring at one for longer than the rest. The one the Helmsman wore.

The Foremen have always worn these symbols. I've just never noticed before. Or maybe I never cared enough to.

Now I can't stop noticing. How much I've missed. How much I've been blind to.

I find the map again and my eyes land on the square drawn in the distance from the compound. The one I'm sitting in now.

I trace a path with my finger until I reach the tiny house marked close by. My gaze shifts to the shelf of unused lanterns, then back to the page.

I rotate the book in my hands, same as last time, and turn the page—the same wavy lines with the black smudge above it. I still don't know what it means.

The info on the pages that follow is still the same as before: Sebastian Fray, Air. Frederick Jameson, Fire. Tamra Adjórde... Space?

What about earth and water? There's no mention of anyone tied to those elements. Are these the only people who can control them? Or are there more?

I think about the strange things I've seen these past few days.

Joll shoving me back without ever touching me. Kahra steady on the ice in her mukluks, more sure-footed than one might expect. Shosk, growing colder and more distant after becoming a Junior Elder, as if some part of him had been sealed away, and even the ease with which he moved across the ice.

I think of Kerr's scarred hands, the skin marked in ways I can't explain. And me, those moments when everything slows, when the air feels heavy and pressure folds in around me and anyone close enough to be caught in it.

What does it all mean?

I push the thought away before it can root itself. It's easier this way. Safer.

I decide to close the book, telling myself it'll be for the last time.

There's nothing new in here.

Just a bunch of numbers and diagrams I've never understood. Sketches of parkas and mukluks. And that strange long pole again, its surface etched with markings. Beside it, the word conduction written in neat, careful letters.

As I close it, the back cover bends slightly, and I notice the edge of a pocket worked into the inside, right between the spine and the last page.

It's the kind you could slide something into, hidden unless you knew to look for it.

I press the cover open a little farther and the pocket parts just enough for me to slip a finger inside.

Tucked within is a tiny folded piece of paper, the edges yellowed and soft. It feels as old as the book itself.

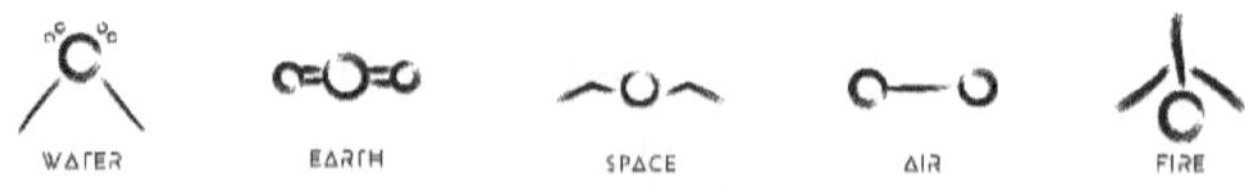

I ease it out and set the journal aside. Then I unfold it with more care than I've ever given anything in my life.

There's a letter. And on it, it reads:

I have given this matter more attention than anything else in my life. My work was conceived to reshape history, to thrust mankind into the future, and to grant access to understandings once believed beyond our reach. Instead, I brought about chaos and destruction, an outcome far removed from my intentions. An experiment that failed led to a discovery of unprecedented scope. It revealed possibilities I could never have conceived, yet it also set in motion a civil war.

Closing the hole, the portal I opened, will require an immense concentration of power. My proximity to it at the time of its creation has altered me in ways no one else has experienced. This is my greatest fear. What I have done can only be undone by my own hand, unless another should emerge with the ability I possess. It is the ability to manipulate ether, and the strength to fold space with sufficient force to seal the wound in the sky. Without such power, the hole will remain, and it will destroy our planet, Earth, and everyone on it.

Dr. Tamra V. Adjórde

I fold the letter and slide it back into the pocket, then tuck the journal into my mukluk. I pull the boot back onto my foot and sit on the edge of the bed, leaning forward with my face in my bare palms.

My head hurts from trying not to think, but the thought slips through anyway. That I might be more like Adjórde than I've wanted to believe.

The idea grips at me, refusing to let go.

Without realizing it, my leg bounces against the floor, my heel tapping the metal with each movement. *I wish I still had more of Batkins' medicine or something stronger, even.* Anything to take the edge off right now.

I start rocking forward and back, letting the motion settle me until my chest loosens. Then I stop fighting it.

The familiar feeling rises in my spine, uncoiling and creating a warm, heavy sensation that spreads through my body.

By the time it reaches the base of my neck, I lift my head and open my eyes. The colors set in instantly, swirling in the edges of my vision. I push myself to my feet and drift around the room, waving my hands in front of my face.

Red, orange, and green trail from my fingers, stretching and bending in ways they shouldn't.

My shoulders drop and my movements seem to slow, as if the air itself is holding me in place.

I think of Barrack 10. Of yesterday with Abhishek on the way to the Mess Hall. Our fight.

The pressure in the air thickens and my hands curl into fists, pulling at something I can't see but can feel all around me. *It's too much.*

The air thins and my lungs lock. I try to pull in a breath but can't. I stagger sideways, slamming into the wall of tools. The clatter rattles through the small room.

My hand fumbles for something to hold and closes around the cold wooden shaft of a pike pole, Adjórdean steel running from top to bottom throughout.

The moment my fingers curl around it, the world snaps back. The colors vanish. The weight lifts.

I'm standing there, breathing hard, gripping the pole like it's the only thing keeping me here.

I struggle to my feet and fall back against the bed, the pike pole still in my hand. The only thought that cuts through the haze is whether this is really happening. And if it is, why me?

It takes a while for the room to fully come back into focus. Everything spins, both from the experience and from fear. My chest heaves as I fight to keep my mind from running wild.

When I'm finally able to sit up again, I realize I'm hungry. Of all things.

I've had access to three meals a day every day since I've been on Adjórde, and it's surely past dinner by now. I haven't eaten or drunk a thing.

I think of Kahra, who wanted off this planet as much as I did, being treated like dirt for another three years, still getting pushed around and outcast because she's different. The way the other Junior Elders speak over her. The way people push past her like she isn't even there. And the way the rest keep her at arm's length, polite when they have to be but never letting her in.

And Faeya, who'll probably get dragged into my mess one way or another. If not by the Elders officially, then by the other Miners behind her back, teasing and accusing her of things that aren't true.

My plan to escape, my carefully crafted plan with Kahra that was surely too good to be true, will never happen. By the time I'm out of here and back on the compound, I'll have no choice but to begin Junior Elder training and fall back into

routine, pretending nothing's any different than it ever was. And I have no idea how to live that lie.

I look over at the lanterns again, the unused ones.

Kahra was supposed to take two, fill them with oil, and sneak them into a cave. Then today, on Off-Day, I was going to get them and meet her by the water tower. From there, we'd head for the ships.

Since she still had to bring provisions to Tibbs, it gave her an excuse to leave the compound overnight, given the distance and the time it takes to get here and back on foot.

For me, it would have taken a while before anyone noticed I was missing or even cared enough to say anything.

Kahra said that since my barrackmates knew I was supposed to be becoming a Junior Elder, they'd probably assume that had already started and that that's where I'd be. And with the Foremen leaving and Dmitry knowing the timeline and the way it all works, it's likely Gardley knew, and Abhishek too.

The Elders almost never do barrack checks when we don't work. It's mostly an Off-Day for them too. No one would have noticed me missing until breakfast, tomorrow.

And by then, we would have been too far ahead for them to catch us, with the Foremen, snuck aboard a ship.

I stand, feeling better now than I had a few moments ago, and hang the pike pole back on the wall, clearing the rest of the mess after I do.

I blow out one of the lanterns, since I have no idea when Joll's actually going to return. I'm stuck on Adjórde at least another year, and that thought is eating me alive.

Tears swell behind my eyes and I swallow to fight them back, though I don't know why. Maybe I don't want to cry again.

My stomach growls and I grab it. The feeling is uncomfortable because it's unfamiliar, and I have no choice but to bear it. The Second Moon should be setting soon, I guess, which means everyone will be in the Mess Hall, heading toward it, or just about to leave.

I lay back on the bed and close my eyes. I don't know how long it is before I drift asleep.

***

A sharp rap at the door jolts me awake. The sound of a key jiggling in the lock follows, then a few hard pulls before it swings open.

Moonlight spills into the room, and in the doorway stands the last two people I'd ever expect to see together.

Faeya. And Kahra.

22
THREAD OF TRUST

Neither of them gives me a chance to think or ask questions.

"Ready?" Faeya says, looking at me from above Kahra's head.

I start to stammer, but Kahra lifts a hand, cutting me off. "We must go. Now."

Her tone leaves no room for doubt, slicing through the fog in my head.

The pressure from earlier still lingers in my chest, like a shadow of what I'd tried to do. My hands feel clumsy as I turn and head for my parka on the wall hook.

Both of them are already dressed for the cold, pants tucked into mukluks, hoods up, scarves hiding their faces. Gloves on Kahra, mittens on Faeya.

I pull my parka on over my head, wrap my scarf, and tug my hood up to match them. My gloves go on last.

Kahra steps in behind me as I'm fixing my boots, my fingers fumbling, breath heavy.

"I need help with this," Kahra says.

I glance over my shoulder as Faeya moves to join her. Together they pull the bed away from the wall. A dull scrape cuts through the air, revealing a built in metal compartment near the floor.

Kahra kneels and rifles through the keys in her hand until one slides into place.

Inside are several bottles, identical to the one Stokes showed up with at our barrack with the extra ration of oil. She hands one to Faeya, who moves with quiet precision to the shelf, takes two lanterns, sets them on the floor, and begins filling them.

Kahra leans deeper into the compartment and pulls out an old brown bag, nothing like the ones I've seen before. She already has her Junior Elder satchel across her shoulder, but this one looks different. Heavier.

She presses it into my hands. "Hold this open." Then she steps just outside the barrack again, into the cold, and comes back with another, like the one Batkins gave me days ago as I was leaving her hall. "Food," she says, dropping it into the larger bag I'm holding. "From Joll."

I nod, glancing at Faeya as she puts the top back onto the oil bottle and hands it to Kahra. *He sent Kahra to me in his place.*

The oil goes in beside the food. I hope it doesn't spill, but they're both moving with a purpose I don't want to interrupt that feels like it's already been set in motion.

Faeya grabs the blanket from the bed, folds it tight, and shoves it into the bag, nearly filling it.

"Put it on," Kahra says, glancing at me briefly before looking away.

I hesitate, holding the bag up. It has two straps, not like the ones Elders wear. I look at Faeya for help, but she only shrugs and glances at Kahra.

Kahra steps forward, takes the bag from my hands, and holds out one strap.

"Put your arm through here."

I do, and she moves to my other side, which presses the bag against my back.

"Now this arm."

I bend awkwardly to get under the second strap. The bag locks snug against me. I jump a little, it shifts but stays in place. Kahra fastens it, then heads for the door.

"Let's go," she says, stepping into the night.

Faeya picks up a lantern in each hand and falls in behind Kahra.

I start to follow, but something holds me back. My eyes catch on the wall of tools, the rows of metal glinting in the lantern light.

I grab a pike pole from its hook, swing the end over my head, and guide the handle down my back until it's pinned tight between the bag and my parka.

It stays in place, steady and unmoving, grounding me again in a way I didn't know I needed. Then I head out the door behind them.

I know where we're going. I just can't make sense of the two of them being here. Together.

We walk for what feels like hours, and the Second Moon has nearly set. I can only just make out the dark silhouette of Faeya in front of me, and I can't see Kahra at all. My calves burn and my mouth is so dry I can't swallow. My chest aches,

and while Faeya and I have both started to slow, Kahra keeps a pace we can't maintain.

"Kahra," Faeya says between ragged breaths. "We need a break."

She stops and looks around. "We'll need to light the lanterns soon."

Faeya turns toward me and puts out a hand, feeling through the dark until it brushes my shoulder. When she finds it, she rests it there and lets out an exasperated breath. "I'll fill you in."

Her grip lingers, warm even through layers of fabric, an anchor against the dark. Then she lets go.

The feeling of something coming up behind me makes me flinch, and I turn too fast and nearly fall.

"It's me," Kahra says, her voice coming from just below eye level. "I need the blanket from the bag."

I turn again, more carefully this time, until my back is facing her. I feel her tugging as she works the blanket free from inside.

"Guys," Faeya calls from a short distance away, a tremble in her voice that's thin with fear. "I can't see."

I squint into the dark, trying to spot her, but she's gone from view.

When I look back, I can only make out the fur around Kahra's face because of how close she's standing.

That's when it hits me—we're farther from the compound than I've ever been, farther than I ever imagined going. The Second Moon has almost set, and the moment it's gone, we'll be swallowed in complete Adjórdean darkness.

The thought shakes me to my core, the weight of the black sky pressing down.

Kahra walks past me in the direction of Faeya's voice. I follow, afraid that if she goes too far, I'll be feeling around in the dark trying to find them.

Right before the Second Moon had begun to set, the path ahead of us was clear. Nothing but flat endless icy terrain that seemed to stretch on forever. Like we were walking toward nothing and going nowhere.

I stand close to Faeya, and she moves in, pressing the side of her arm against mine while Kahra shuffles around on the ice. "Come," she says.

I feel Faeya move like she's being pulled. She reaches for me and brings me with her, and as she bends, so do I. The handle of my pike pole hits the ground before I do, so I remove it and place it flat, next to me, then sit.

The blanket is beneath us, and we all crouch together as close as Kahra will allow.

The more Faeya and I inch toward each other for warmth and to fit on the blanket, the more I feel Kahra pull back, sinking into her own space where I can't feel her near.

"Wha—" I cough to clear my throat, realizing I haven't spoken real words since we left the Isolation Box. "What's going on?"

I hear Kahra rummaging through her bag, shifting in place. A match strikes, then flares as she lights the lantern. The oil fed flame swells, spilling light between us, bright enough to catch their faces and throw sharp shadows onto the ice.

"Kahra found me at lunch today... in the Mess Hall," Faeya begins. "Said people were talking about you and Abhishek getting into a fight. We didn't know where you were for sure. Then Tibbs showed up."

I shift, readjusting myself on the blanket. I look up at Kahra, who's staring down at the lantern, her knees pulled to her chest, arms wrapped tight around them. Like usual.

Faeya glances at her too, then back over her shoulder at me. "She told me what you were planning, what you both were. It's crazy, Akasha." She lets out a short chuckle, more nerves than humor. "Then she told me what happened with her, and why she wanted to come with you. To leave this place."

Kahra rests her chin on her knees, looks up at Faeya for just a second, then back down again. Faeya gives her a reassuring look.

"I—" Faeya stutters. "I couldn't let her come alone. And I couldn't let you do this without me."

I don't know what to say, so I just let her words sink in and wait for something to come to me.

"They won't notice us missing until morning meeting," she adds. "But by that time, the first wave of Foremen will be back on their ships, headed for New-Earth."

"Us too," I say.

She nods. "Exactly. But when I don't show up for Morning Meeting and Kahra doesn't return, they'll know something's wrong."

"So, now what?" I ask. "I have no clue where we are or where we're going."

"We have to head to the sea," Kahra says.

I frown, and Faeya glances at me like she already knows what I'm about to ask. "The Adjórdean Sea," she says.

"Like an ocean?" The confusion in my voice comes through hard. "On Adjórde?"

"Yes." Kahra doesn't hesitate.

All I've ever seen here is ice, and the bit of water we have in the caves, barracks, and outhouses. But an actual sea?

"That's where the Foremen ships dock," Kahra adds. "On the shore of the Adjórdean Sea, which we won't make it to in time if we don't start moving now."

I sense the urgency in her words, but need answers if I'm going to keep going. "How do the Foremen get there?" I ask.

"Trucks," Kahra says.

"Trucks?" I repeat.

"They have trucks," Faeya says, "with chains on the tires to stop them from sliding around on the ice... according to Kahra."

I look up at her, confused. "Where do they keep trucks?"

"Just beyond the border," Kahra says. "Not far from Barrack 11. Which is why Miners aren't allowed to travel beyond it without permission... and an Elder."

It all starts to make sense now.

The rules, the schedule, the routine. The Junior Elders, even the layout of the compound. It's all built to keep us hidden in the dark, in every way.

Even the Foremen carry their own secrets, tucked into crests and quiet nods only them and the Elders seem to understand.

No one questions. No one challenges. How could they? No one knows any better. *We* don't know any better.

"So who are the Elders?" I ask. "Really?"

I look at Kahra, my expression demanding an answer.

"Elementalists," she says.

She lets go of her knees and relaxes, extending her legs until they're flat against the blanket. She takes a breath like she's bracing for a long speech—or a heavy one.

"Elementalists are people who can control the natural elements." She takes another breath. "Seven hundred years ago, a physicist on Earth accidentally caused a hole to open in the atmosphere. It changed her instantly. She could manipulate the element of ether, or space, as most people call it. A year later, others started showing the same kind of abilities with water, earth, air, and fire."

Faeya tilts her head. "All of them? Or just one?"

"One per person," Kahra says. "Today, Elementalists inherit the gene from their parents. They call it *Potential*. It's passed down, and the chance is higher if both parents come from the same faction. Otherwise, you might not have any at all." She pauses. "But every Elder does."

I glance at Faeya, trying to wrap my head around it, and see the same look on her face. A hundred questions run through me, but only one makes it out. "And the Junior Elders?"

Kahra shifts, uneasy. "You can't be a Junior Elder unless you can manipulate an element."

Faeya lets out a sigh. "So you're an Elementalist, Kahra?"

She nods. "Water."

Faeya and I look at each other.

"Shosk is a Water Elementalist as well," she adds.

The words hit me hard. *Shosk*. An Elementalist.

My mind reels, and for a moment I can't think straight. How could he keep something like this from me, when we once shared everything? I think about the last time I saw him, searching for some sign, anything I missed. But there was nothing. Just silence. Then he vanished, without a word.

"What about Kerr?" Faeya asks.

"Fire," she says without pause. It gets quiet for a moment. "I am curious about your Potential, Akasha."

I furrow my brow when she looks up at me.

"You were chosen to become a Junior Elder. All Junior Elders are Elementalists."

"I... I don't know," I say, shaking my head. "Kerr must know something I don't." *But how?* I glance at Kahra. "Did you ever say anything to him about me?"

"Yes," she says. "I told him you were asking about Shosk."

Faeya shoots her a sharp look, then flicks her eyes at me like she's saying *I told you so.*

Kahra goes on. "He said if you asked about Shosk, I was to let him know."

The words sink in. Why does Kerr care so much about me and Shosk?

Faeya gives me another look. I shake my head, telling her to let it go. It's not important anymore.

It goes quiet for a while before someone speaks again.

"I think I'm an Elementalist," Faeya says, catching both me and Kahra by surprise.

"Fire," she adds, her voice shaky again. "My hands... they've been burning. Especially when I'm scared... or upset."

To our surprise, Kahra cracks a half-smile. "That's funny," she says. "Most people with red hair have Fire Potential. Not all, but the chances are higher if you do. But Gardley..." She gives a small shake of her head. "Not him. No matter how much he wanted it to be." She smiles again and pulls her knees back in, resting her chin on them, looking far too pleased.

"Gardley?" I say. "The other day I saw Fellows talking to him in our barrack. He seemed down for a while after that."

"Kerr wanted to check, since he has red hair. He called him in to see if he could create fire." She grins again. "I don't like Gardley. He's never been nice to me. Better you than him, Faeya." She looks up at us for a moment before resting her chin back on her knees.

Faeya fidgets, rubbing her mittened hands together like she's trying to keep warm. "Create fire?" she says, more to herself than to us. "I don't know if I want that."

I glance at her. "I understand. It's... it's scary." Then I look to Kahra. "Why have they never told us any of this? What's the big secret?"

Kahra exhales slowly, her gaze settling on the lantern flame. "This was never the plan. The Water Faction was supposed to handle everything, gathering the ice and taking it back to New-Earth. But when Jameson took over after Director Fray, he changed things."

Faeya tilts her head. "How do you know all of this?"

"You learn it, when you become a Junior Elder." Kahra pauses for a moment. "But things are really bad on New-Earth right now with the water crisis, and they need all the help they can get. That's why Shosk was sent back early. They arranged a secret transport for him."

"Why him though?" I ask.

Kahra's eyes flick to mine. "It has a lot to do with how long we've been here and what we're able to withstand. Shosk can also manipulate ice, which is rare—a mutation of a mutation. They needed him to go back early and help on New-Earth, since things are getting worse. To Directorate City."

"Directorate City?" Faeya says.

Kahra nods. "It's the capital, where everything is run and overseen."

"What are the other mutations?" I ask, thinking she means something unusual, or not the way it's supposed to be. *Even though all of this is already strange.*

Her gaze shifts to Faeya, then out into the darkness beyond the lantern's glow. "For Fire, it's absorbing methane, though only one person's ever been able to do it. People with Earth Potential can move soil, rock, and sand, but with the mutation they can also influence plants. For Air, it's having both nitrogen and oxygen Potential. It creates a kind of crossover."

Faeya and I just stare at her, taking it all in. I don't think I've ever heard Kahra talk this much at once.

"What about Space?" I ask, deciding to take advantage of her sudden willingness to share.

She raises a brow. "Only one person was ever known to possess the Ether Potential, and she died over seven hundred years ago. She left the portal open that's destroying New-Earth. There's very little understanding of it."

"Adjórde," I murmur under my breath.

Kahra studies me for a long moment. "Is that your Potential?"

"I don't know," I say, my voice lower than I expect. "I don't know what I can do, or who I am, anymore." I push myself to my feet. "We should go."

Kahra stands too. "We should."

Faeya folds the blanket and tucks it into the bag. I pick up my pike pole from the ground and swing it over my back like it's becoming routine, settling it between the bag and my parka again. Then I grab the unlit lantern.

She looks at Faeya. "Bring the light closer so I can see." Faeya steps forward while she digs into the bag again.

She pulls out a piece of rope a few feet long and no thicker than my thumb. She takes one end for herself and hands me the other, then walks a few steps away until it stretches tight.

"Faeya, hold the middle," she says. "And hold the lantern. The closer we get to the ocean, the more water there is beneath the ice. I've got a better feel for where we're headed now."

Shosk's thin-soled boots suddenly make sense. He needed to be close to the ice, to connect with his element. And now... on New-Earth, I guess he is.

With one hand each on the rope, we move forward under the faint glow of a single lantern and the thread of trust holding us together.

23
FAEYA

We've been walking in the dark for hours.

I can't stop replaying everything Kahra said, and I still can't see where we're going. The lantern in Faeya's hand went out a long time ago, and we haven't lit the other. The rope, with Kahra in the lead, is all we have to depend on now.

For a moment I wonder if this is a setup, if she's guiding us into some kind of trap. I shake the thought away. She wouldn't have told us everything she did if she were still working with the Elders. Unless that's exactly what she wants us to think.

My mind is playing tricks on me. I'm light-headed from walking, and the emptiness in my stomach is gnawing at me.

"Kahra," I say, my voice rough. "Can we stop to eat?"

"Shortly," she answers. "We're almost there."

I can't imagine we're at the sea yet. "Almost where?" Everything feels the same—cold, flat, endless. "Almost where?" I press.

"The cabin," Kahra says.

I remember the drawing of the house, the wooden panels and the triangle roof. She's taking us there, and I wonder why.

We walk a little farther before the rope tugs to the side. I follow the pull, and so does Faeya, as Kahra guides us to turn.

"Here," she says, slowing to a stop in front of us. "I need the other lantern."

I extend my arm to the side, careful not to hit anyone in the dark, and feel the weight leave my hand. Then Kahra shuffles around again, followed by the sharp rasp of a match. A wick catches, and the faint glow pushes back just enough darkness to see again.

Kahra lifts the lantern toward the door, tilting it to catch the metal as she searches for the knob. When she finds it, she pulls out her ring of keys and flips through them with one hand. "I don't know if any of these will work," she says.

I step forward and lean in to inspect it too. I jiggle the handle, but it doesn't move. I glance around, but the light barely reaches two feet past where Kahra stands.

After she tries every key, a thought crosses my mind. I wonder if I could open it with my magic. *Magic.* The word sounds ridiculous, even in my head, and I feel silly for thinking it.

"Let me try," I say, inching closer to the door. I throw my shoulder into it a couple of times, hoping it might give, but it doesn't budge.

"Maybe a window?" Faeya suggests.

"Maybe," Kahra says. She sets the lantern down and walks off into the dark.

I glance at Faeya, who's stepped closer, then down at the frozen ground between us.

Her breath hitches—a sound that tells me she's just as uneasy as I am.

Kahra returns a moment later. "They're up too high for me to reach."

"I'll go," Faeya says, her voice flat and resigned. Like someone has to do it, and since she's the tallest, it might as well be her.

"You sure?" I ask. "I can go."

"It's fine," she says. "If I can't reach it, none of us can."

I hold out the lantern. "Take this."

She shakes her head. "You need it to see."

I can't believe she's really willing to go out there without light.

"Alright. Just... keep your hands on the cabin at all times. If anything happens, Kahra will come for you."

I lift the lantern and hold it to the wall near the door as Faeya puts a hand on the siding, trailing it along as she disappears into the dark.

Out of nowhere, the handle jiggles, then clicks open. Kahra steps back into the shadows, disappearing completely, and whoever's in the doorway lunges at me, knocking me flat onto the ice with a hard thud. The lantern crashes onto the ground and rolls just beyond my reach, its flame still burning.

The bag on my back cushions my fall, but the pole only makes it worse.

I reach for it, trying to pull it from beneath me, something to hit them with, but can't.

"Akasha!" Faeya yells from the distance.

We writhe across the frozen ground, their weight crushing me. Hands clamp around my neck, cutting off my air.

They're bigger, stronger, and I can't break free. I can't even see.

I try to focus, to connect with the space around me and force them off, but I'm too overwhelmed. *I can't.*

Out of the corner of my eye, I see the lantern lift from the ground and swing toward me, then a loud bang as Faeya slams it into the side of their head.

They fall flat and motionless on top of me. It takes more strength than I have to push them off, rolling them onto the ice where they land on their back. Faeya brings the lantern close again, somehow still lit, and holds it to their face. *It's Voiyt.*

"What's he doing here?" Faeya screeches, her voice high with panic as she stares down at him. His body is motionless, a pool of red spreading near his head. "Where's Kahra?" she cries, the lantern in her hand swinging wildly as she looks around, searching for her.

I sit up, trying to steady myself. I've had two fights in less than a day, and they're the only fights I've ever been in. I realize I haven't slept, and it's probably already tomorrow, though it still looks like night. By the time the First Moon rises, we should be aboard a ship, headed for the bridge.

"I'm here," Kahra says, stepping back into the glow of the light. I look at her and can't decide if I feel anger or pity.

I was being attacked and she ran, did nothing. But Faeya actually came back for me.

"Thanks, Faeya," I say, glancing at Kahra, whose eyes stay fixed on the ground.

"Where did you go?" Faeya asks.

"I couldn't let Voiyt see me," Kahra says.

"See *you*?" Faeya snaps. "What about Akasha? What about me?"

Faeya's eyes widen in the shadows. She steps toward Kahra, and instinctively, Kahra steps back, gliding on the ice and shifting her weight onto her back foot, disappearing into the background again.

Then her voice comes from somewhere unseen. "Voiyt is the reason I need to leave."

I watch as Faeya's expression softens, her fury turning into realization.

She huffs, turns toward the cabin door, and walks through, dropping the matter for now, it seems.

I look at Kahra, who's stepped back into sight, but the farther Faeya moves into the cabin with the lantern, the less I can see of her and Voiyt, who's still sprawled out on the ground.

"Do we have any more matches?" Faeya calls back to us.

Kahra steps into the cabin, and I get up to follow, glancing down at Voiyt before I do.

"He should be out for a while," she says. "You hit him hard."

Faeya snorts, then fumbles with a lantern she's found. Kahra hands her a match. She lights it, and the room brightens. We find another and light it too, and the cabin comes into view without needing to hold a flame to everything.

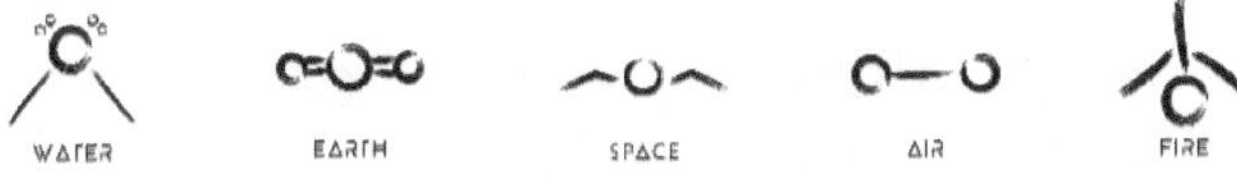

"Three hours," Kahra says, like she's talking more to the air than to us. "That's about how long until the first of the ships leaves."

I have no idea how she's keeping track of time. Everything is blurring together for me. I decide I need to eat.

I take off the bag and pole, pull out the food, and tear into a hard piece of bread, finishing it in two bites. I hand some to Faeya and Kahra before taking more for myself, and we sit on the floor, eating in the light of the lanterns until we're done.

I stand and walk around, taking it all in. Exploring the cabin.

It's old and cramped, and you could probably fit three of these inside a single barrack.

There's only one bed and everything within is made of metal. The wooden floors creak under my feet as I move. Animal furs hang from beams running across the ceiling, and an old burner, like a stove, sits against one wall with a few pots hanging beside it.

There are two windows on each side and one in the back, all too high for me to see out of without standing on something. A bench sits on one side with an old blanket spread across it, making the place feel like a tiny home for one person.

There's a table in the middle covered with papers, and another in the back has a chair and a set of needles and thread like the ones I use in my barrack to patch clothes. A pair of boots sit by the wall—Voiyt's, I'm guessing—and it hits me that he must have attacked me barefoot.

I grab a lamp and step outside, holding it close to his face to check for breathing. Satisfied, I head back in. *He's alive.*

Faeya's sitting with her gaze turned away from me.

"Faeya," I say. "Are you okay?"

She takes a big bite of her bread and shakes her head no.

I sit beside her. "It's going to be alright." I try to reassure her. "You did what you had to."

"He'll be fine," Kahra adds.

I know she means well, but her tone doesn't sound like it, so I give Faeya a light nudge before she can think too hard.

"How long will he be out?" I ask Kahra.

"I don't suggest we wait around to see," she replies.

"Why did we stop here?" Faeya asks, looking up at Kahra with red eyes that are fighting back tears.

Kahra gets up and heads to the back. She starts shuffling through drawers in a way that's hurried but still controlled. She never loses her calm, but there's a rush in the way she moves.

She goes to the stove, opens it, peers inside, then closes it again. Then she stands in place for a moment, scanning the cabin from one spot, looking up and down. Then she takes a knee, removes a glove, and places her hand on the wooden floor. She pauses like she's thinking, then stands and walks toward the door. It's still open, so she pushes it shut.

Behind it, fixed to the wall, is a row of tiny hooks holding keys and other trinkets I don't recognize. She scans them quickly before grabbing something shiny and round.

After turning back to us she holds it out. "This," she says.

Faeya looks up, and I lean in as Kahra comes closer.

"What is it?" I ask.

"A compass," she says. "It shows our direction, where we are, and where we need to go."

"I thought you already knew where we were going," Faeya says, a hint of anger in her voice.

"I did, up until here," Kahra replies. "Past this point, everything's unfamiliar, and there's so much water it all feels the same beneath my feet."

"Three hours," I say, repeating the timeframe Kahra gave us, as both a distraction for Faeya who seems like she might explode at any moment, and a reminder to myself that we need to pick up our pace.

"Yes," she answers, confirming like I'd asked a question.

I grab the bag and put it back on. Then, the pike pole.

"Why do you have that thing, Akasha?" Faeya says. "Just leave it here. It's more trouble than it's worth."

I shake my head. "No, I need it." Then I walk to the door with Kahra close behind.

Faeya is slower to follow but ends up in front of me as we take hold of the rope and set out into the dark again, two lanterns now and the single line connecting us. In front of me, she keeps her eyes straight, never glancing down at Voiyt as we pass. He's still breathing, so that's worth something.

"What if he tells?" I ask.

"By the time he makes it back to the compound, we'll be gone," Kahra says.

"If this even works," Faeya adds.

I don't say anything, and neither does Kahra—not that I expect her to. Faeya never wanted to do this in the first place,

and I feel the weight of her actions, especially knowing she only did it to protect me.

"What was he doing there?" Faeya asks.

"I don't know," I say. I answer her only in case Kahra doesn't, just to fill the space with something other than whatever she might be feeling.

"He's waiting for the new furs," Kahra says. "The Helmsmen should be back on the ships by now and will send out the final provisions. The furs and tools are the last to come."

"Why don't they bring it all at once?" I ask.

"They work in teams and shifts," she explains. "They start at the compound and work their way back. It's more efficient. They can't carry or transport everything in one trip, even with the Elders and Junior Elders. They can't all go missing from the compound or ships at the same time."

It actually makes sense, and it explains why we never really see them working, moving supplies, or bringing in new stuff. They work at night and in the distance.

"Now what?" I say.

"Now, we figure out how to work the compass."

"You don't know how to use it?" Faeya's tone is sharp.

"I opened it, and it's not working. The arrow should move and tell us the direction we're going, but it's not."

I stop, holding the rope tight enough to bring both Kahra and Faeya to a halt in front of me. Then I walk up so I'm standing between them.

Faeya lifts her lantern to my face, and I hold mine up to Kahra.

"So we're just walking wherever now? With no clue where we're going?"

"We can't turn back," Kahra says. "So I'm feeling my way forward."

Faeya's jaw tightens. "I thought you knew what you were doing."

"I did," Kahra says, her voice even. "I didn't expect the compass to be broken."

"Which way do we need to be going?" I ask.

"Southeast," she says. "That's where the Foremen arrive, where the bridge is. I know the sea is in the direction we're heading, but I can't tell if we're going south, southwest, or southeast."

Faeya exhales sharply, her breath visible in the cold, even through her scarf. "I wish I'd never come."

The words land heavy, and I feel a twist of guilt in my gut.

Kahra stays calm, though her eyes narrow slightly. "We can't go back."

"That's the problem," Faeya says, glaring at her through the lantern light. "If we can't figure out which direction we're going, then what are we supposed to do?"

I step forward again, trying to keep the rope from pulling too tight between us. "Then we figure it out together. We're not going to solve it standing still."

No one answers right away. The silence feels tense, each of us stuck in our own thoughts, the night pressing in from every side.

"I'm doing my best," Kahra says.

Her words are steady, but the faint tremor in her voice betrays the weight she's carrying.

I realize we've been hard on her, and this was my idea in the first place. I've probably been the least help this whole time, doing nothing but asking questions and doubting while we've both been depending on her.

"Let me see that," I say, holding out my hand for the compass.

She passes it to me, and I give her my lantern. They both stand close, holding up the light so I can see. I pull off one glove and turn the compass over in my bare hand. The bottom of the brass casing is scratched and dulled with age. Then I flip it upright onto my gloved hand. The glass face is cloudy at the edges but still clear enough to see the worn markings and the needle resting inside.

Kahra inches closer, but not too close. *I've been starting to understand she doesn't like to be touched or too near people.* She points at the face of the compass, toward the needle. "It should move and turn as we do, showing us which way we're going."

Faeya leans in too, trying to get a look. Kahra rotates the compass in the palm of my gloved hand, then points again, this time at the faded SE letters on one side. "If we were headed in this direction, the arrow would point to it."

I take the compass between two fingers and give it a gentle shake, then a light tap before setting it back on my glove. Looking out into the dark, I catch a faint glow on the distant horizon.

Faeya turns to follow my gaze. "First Moon," she mutters.

"We have to start moving again," Kahra says.

"Here." Faeya hands Kahra her lantern. She pulls off her gloves and tucks them both under one arm, then takes the compass from my hand and sets it flat on her palm.

Holding it out toward the light, she moves it around slightly, shifting her hand from one point, to another. "The needle should spin when I do this, right?"

"It should," Kahra confirms.

Faeya tilts her hand one way, then the other, giving the compass a little shake. She turns her body slowly in a half circle, watching the face for any change. Still nothing. She exhales through her nose, a short, frustrated sound, then gives it back to me. "Maybe it needs batteries? Like Kerr's megaphone."

I lift the compass once more and turn it over again. On the back, engraved into the metal, I spot the words *Property of Tamra V. Adjórde.* I look up at Faeya and Kahra. "This was Adjórde's."

"Yes," Kahra says. "She used it to navigate between the bridge and her cabin."

"That was where she stayed?" Faeya asks. "Over seven hundred years ago?"

"Yes," Kahra says again, leaving it at that.

I pull off my other glove and shift the compass so its base rests flat in the palm of my bare hand.

The moment it touches my skin, the needle jolts and begins to move.

24
KAHRA

Kahra moves carefully across the ice, each step measured, each shift of her weight deliberate.

The First Moon is in the distance, giving us just enough light to see in the darkness we've grown used to—without our lanterns.

Her gaze drifts over the surface as though searching for something hidden just beneath. She pauses, tilts her head, then takes another careful step. Faeya and I watch in silence, caught between curiosity and awe. Then she stops.

She crouches, bare fist pressed knuckles down against the ice. Slowly, she twists her wrist. *Crack!*

Another turn. *Crack!*

The sound is sharp and purposeful, like she's following a rhythm only she can hear. There's no sign of strain, only focus.

The ice holds until—CRACK! A spiderweb of fractures bursts outward from beneath her fist. She lifts her hand, revealing a shallow dent at the center of it all.

Spreading her fingers, she sets them lightly over the spot, encircling the opening. Her hand moves inward, almost closing around something invisible.

Inch by inch, the cracks darken and water begins to well up, then flow, spilling across the ice.

In one motion, she pulls a small tin cup from her satchel, slides it beneath the stream, and presses her thumb against the ice. The water climbs into the cup as if pulled by invisible threads, filling it to the brim.

When it's full, Kahra rises and offers it to Faeya. She hesitates, glancing at me as if unsure it's safe. Her shoulders tighten like she's bracing for poison. I take the cup from her hand and drink first.

The water is cold and clean. It runs sharp down my throat, biting at the edges of my chest. When I hold it out, Faeya finally lifts it to her lips and takes a careful sip.

Kahra doesn't move to join us.

"I'm not thirsty," she says, but something in her voice makes me think it's not thirst that keeps her from drinking. Her hand lingers too long near the satchel, as if guarding it with her life. I can't shake the feeling she doesn't want to share the cup with us.

The First Moon is high, casting enough light across the ice that we can see without the lanterns. Out here it seems brighter than it ever did back at the compound, the pale glow stretching farther and much sharper.

"I thought you said you couldn't control ice," I say.

Faeya hands the water back to me. I finish what's left and pass the cup to Kahra, who tucks it into her bag before answering.

"I can't. I drew the water upward and guided it until it broke through the surface on its own," she says.

I think about the cracks, the sharp way they split, extending in every direction.

I picture the water forcing its way out, almost like a weapon, breaking through the thick sheet beneath our feet.

For a moment, I look at Kahra, impressed. Her calm makes me feel small, like I've just watched a secret I was never supposed to see.

She looks unfazed, like this kind of thing happens every day. Then she says, "How long have you known?"

I frown. "Known what?"

Faeya glances at me, and I give her the same confused look. She makes a face that says she knows exactly what Kahra means—and that I should, too.

"Oh," I say. "Um... not long. Just a few days."

"How did you first find out?" she asks.

I take a second to think, eyes on the ice at my feet. "Faeya and I snuck into Barrack 10. I got scared and hid between a bunk and a dresser." I glance at Faeya. "She came in and should've seen me when she walked to the back, but later said she didn't."

The memory sits heavy for a moment before I continue. "Then I found out Adjórde could fold space around herself and hide in plain sight. At first, I didn't believe it." I shift my weight, feeling the cold through my boots. "But then

something happened with Abhishek, before our fight, where time felt like it slowed and a black hole started to form near him."

Faeya looks at me, surprised. She's hearing this for the first time. Her lips part beneath her scarf, but no words come, only a sharp breath.

"How do you know that about Adjórde?" Kahra says.

"I... read it in a journal," I stammer. "A journal Shosk told me about and left in Barrack 10. That's why we were there." I stop. "I mean, that's why I was there."

"*We* were there. Together," Faeya says, her eyes cutting toward me. Heat flashes in her voice, like she wants Kahra to hear the whole truth.

Kahra nods and drops it. "We have to go," she says. "And we have to move fast."

As we're getting ready to leave, the ground shifts beneath our feet. A low rumble rolls through it. Kahra moves the way she always does on ice, sweeping her right foot behind her body and rotating sideways. She looks up, toward the distance. Faeya and I follow her gaze.

At first, what I see is small, but I know what it is. A truck. Just like the one Joll brought me in when he took me to the Isolation Box. It grows larger as it moves toward us. My heart drops. The sound of the chains grinds against my skull, familiar and merciless. Faeya gasps, taking several steps back like she's about to run.

We're caught, and there's nowhere for us to go.

Faeya bolts, or tries to, but her feet only shuffle against the ice before she slips and goes down hard on her shoulder. She cries out, rolling onto her back and clutching it.

I drop to my knees beside her to help her sit up. Her face twists, teeth clenched against the pain. When I look back at Kahra, she hasn't moved. She's still standing sideways to the approaching truck, right foot behind her, both hands angled toward the ground, her eyes never leaving it.

We can't run. Faeya's hurt, and Kahra won't move.

The ground shakes harder. Then it cracks—not like when Kahra pulled water for us to drink, but a deep, violent break that splits the foundation beneath us. Like the night I saw her, Joll, and Fellows, then felt the ground move under me... only much worse this time.

I'm thrown back, landing beside Faeya and sliding several feet. I push up to my knees, trying to steady myself.

The truck is closer now. I can see the chains wrapped around its tires. Like the ones Faeya told me about.

The ground moves again, even harder.

One last time, the ice shifts, then cracks wide, splitting into a pit so deep that water bursts to the surface, spilling across the terrain.

I tear my eyes from the truck and focus on Kahra. *It's her.*

One arm is extended toward it, palm flat, fingers pressed tightly together. The other hand is near her side, palm down, fingers just as straight. Her gaze is locked, her body still. She moves the water. She breaks the ice.

In one sharp motion, she rotates the hand near her side, like turning a lock into place. The front end of the truck plunges into the water fifty feet ahead of us.

She shifts her stance, switching her weight to the other foot, bringing her opposite shoulder forward. Her hands

mirror the previous position. Another turn of her lower hand, and the ground beneath the back tires opens, sending the rest of the truck into the water.

Only the fractured ice beneath its body keeps it from sinking completely, but it's trapped. It isn't going anywhere.

Two doors slam open, one on each side, and two figures dash out onto the broken bits of ice, barely avoiding falling into the water.

On the left is the woman with the scarf wrapped around her head, the same one I saw meeting with Kerr before. Helmsman Iman. And on the right is the last person I'd ever want to see again. *Joll.*

25

UNCHARTERED TERRITORY

Helmsman Iman's hand goes to the stick at her waist. She slides it free from its holster, the motion quick and practiced.

She's got a glove on her free hand, not one like ours but one that matches the uniform she's wearing. None on the other.

She and Joll close in on us. I stand, pulling Faeya up with me. Kahra hasn't moved, but with whatever Iman's holding and the look in Joll's eyes, there's no way she can handle this on her own.

Joll yanks his hood back, then tears the scarf down from his mouth.

The sight of him uncovered sends a ripple through the air around us, like the threat is more real now that it has a face.

I can feel Faeya's heavy breathing beside me as much as the tingling starting to rise in my spine, fingers, and arms. It stops at my neck and sits there, pulsing. Her eyes flick over to me, and she shifts to the side and out of the way.

Iman's expression goes wide when she sees me, and she glances over at Joll as they come to what seems like a quiet understanding.

He drops his chin, his gaze locking on me like we're the only two here, his face going paler than it already is.

The ice creaks under our boots, a reminder of how thin the line is between standing and falling.

Kahra looks back at me, blinks, then turns to Joll again, resetting her stance.

Joll takes two steps forward, his eyes still locked on me behind Kahra. He pushes both arms out in front of him, palms facing forward, then in one slow, continuous motion pulls them back toward his chest, rotating them and rising with the movement, before stepping forward again and throwing his hands out at us.

The air starts to move, slow at first, then whipping fast and hard enough to shove us across the ice.

Faeya and I grab onto each other to keep from falling. Kahra holds her ground, no doubt locked to the water under her feet.

I try to push forward to reach her but can't. The wind steals my breath, forcing my head down.

Faeya slams to the ground again, crying out. The sound cuts sharper than the wind itself, pulling at something deep in me.

Behind Joll, Iman stands untouched, a sinister grin on her face. Everything behind him is still. The chaos is aimed at us, and only us.

I slide and fall on the ice, crashing into Faeya before rolling off to her side and onto my stomach.

From the ground, I look up at Joll. His hands ball into fists, and the air closes in, pressing us tighter together. I gasp, but no breath comes.

Faeya rolls toward me, clawing at my coat, her eyes wide and bulging, lips turning blue. She grabs at her own neck, yanking at her collar. Her mouth opens, but nothing comes out, no breath from either of us.

The world narrows to the frantic drum of my heartbeat and the burning in my chest.

Kahra turns toward us and looks down, her face and lips the same blue as Faeya's. She stares for a moment, and the usual emptiness in her eyes drops away.

She leans into the wind, forcing herself to turn back to Joll, fighting against the current with everything she's got. She raises both hands high above her head, palms flat, and slams them down toward the ice.

Her hands hit hard, the impact rippling out beneath us, leveling the surface and sending all of us, Joll and Iman included, into the water.

I panic. I don't know how to swim.

The cold hits like knives, stabbing through my coat and sinking straight to the bone.

Faeya and I grab at the larger broken pieces of ice, pulling ourselves toward a nearby stretch that's still whole. We haul ourselves up, water streaming off us.

Out of the corner of my eye, I catch Joll and Iman doing the same.

When she comes out of the water, the scarf around her head has slipped back to her neck, exposing hair as white as the Adjórdean moon. Joll turns to her, and she scrambles to

pull it back over her head, searching for it with frantic hands. For some reason, he looks away, like he's seen something he shouldn't, and locks his focus back on us.

The strangeness of that moment lingers, even in the middle of the fight.

When my vision clears, Kahra is kneeling on a big chunk of ice floating in the water. When it turns and starts heading for us, I realize she's moving it. Steering it.

Iman pulls her scarf back over her head as best she can, tucking it in place with quick, rough movements.

She crouches low, raking her hands through the water until her fingers find the stick she'd been holding before she fell in. She grips it tight, then straightens and takes off with Joll in our direction, leaping from one block of ice to the next until they land on the solid, unbroken foundation, feet unsteady on the ground beneath them.

When Kahra crashes into us, we're shoved onto the solid ground on the other side.

"We can't run," she says, never taking her eyes off them.

She's right. I look over at Faeya and push myself to my feet.

Joll and Iman are halfway to us when I decide to let go, just like in the Isolation Box and just like with Abhishek outside and in the barrack. *Fear has held me back long enough.*

My hands go numb, the tingling flooding up my arms until it's in my chest, my neck, my head. The air feels heavier, bending around me, pulling in tight like the world is folding over itself. My vision sharpens and narrows at the same time, every sound muffled except the pounding in my ears.

The ground under my boots seems to shift, as if something beneath it is answering me. It feels alive, like the planet itself has been waiting for this moment.

I watch as Joll starts to bring his hands to his chest again, but before they get there I step back, slipping into the same darkness I once sat in inside Barrack 10. Back then, I was crouched in a corner, hiding in fear. This time, I don't hide.

I lean into it and let myself get lost. The colors return, and I watch as Kahra and Faeya look around, wide-eyed, like they've lost me and can't seem to find me. Faeya is panicked, and though Kahra can't see me either, she stays her usual unwavering self.

Joll and Iman glance at each other, then back at us.

I decide to take a step.

When I lift my leg, it's like I'm floating. But I'm not. I try to steady myself, to get a grip on the feeling.

It's weightless but heavy at the same time. I have to stay focused, to hold onto that almost lifeless sensation I know keeps me shrouded.

I take another step, same focus, same feeling, then a few more until I'm standing beside Joll.

I don't know what to do, so I lift my hands to push him, planning to send him toppling into the water nearby. But instead, he flies across the ice, skidding hard and slamming into the surface so violently his head bounces.

The shock of it rips me back into view, and Iman turns toward me. The stick in her hand bursts into flames, the fire stretching far past its length.

Kahra and Faeya take off in my direction.

She swings the stick toward me again and again, and I twist and sidestep, weaving away from its fiery blade. I feel the heat every time it sweeps past my face.

She raises her gloved hand in a tight fist, and it ignites. She pulls back, ready to drive a fiery punch at me.

The heat stings my skin before she even lands the blow.

In the background, Joll drives toward us, another wall of wind coming with him. But he can't avoid Iman this time. She's in the line of fire with us.

She opens her hand and grabs Faeya by the hood. Smoke rises from her parka, the fur lining catching fire.

Kahra shifts her weight, and the ground moves beneath us again as we all fight to stay upright.

Faeya claws at Iman's hand, trying to rip it away, but her mittens ignite, burning holes straight through them.

The ground shifts again, Joll's wind pushing at us, forcing Iman to release her.

Faeya pulls away, but her hands are now on fire.

Iman goes pale. "The bitch burns!" she shouts, a wild look crossing her face.

Faeya screams and drops to the ice, plunging her hands into the water until the flames sputter out.

The hiss of steam fills the air, as sharp as her cry.

Joll reaches Kahra and grabs her.

I step aside, take the pike pole from my back, and pull it free. I swing it up over my head, and as it comes around my body—aimed at whichever of them it may hit—I feel it. The same black hole I made appear around Abhishek takes shape behind me.

It hits like a wave, a surge of tangled emotions mixed with clouded, dark thoughts. It's dense and heavy, and I feel the head of my pike pole cut through it as it arcs behind my back, circling over my head, sending a rippling sensation down the handle and into my body, like it's been charged.

Joll ducks, almost avoiding it, but Iman doesn't move. The pike pole slams high into her shoulder, the impact nothing like when it hits the ice.

Out of habit, I pull back the same way I would with the saw, the same way I'd lift the it from a block of ice. She topples forward over Joll, grabbing him as she goes, and they crash into the water together.

Kahra's eyes shine with tears as she looks over at us. She takes a deep breath, presses the first two fingers of each hand together, and starts moving them in slow, deliberate circles, one after the other. The thin layer of water floating just above Joll and Iman's heads begins to swirl, spinning so hard they can't break through. Iman manages to get a hand past it, but the current catches her and drags her back down. I glance at Faeya, then back at Kahra, then down at Joll and Iman as they thrash, fighting to reach the surface again.

Kahra never takes her eyes off them, watching as they punch against the water and her hold on it. Faeya and I stand off to the side, as she works, keeping them under without a flicker of hesitation. We glance at each other again, then back down at the water. *It's stopped moving.*

The moment it stills and they stop fighting, Kahra clenches her fists, pulling them to her body like she's lifting something, and takes several steps back.

Both of them rise. Her shoulders strain as she hauls their weight upward until they flop onto the ice, motionless. She spreads her hands wide, one over each of them, and water gushes from both their mouths and noses. Joll coughs. Iman's chest lifts. But neither of them stirs.

Without a word, Kahra turns on her heel and starts walking again in the direction we'd been headed before Joll and Iman showed up.

Faeya falls in step behind Kahra. I sling the pole onto my back, glance down at them one last time, then follow after her.

26

A PLOT. A PLAN. A DEVICE.

We walk fast until the ground under our feet starts to change. The ice goes from dense to thin, and eventually turns dark brown. Frozen. Hard. And unmistakable from photos I've seen. *Dirt.*

As much as I want to stop, to dig my fingers into it and tear up handfuls until it crumbles in my palm, I don't. Faeya stares at it as we walk, her gaze locked on, glancing back at me every so often. We come to a silent understanding: shock.

"The sticks," she says, "on the map." She jerks her chin toward the distance.

I turn to look. *Trees.* Leafless, white with dark gray markings, branches reaching out in every direction.

At least a dozen clusters in sight, scattered on both sides of us, stretching farther than we can see. I can't wrap my head around it. Who knew Adjórde had earth on it. Who knew it had trees.

We move faster now. The rope is long gone, left behind with the dark. Joll and Iman's lifeless bodies flash through my mind again.

Kahra picks up a light jog, and for the first time in my life, I do too.

Running on dirt feels impossible to describe. On ice, every step is measured, my balance shifting with the smallest movement, every footfall placed like it might be my last. Here, the ground grips back.

It's solid under me, steady and unyielding, so I can push harder, take longer strides, almost launch myself forward. The dirt crunches under my boots and catches me each time I land.

I still feel unsteady, but not because of the ground. It's the air. My body lifts and falls, and I'm careful to make sure each foot touches down exactly how it left.

Faeya runs ahead, her hands flailing at her sides, her steps clumsy but sure.

Her laughter slips out between breaths, raw and strange, the kind that comes from feeling something new for the very first time. We run until we can't anymore. Slowing down, wheezing.

Running is hard. Harder than working the caves. Years of sawing, hauling, and moving ice haven't prepared me for this. We come to a stop and I lean over, clutching my sides. Pain shoots up my legs. Faeya bends forward and vomits the little food and water we'd managed to put down earlier.

Kahra walks up beside her, and for a second I expect her to help. Instead, she holds out the small cup we drank from

earlier. "Here," she says. "If your hands catch fire again, hold on to this."

Faeya looks up, and for a moment I think she might just lunge at Kahra. She stands, breathing hard. "Why would I need that?" She takes deep, staggered breaths, then heaves again, but nothing comes out. There's nothing left.

"It's made from Adjórdean steel," Kahra says. "It will help ground you when you combust."

Faeya glances at me. I shrug.

She takes the cup from Kahra, turns it in her hands a few times, then shoves it into her pocket.

I decide to take the moment to look at a tree nearby. As I pass Kahra, I ask how much time we have left.

"The first ship should be leaving in about thirty minutes," she says.

Faeya spits, her voice sharp. "How do you know what time it is?"

"The moons," Kahra answers. "Their positioning in the sky. They shift slightly every thirty minutes or so." She says it so matter-of-factly that I feel stupid for never thinking of it myself. But I never needed to tell time. The Moon-Cycle Bell and the Elders always told me when to come or go. I only know when one will set and the other rise because I can see them in the sky, but never thought to track their changes.

I walk toward the nearest tree. When I reach it, I pull off my hood, and stuff my scarf and gloves into my front pocket. Then I touch it.

The bark is smooth but faintly gritty, with shallow ridges that catch against my fingertips. It rises straight out of the ground, the base disappearing into dark soil I've only

ever seen in books. I look down and trace the uneven shape where trunk meets earth, noticing small cracks in the dirt where thin roots push through.

The smell rises faintly, damp and foreign, making my chest ache with something close to homesickness for a place I don't remember.

I walk back over to Faeya and Kahra.

Faeya is crouched on the ground, chewing at a piece of bread she must have taken from Kahra's satchel. Kahra stands in place, staring off into the distance at nothing in particular. Neither of them speaks.

Faeya looks defeated—quieter than her usual self.

"We need to talk about what happened," I say.

Faeya looks up at me from the ground, her expression twisted with disgust. Then she glances over at Kahra, who doesn't seem to notice us at all.

"Joll. Iman," I say, stepping up beside Kahra. "Will they live?"

"Voiyt," Faeya adds.

Kahra exhales—a heavy, drawn out sigh, the kind she does when talking about something she'd rather not. "I can't say for sure what will happen to any of them. I can only say it was not my intention for anyone to die."

I look back at Faeya. She turns her head away.

"How did you learn to do that?" I ask. "To control your Potential that way?"

Kahra looks at me, making direct eye contact for maybe the second time ever. "We do not control the elements. We are honored to wield them."

The conviction in her voice rattles me more than the fight we just survived.

I shake my head, and she shifts her attention back to the distance. "The elements are an extension of who we are. I am never fully sure of what I can do until I do it. I release, set my intention, and trust."

"Your intention?" Faeya cuts in, her voice sharp. "So you just *mean* to do it and it's done? Because I definitely don't mean for my hands to catch fire. I'd actually rather they didn't."

Kahra turns away from me, toward Faeya. "It is most difficult for people from your faction," she says, her voice flat. "You need something to channel your fire through. Something that can withstand its power. Like Adjórdean steel."

My mind goes to the pike pole on my back, the way it grounded me when I grabbed it and how I felt it charge in my hands when its metal head passed through the energy surging behind me when fighting off Joll and Iman.

I walk over to Faeya and kneel beside her. "Can I see?" I hold my hands out.

She glances up at me, hesitates, then sets the bread on the ground and places her hands in mine. Her gloves are burned, and through the holes I can see patches of red skin, small blisters rising to the surface. My stomach drops.

"I'm sorry, Faeya," is all I can say as I look back up at her, her eyes swelling with tears.

"I didn't ask for this, Akasha."

"None of us did," Kahra says, and I realize she's been listening the whole time.

"Just..." I pause. "Keep the cup near." I don't know what else to say. I don't even have a hold on my own Potential, let alone the right words to encourage her or make her feel better.

"Intention?" I say, looking back at Kahra. I stand and move to a spot halfway between her and Faeya. *It makes sense.* Every time I've cleared my mind and let go of worry or lingering thoughts, that's when I've felt most in control—or most aware of the power running through my body.

I could feel the world around me, and it was like isolating the one thing I could reach for... *ether.* Invisible, like air, but almost impossible to move. It's like striking a cave wall that refuses to break, over and over, until you give up and accept the wall isn't there. Then it shifts.

Or maybe it's me that actually gives—and that's what allows me to move, to become one with it. So many things have happened since I first felt this power. The colors. The folding of space around me. The way time seems to slow, and the gaping holes that tear open in thin air.

I notice Kahra and Faeya staring at me. I don't know how long I've been frozen here, lost in thought.

"Thirty minutes isn't enough time," I say.

"I know," Kahra replies.

"So if you know, why did you keep counting the time?" Faeya snaps.

I look at Kahra, the same question now sitting heavy in my mind.

"If we miss the first ships, we'll have to get on the next set," Kahra says. "By then, the whole compound will know we're gone—especially if Joll and Iman don't return."

Faeya and I trade a look. She swallows hard, and I can't help picturing their still bodies laid out on the ice.

"If they do return," Kahra continues, "they'll have told the Foremen. And none of the ships will leave until they find us."

I nod. "Well, we're not going to make the first," I say. "So I guess that's it."

"They're going to kill us," Faeya adds.

I keep my gaze forward. Her words feel true. What we've done goes so far beyond the rules, there's no way they'll let us back inside the compound. They won't send us to New-Earth either. I figure they'll keep us in the Isolation Box for the rest of our lives. Separate us. Maybe send Kahra back, since her potential is worth more to New-Earth.

The weight of it presses on me harder than Joll's wind ever did.

A sudden thought hits me, and I decide to ask—just to see what she says. "What do you know about Adjórde?" I say to Kahra.

"I've already told you what I know."

I walk up to her. "What do you know about the bridge? The hole. And what it has to do with her?"

Kahra steps away from me, pacing, still staring into the distance. I follow her gaze but see nothing—just trees jutting out of frozen dirt, stretching far beyond sight.

"It was an experiment gone wrong," she says. "She went against what she was told—to stop working with ether and the idea of interdimensional transit. Wormholes. She didn't listen. She kept going in secret, and it went terribly wrong,

tearing a chasm in Earth's atmosphere so big she couldn't close it."

"So it's her fault we're all here," Faeya says, more an afterthought than a question.

Kahra looks at her but neither agrees nor disagrees.

I take in her words, thinking about how I share a part of the woman who caused the chaos we're living in.

"The tear remains open," Kahra continues, "and through it, water from New-Earth's surface has been slowly evaporating. As I understand it, there's one body of water left, on the opposite side of the portal we're going to."

I study her words. "What do you mean, the portal *we're going to*? Is this not the only opening?"

Kahra shakes her head. "Adjórde opened the one that leads to this planet after the first was already there."

Faeya shifts her weight, standing. "Her solution to the problem was to create another?"

"We're taught," Kahra says, "that opening the second actually stabilized the first and slowed the water's evaporation. The two polarities created a balance—with the water moving toward the portal on Adjórde while the other pulls it back, for evaporation."

I try to follow what she's saying, but some of it gets lost in the way it sounds. It's like she simply echoes back things the way she's learned them.

Kahra sighs again. She looks at Faeya, then at me. "Adjórde died here. By choice."

"What?" I say. My expression shifts.

Faeya looks just as confused.

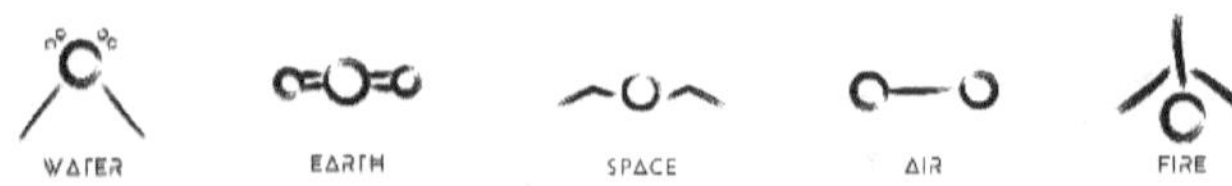

"The two portals create two opposite polarities," Kahra says. "Like a push and pull. There cannot be a third." She turns toward me, eyes me for a moment, then walks away.

I look over at Faeya, then off into the distance.

"The compass," Kahra continues. "When you put it in your hand, it activated, but it pointed in the opposite direction. She takes a few steps forward. "If you return to New-Earth, it would throw off the balance between the two portals. There's no telling what would happen. Adjórde chose to remain here to protect the planet from what she had done. If you go back..." She stops.

I reach for the compass, pull it from my pocket, then rest it in the palm of my hand. The needle jumps, spins in place, then stops. Its arrow points in the direction we're going. I turn to Faeya and show her.

"The needle," I say, loud enough for Kahra to hear. "It's pointing toward the bridge. The direction we're going."

I'm flustered, trying to make sense of what she's saying... what she could be implying.

She never turns her attention to me. "What color is the side that's pointing the way we're headed?" she asks.

I lean in over the compass and squint, tilting my hand so the light catches what little color is left. "Red," I say. Then I look up at her.

"We've been traveling south, but the compass is pointing north—meaning you're the magnetic opposite. The magnetic opposite of this portal. True North."

To make sense of what she's saying, I turn in the opposite direction, the compass still flat in my palm.

I watch the needle jolt again, then rotate, its red end settling in the direction of the compound—like it's warning me to stay away from the bridge.

Instead of directing us, it's trying to direct me.

"Why would they teach you all of this?" Faeya says, her voice shaky. She looks at me, her eyes flashing with concern as she starts to understand what Kahra's saying too. "Why would they give you all of this information?"

Kahra turns and walks back, joining us, forming a loose triangle. "New-Earth is dying," she says, "and they don't have long left. They've got everyone working on a solution—even the Junior Elders. Especially those of us with water Potential. It's no longer about secrecy. It's about survival."

"Then why not tell the rest of us?" I ask.

"To avoid panic," Kahra says.

"No," Faeya adds. "To maintain control."

I deflate. If they were able to solve this problem on their own, would they have even told the Junior Elders? Would they have let us go afterwards—or would that have exposed whatever they've been doing here, for however long they've been doing it?

"You're right," I say to Faeya. "They want to protect their secret, not us."

"So what now?" she says. "You just... stay here? And don't go back with us?" She looks at Kahra. "We're supposed to just leave without Akasha?"

Kahra keeps her eyes on the ground. "I just need you to be aware of what you'd be risking by crossing through the bridge, Akasha. I don't know what would happen if a third

singularity were to appear on New-Earth. Especially right now."

The word "singularity" runs through my mind, but I let it go.

Faeya huffs. "But if Adjórde opened it, then maybe Akasha could close it?"

Her words hit me like a block of ice, and the world spins out of view. I can barely handle sneaking to the bridge. How am I supposed to go to New-Earth, find the portal and somehow close it.

I don't even know what I'm doing.

A shock runs through me as I process it all.

If Adjórde herself couldn't close the portal—and it's been open for seven hundred years with no one being able to—how am I supposed to? I look at Faeya, then at the ice.

"I don't know how that would work," Kahra says. "I was only taught that people have tried, but no one can get close enough. Even when traveling through the bridge between New-Earth and Adjórde, the Foremen take shelter deep within ships made of Adjórdean steel to safely travel through, and they don't surface again until they're far enough away on the other side."

"But..." Faeya starts, "you said Shosk went back because he can get near it. So surely someone else can."

"Shosk would not be the first person to try. Many have not survived. Even in the ships, you can't linger too long— they only provide temporary safety, just long enough to cross through. Only Adjórde could get near and travel through it unharmed."

Faeya looks at me again, and I don't know what to say. I shake my head and think on everything. Kahra clasps her arms behind her back, and Faeya folds hers across her chest.

"Then I'll stay," I say. "But I'll make sure I get you two there safely—and I won't leave until I see you off."

"We're not leaving you, Akasha." Faeya turns toward me. "Not after all of this. Not after everything we've been through."

I know "we" includes Kahra now too, but a big part of that we means us. I can hear it in the rasp that rides her voice.

"I'll help you to the second wave of ships," I say. "And if I have to, I'll do what I can to distract them until you get away."

"We're not leaving you," Faeya repeats. "We will figure this out."

I just look at her, and my heart sinks. I don't want to leave them either. I want to be there with them, on the other side, but not if it's going to do more harm than good.

"You're right," I say. "We have to stick together." I lie.

Kahra drops her head. "Two hours," she says.

I nod. "Let's go then."

Faeya perks up, as much as she can after everything that has happened. We collect ourselves and keep walking, and in my head, I start making my own plan to get them both back... safely.

27
POINT OF NO RETURN

"This is the last of it," Kahra says, pulling out one-and-a-half pieces of bread and a few dried berries. She hands them to us, and we split them.

We don't talk about me staying anymore. That was decided already, and nothing's changed as far as I'm concerned.

Faeya walks up beside Kahra and says something low enough that I can't hear. Kahra glances at her, then nods. The two of them walk off toward a small cluster of trees. The way the trunks lean together makes a kind of wall, hiding them from view.

I watch them go, curious, but don't call out. When they slip out of sight, I squint, trying to see between the gaps, but the angle's no good.

After a moment, I turn and head for another set of trees a little farther away. Using the bathroom with girls around, especially while on the run, has been awkward. I figure they probably feel the same. Chances are, they're doing exactly what I'm about to do.

When I get back, Kahra's already there, sitting on the ground and finishing the rest of her bread. She doesn't look up, just brushes crumbs from her hands and keeps chewing.

I tore a strip of fabric from the bag and used it to tie back my hair, which kept falling into my face and blocking my view.

The air is still cold, but nothing like it was back on the compound. Out here, the chill doesn't bite the same way. It settles instead, the kind of cold you notice but can move through.

When Faeya returns, she gives me a quick look from the corner of her eye as she straightens her coat. Her fingers run over her hair, pressing it down where it's still sticking up from when we fell in the water.

She's taken off her gloves, scarf, and hood, same as me.

Kahra looks up as Faeya walks past and sits beside her, then glances down at me before turning back to what's left of her food.

I lean forward, elbows on my knees, and think about how I'm going to pull it off—getting her and Faeya on the ship without them realizing I'm not going.

I picture them climbing aboard, the gates closing, the engines starting. Safe. Out of reach. And I'm still here.

It's not just getting them on that worries me. It's what happens after. Them... without me.

The Elders won't be there, but Earth has its own dangers. *New-Earth* means new dangers.

I pull the compass from my pocket again and place it in my hand. The arrow swings and the red side stops, still

pointing in the direction of the bridge. A not-so-gentle reminder that this isn't right.

I glance over my shoulder, back in the direction it's pointing. The compound lies that way.

Maybe that's the truth of it—my job is to stay here. To go back. Maybe I'm meant to help the other Miners, the ones still living in the shadow of the lies the Elders have wrapped around them.

I decide to ask Kahra how much time we have again. She looks up at the sky, both moons present, and studies them for a brief moment. "One hour."

I look up and try to make sense of it myself, but can't. Again, I wish I'd taken time to pay more attention to things like this. To learn more.

"How far are we?" I ask.

Kahra doesn't say anything. I know that means she's thinking now, not ignoring me. She just doesn't show it the way I do when I need someone to know I'm pausing to make sense of something.

"About thirty minutes."

Faeya speaks. "Have you been here before? To the sea?"

Kahra shakes her head. "No."

Faeya looks at me before asking, "So how do you know how far we are?"

"Maps," Kahra says. "We study and are required to memorize them." She looks around. "But they're not as detailed as this." She taps at the dirt beneath her where she sits.

I ask, "But you knew we were supposed to be heading in this direction though? Southeast?"

"Yes, Akasha," she sighs, shifting and then rising to stand. "But the map is a flat view, and being on the ground is very different. Bearings are necessary." She glances down at the compass still resting in my hand, the red arrow screaming at me to go back.

"We should start moving again," I say, standing up. I tuck the compass back into my pocket, then walk to a nearby cluster of leafless trees where I decide to hide the scarf and gloves I'd stuffed there, leaving them behind. Faeya does the same.

We both look at Kahra, who stares back at us, or maybe through us, her hood still on, gloves, and scarf packed into her satchel.

Faeya shrugs, and we head off in the direction of the sea. "This has to work," she says, out of nowhere, cutting through the silence as we walk. "I can't go back." Her voice cracks on the last word, the sound sharper than the cold wind.

The silence lingers.

I'm about to reply when Kahra speaks first. "When we get to the sea," she says, "we'll have to climb down the side of a cliff to reach the shore."

"A cliff?" Faeya says.

"A big hill, if that makes more sense to you."

"How do they get the supplies and Foremen up the cliff?" I ask.

"They don't," Kahra says. "They pick them up in trucks and drive around. Which is why we haven't run into them bringing their last rounds of supplies."

"No," Faeya says. "Just Joll and Iman."

"They came looking," Kahra says. "Probably sent in secret."

"Kerr," I say. "He probably doesn't want to raise an alarm."

"He doesn't want to look bad," Faeya adds. "But I don't understand why he'd send that Helmsman lady."

"They're close," Kahra interrupts.

"Close?" I ask.

Kahra speaks, but not to answer me. "There." She points into the distance.

Faeya and I stop beside her. Far off, a horizon stretches further than my eyes can see—a line that marks a body of water more vast than anything I've ever imagined.

The Adjórdean Sea. Something I didn't even know existed until just hours ago. From here, I can almost see it moving, the waves curving upward and downward like the image in the book. I take it in, and so does Faeya.

The endless shimmer of it steals the breath from my chest.

"I want to show you something," I say to Kahra. I kneel on one knee and take my boot off, pulling the soaked journal from the bottom. I hold it in my hand—as lifeless as Joll and Iman were when we left them. I already knew it would be destroyed when we fell into the water, but what could I do about it?

Faeya's mouth drops; she hadn't considered it being damaged. I look at her and grin.

"We got what we needed," I say, grinning back at her assuredly.

Kahra eyes it, and when she doesn't say anything, I speak. "Adjórde's journal. Details about what she learned and knew while she was here."

Kahra cocks her head to the side and looks at me and Faeya from the corner of her eye. "So you knew before I even told you?"

"No," I say. "We only knew something was off about Adjórde, and that we weren't being told the truth about why we were really here. But we had no idea that any of this was even real." I hold out my hand and gesture to the surroundings, then downward at Faeya's hands.

"Why didn't you tell me?" Kahra says to Faeya.

Faeya squints back. "It wasn't my secret to tell. The book is Akasha's."

"Shosk left it for me," I say. "Told me where to find it."

"In Barrack 10?" Kahra says. "That's the book Evan told you about?"

I nod.

Kahra shoots Faeya another look, and Faeya seems taken aback. She's still looking at her when her voice sharpens. "You kept that from me?"

Faeya frowns. "What are you talking about?"

"The book," Kahra says. "Why wouldn't you tell me?"

"It's Akasha's journal," Faeya says. "And I didn't know if we could trust you."

"I trusted you," Kahra says. "When Akasha was sent to the Isolation Box, I went to you. I told you what was happening. I risked everything to leave the compound with you to find him. Then I told you both everything I know about Adjórde. About the Elders. About the bridge. I answered

every question." Her voice falters, and the sound feels heavier than any storm we've faced.

It catches for a second, like a stutter. It's the first time I've ever heard her sound like this. Her body tenses and I think she might cry. I watch her, trying to read the situation, but I don't want to make the wrong move and do something that could make it worse. The air feels still, like it's waiting to see what she does next.

Faeya crosses her arms. "You're acting like I lied to you."

"You didn't tell me the truth," Kahra says. "This isn't a regular book."

"It wasn't my place," Faeya says. "Sometimes trust means keeping your word."

Kahra's eyes narrow. "Sometimes it means not making the person you're with feel like a fool."

"You're not a fool," Faeya says. "But you're acting like one right now."

The words land hard. Kahra's shoulders pull back and her hands curl into fists. I glance between them. This is not just anger. It's hard for Kahra to show anything like this. And Faeya doesn't back down.

For a moment neither of them moves. The space between them feels like a stretched wire ready to snap.

Kahra's voice hardens. "You wouldn't even be here if I hadn't told you about the plan in the first place. Akasha and I would have been long gone if we didn't have to carry the weight of an extra person."

Her words slice clean, sharper than her single-blade plow.

Something in me shifts. Up until now I thought I could just let them work this out, but I can see it's heading somewhere worse. Faeya shakes her hands out once, quick, then clenches them together the way she does when her Potential starts to rise. She's holding herself back, hiding it from Kahra, not wanting to show weakness.

Kahra shifts her weight, planting her feet the way she does when she's bracing for something. I step in closer, standing between them.

Faeya fumes. "You were an afterthought," she says to Kahra. "Akasha only came to you as a last resort. Otherwise, you wouldn't even be here."

I look over at Faeya, and out of nowhere her hands ignite, flames climbing up her fingers. She screams and drops to the ground, writhing in pain. There's no ice or water in sight. Only hard dirt and bare trees.

I remember the cup Kahra gave her and rush to reach into the front of her parka as her screams grow louder. She looks like she wants to bury her face in her hands but hesitates, catching herself before she does.

She calls my name, looking into my eyes, and I pull the cup out, place it in her hand, and grab her other wrist.

My skin burns where it's too close to the fire for too long, but I don't let her know. I rub my hand down the side of my parka hard to push the pain away.

Faeya wraps both hands around the cup, leans forward until her head touches the ground, and sobs.

When I look over at Kahra, she's standing straight now, both hands at her sides, looking down at us.

I get back up and look between the two of them. There's no way they'll make it there or even survive on New-Earth like this.

"This has to stop," I say, as calm as I possibly can. I look around at us, standing in the middle of nowhere. Joll and Iman's bodies flash through my mind again. So does Voiyt's.

I look over at Faeya, her grip fiercely tight on the cup. A small, faint flame rests just inside.

Tears stream down her face as she watches it, the flame waving back at her. Her hands are red, bruised, and not likely to heal... like Kerr's. A reminder of everything she's had to do for us to get here.

Every sacrifice she's made to help me find out what happened to Shosk, and the pain she's caused others and herself. I bear the weight of that.

And Kahra too. If I hadn't gone to her in the first place, she wouldn't be here with us. I've pushed her far outside her comfort zone. As strong as she is, as distant and emotionally removed as she can seem, she feels and cares just as deeply as we do.

When my head stops reeling, I add, "We're almost there. Look how far we've come." I look to Faeya. "You're right. We can't go back from here." And when I say we, I know I mean them, but now is not the time to explain this. "So we have to keep going forward."

I help Faeya to her feet. She winces as she rises, the cup still in her hand. I pull her close from the side, a hug that won't hurt her hands. "I'm sorry," I say. "This is my fault, and we'll finish what we started that night in Ten." I nod at her.

"Kahra, we wouldn't be here without you," I say, looking over to her. I slowly approach, pulling Faeya with me. "The only way we make it off this planet is together."

Kahra lifts her gaze to me. Her eyes get wider than usual and lock with mine. "You're right."

"I should have told you about the journal earlier," I say. "Exactly what it was. But it didn't seem relevant until now. And honestly, you've been more helpful than it has anyway." Her expression warms just a bit, only enough for me to no-tice.

"Faeya, from day one, you've had my back and I've had yours." She tries to smile through the pain, and I know she hears me. "We've got this," I say, looking to both of them.

I let go of Faeya, the compass still clutched in my hand, closed from when I secured it while digging into her pocket for the cup.

I open it. The needle tells me to go back, but I push forward in the opposite direction, with Kahra and Faeya in tow, determined to get them to safety and their freedom.

28
FROM THIN AIR

The ground changes under our feet again.

The frozen dirt softens, each step sinking just a little. Patches of green push through, spreading until the hard earth is covered in grass. Trees here are different—thicker trunks, their bark dark and rough, and small leaves beginning to sprout at the ends of their branches.

We slow without meaning to. Kahra steps ahead and crouches briefly, running her hand over the grass. She rubs her palm against her parka before straightening. Faeya lingers, looking down at it but not touching, her hands still raw and marked even without the cup in them.

I kneel and press my palm flat against the blades, letting them bend under my skin. They're soft. Cool in a way that feels alive. I close my eyes for a moment, taking in the texture, the faint scent rising from the soil.

When I look up, Kahra is already moving again. Faeya glances at me once before following. I give the grass one last sweep of my hand, then push myself up and trail after them.

It thickens as we move, the green stretching out between the trees like a carpet. The air is different here too. It still holds a bite, but it's softer, carrying the faint smell of damp soil. Somewhere above, a branch creaks, the sound deeper and heavier than the brittle cracks back in the frozen part.

The ground gives slightly under each step. My boots leave shallow impressions that spring back almost as soon as I lift my foot. The trees grow farther apart, their trunks wider, their roots twisting together in ridges just beneath the surface. Tiny buds hang from the thinner branches, pale against the dark bark.

It feels strange after so many days surrounded by ice and hard dirt. My eyes keep going to the green, scanning for more of it, letting the color pull me forward.

Kahra doesn't speak. Her pace stays steady, and every so often her head turns, like she's checking something only she can see. Faeya keeps her eyes forward too, her hands hanging stiff at her sides.

We move in silence, the quiet thick enough to notice every sound. The rustle of leaves in a small breeze. The dull thud of my boots against the softer soil. The faint click of something settling far off.

For the first time in my life, sweat gathers on my skin. *Real sweat.* Beads slide down my face, and I wipe them away with the back of my bare hand.

I think this might actually work. But the thought drags another with it. How am I going to get them to leave without me? And what happens when they actually make it to the other side? To New-Earth.

"Can we stop for a minute?" I ask, slowing my steps until they notice.

"Not really," Kahra says without looking back.

"It's important," I tell her. "We need to talk about the plan. For when we get there."

Kahra stops, reluctantly, and Faeya pulls up beside her.

"Can't we figure it out when we get there?" Faeya asks.

"No," I say. "We need to talk about it now."

My voice comes out firmer than I expect, the urgency shaking through my chest.

I turn to Kahra. "What's on the other side?"

"Water," she says.

"That's it?" I ask.

The sigh comes. "We're taught that a renegade group, ones who broke from the original treaty meant to unite the Water Faction under one crest, have been guarding the last body of water on New-Earth. That body of water lies just beyond the bridge, on the other side of here."

"Why did they break the treaty?" I ask.

"They didn't agree with what they were doing here," she says.

I sigh. "We were never meant to be here." I remember what the book said about the original water faction rotation schedule and how things were supposed to be done with the ice harvesting.

"Exactly," Kahra says. "Under Frederick Jameson's leadership, and with the approval of representatives from the Board of Directors, they agreed on a new plan. One that lessened the burden for them but raised it for unsuspecting families on New-Earth."

Faeya looks at me and screws up her face. So many questions we've never thought to ask, and answers that may or may not lie on the other side of the bridge.

"So, there will be people on the other side?"

Kahra nods. "Yes. Not directly, but as I understand it, on an island nearby."

Faeya speaks, finally adding to the conversation. "But they're from the Water Faction, or at least they're Water Elementalists?"

"They are," Kahra says. "Ancient tribes whose customs run deep and strong. They believe in something called mana and tapu. The interconnectedness of all people and the shared responsibility they have for the greater good of the world... or worlds." Her voice drifts off.

"Tribes?" I say.

"The Māori," Kahra says.

I don't really understand what she means, but at least it sounds like they won't be enemies or out to get us. If they run into them, they might even help.

The idea of allies—real ones—flickers in me like a fragile flame.

I feel a little better knowing they'll be safe if they find those people. Especially with Kahra being from their faction, in a way.

The rumble of another truck cuts through the air. My chest tightens. No time to think, only move. We run, the ground catching our feet, gripping hard with each push. No ice to slip on now. The grass and dirt give us speed, but the roar behind us grows louder. It's too fast.

Kahra stumbles, her body pitching forward into the dirt. Faeya and I double back, breathless.

"Should we split up?" Faeya shouts.

"No!" I yell, my voice cracking over the growl of the engine.

The truck screeches, dirt spraying as it skids to a stop in front of us. A door slams open. Joll climbs out, storming forward, each step heavy with rage.

Something swings in his fist. I blink, stepping back, tripping over Kahra's legs before I see it clearly. *A scarf.* Iman's scarf.

Joll's face is twisted, red eyes wild and wet like he'd been crying. He lunges, one hand snapping around Faeya's neck. She gasps, flames erupting over her fingers, wrapping around his wrist. He doesn't even flinch. His roar shatters the air. Faeya collapses to her knees, choking.

The other truck door slams. Voiyt steps out. Kahra stiffens beneath me, her body sinking into the dirt as her fingers claw into the soil. She twists, shoving my legs off and rising, steady, armed with nothing but herself. Her eyes lock on Voiyt.

I scramble up, heart hammering, and launch myself at Joll. His grip is iron, Faeya's flames crawling over his skin like they're nothing. He screams, a sound that rattles my bones, and Faeya crumples, coughing, fire dying in her hands.

Her eyes go white, the color draining from them completely. The fire in her hands vanishes like it was never there.

"Faeya!" I shout, panic cutting through my throat. Joll's grip doesn't loosen. I claw at his arm, trying to pry him off her, but it's like pulling at stone.

"Faeya!" I yell again, louder, desperate. My hands slip against his wrist, useless. I can't focus. I can't fight.

The weight of losing her crashes in, heavier than the world itself.

From the corner of my eye, Voiyt moves. He steps toward Kahra, matching her stance exactly, one hand raised, the other at his side, both palms now turned upward to the sky.

Kahra doesn't move. Her gaze is locked on him, steady, unbroken.

"We've got to finish what we started," he says. His voice comes out as a sinister hiss, nothing like I've ever heard before. His whole presence has shifted. Whoever he was back on the compound, that's not who stands in front of us now.

Kahra adjusts her footing, her hands moving back into the same position as before. Voiyt hesitates, then grins.

"Little girl," he says. "Put your hands down." His laugh cuts sharp through the air.

I wrench my eyes back to Joll. Faeya isn't breathing. Her body hangs limp in his grip, her chest still.

"She's dead!" he shouts. "Iman is dead!"

My heart drops into my stomach. I throw my arms around his back and pull, but it's useless. He's too far gone, too strong. Faeya's eyes are blank and staring at the sky, her mouth open, frozen in silence.

All I can do is cling to Joll, helpless, while Voiyt steps closer to Kahra. Then—her hands ignite again. One instant

they're bare against the cold, the next they're swallowed in fire. The flames crawl up her sleeves, searing holes through the parka, blackening the fabric. Then—out. Gone as if it never happened.

It happens again. The fire surges back, racing to her elbows, heat rippling across her sleeves. *Out.*

Again. Like a heartbeat. A pulse. Each time the flames return, the air is pulled tight around me, drawn in as though she's stealing the breath from the world, then shoved back out in a wave of heat so sharp it stings my skin.

Joll screams. The sound is raw, panicked—nothing like the controlled voice of an Elder. He lets go, stumbling back.

Faeya falls forward. Her face is pale, her body trembling, but her eyes don't close. Her hand shoots out, catching the scarf as it slips from Joll's grip.

The fabric flares. Fire leaps from her palm into the cloth, racing along the weave until it's a stream of living flame, coiling and twisting in her hands. Not burning her, not devouring her—answering her.

Faeya wraps her other hand around the end of the scarf. The flames rush inward, pulled from her body and funneled into the fabric, and she gasps as if it's stealing her breath. Then she whirls, swinging the burning scarf wide at Joll. He scrambles on his knees, arms up, trying to fend it off.

From behind him, I yank my pike pole from my back. I swing it hard, the blunt side connecting with his head. His body goes limp. He collapses forward into the dirt and doesn't move again.

Faeya staggers, clutching the scarf as the fire dies down. She tries to steady herself, but I'm already moving toward Kahra.

She glances at me, shaking her head. "No, Akasha. This is my fight."

The words land like stone, leaving me stuck in place.

I drop my guard and step back, my eyes shifting between Voiyt and Kahra. The air clears, leaving only the two of them.

Voiyt strikes first. His movements mirror Kahra's, but bigger, wider, sharper. There's no water in sight, yet droplets seem to form from nothing as he weaves his arms, one hand over the other in steady rhythm. Each step forward pulls more from the air, until wind stirs faintly and threads of moisture twist at his command.

He stops in front of her, palm raised. He exhales. A cloud of condensation swells around Kahra, clinging to her skin, her breath, her hair. Frost creeps over her lashes. Her lips pale to blue. She stiffens, her arms heavy, her breath unsteady.

I want to step forward. I want to help. But something about this moment feels like it belongs to her alone.

Her arms tremble. Then, with effort, she lifts them. Slow at first. Then faster. She breaks through the freezing haze, pulling her hands high above her head. Two fingers on each hand touch, delicately, like the opening steps of a dance. She taps them together once, twice. The ground shifts. Barely perceptible, but enough.

Voiyt falters, glancing down. His guard drops.

Kahra seizes the opening. She lowers her arms, then draws them up tight to her chest, fingers still pressed together. Her gaze sharpens into something lethal, fixed entirely on him.

He gasps. His body locks. He cannot move.

Her hands twist inward, slowly and deliberately, like turning a knob. Clear fluid seeps from his nose. Then more, spilling from his mouth. His chest convulses as water drowns him from within.

Her eyes burn with focus, relentless, until she turns her wrists as far as they can go. Then—snap. She yanks her hands back into place.

Voiyt crumples. His chest is still. His eyes remain open, staring blankly into nothing.

I look at Kahra. If I ever doubted her before, I know now: I will never doubt her again.

I look over at Joll. He stirs, just barely, but I decide it's best we don't wait around to see what happens.

One more glance at Voiyt's body, then I reach out and grab Kahra, caring less about how she might feel about me touching her right now. I pull her with me toward Faeya, scoop her up by the collar, and take off again—running into the horizon.

29
ILLCREST CLIFF

We run.

I decide we'll keep running until we can't anymore. Until I see Foremen ships with my own eyes.

Every step I take, I picture Joll back on his feet, climbing into the truck, driving it straight for us. The thought pushes me faster.

I'll deal with him myself when I get Faeya and Kahra out of here.

The ground is no longer icy. It's only cool beneath us, patches of dirt and wiry grass crunching under our boots. My breath burns, my chest seizing with each inhale, but I keep moving.

Faeya stumbles ahead, weak, and barely upright. I press my hand to her back, pushing her forward each time she slows. Her steps are uneven, her shoulders sagging, the scarf trailing loose from her grip.

Kahra lags behind. Her strength is fading, her pace faltering. She grits her teeth, determined, but her strides shorten, her arms heavy at her sides. I glance back at her, then push Faeya harder, forcing all of us to keep moving.

The horizon wavers, but I tell myself the Foremen's ships are out there. They have to be. The thought is the only thing driving me forward.

And if Joll rises again, if he does come for us in that truck, I'll deal with him like she dealt with Voiyt.

Then Kahra drops. Her knees hit the dirt, and she falls forward onto her hands. I slow, ready to reach for her, but she's already pushing herself back up. She sways, unsteady, her breath quick and shallow.

I hover close, torn between grabbing her and letting her fight through it. She catches my eye and straightens, just enough to make her point.

She's not asking for my help. Not yet.

Faeya bends at the waist, bracing her hands on her knees. Her shoulders rise and fall as she fights for air, every breath ragged.

I stop with her, lifting my head toward the sky. The moon hangs above, cold and bright. I stare at it as if I can do what Kahra does, read its place, tell the time, but the truth is, I can't. It's just light to me.

I look back to the horizon. The line of water I thought I saw before is gone. No shimmer, no reflection, nothing but land stretching out endless and flat.

But the smell lingers. Damp, earthy, undeniable. The water is near. I can feel it.

"We're almost there," I say.

I lower myself to the ground beside Kahra, not too close, just enough that she knows I am there.

Faeya lowers herself as well, sitting cross-legged with her elbows resting on her knees. Her hands tremble as she turns them over, palms up, then palms down again, studying the skin as if it belongs to someone else.

The burns are there. Red, blistered in places, but no worse than before. After what she just did, I expect them to be torn open, charred beyond repair. But they're not.

The scarf rests across her lap. She lifts it carefully, letting the fabric slip through her fingers. It's fine. No burns, no holes, not even a singe along the edges. It looks impossible after what I saw.

Her brow furrows. She touches her hands together, then pulls them apart, waiting for something to spark. Nothing comes. Her lips part, but no words follow.

I watch her. The way her fingers linger on the scarf, the way she stares at her own palms like she is both afraid of them and unwilling to look away. She exhales hard, a shudder running through her.

"It was fire," she whispers at last, her voice thin. "It was me."

The words hang between us, fragile and terrifying all at once.

Kahra has steadied her breathing, her voice quiet but sure when she speaks. "Faeya... what do you know about Primus Raisa Fold?"

Faeya blinks. "Who?"

I look between them. "What is a Primus?"

Kahra's eyes shift to me. "The faction founders. The first recorded people to manipulate their faction's element."

Faeya shakes her head. "I don't know anything about any of that. Why?"

Kahra studies her for a moment before answering. "Because Primus Fold wasn't able to create fire. But she could extinguish it. She was the only one known to be able to do this. Everyone in the Fire Faction needs a grounding device to channel their fire through, because once it starts it causes damage if it is not directed. That's why they use things like Adjórdean Steel... or the Helmsman's hijab, which is fire-proof."

She points at the scarf in Faeya's lap. Faeya and I both stare at it, confused.

Kahra doesn't pause. "But they wouldn't need grounding devices if they could control the flames themselves. If they could combust and extinguish fire on their own."

She looks up at Faeya, her gaze steady, then back down again.

Faeya lifts her head toward me.

The weight of it shows in her eyes—fear, wonder, and something else neither of us can name.

We move again.

Every step is harder than the last. My legs ache, my throat is raw, my stomach twists with hunger. Faeya drags her feet, the scarf clenched tight in her fist. Kahra keeps her eyes forward, her jaw locked, but her pace is slower with each stride. None of us speak. We don't have the breath for it.

The smell of water thickens as we push on, wet and heavy in the air. It fills my mouth until I can almost taste it. My tongue feels swollen, my lips cracked, my body screaming.

The ground rises beneath us, uneven and jagged, until we climb higher and higher without realizing it.

Then, the world drops away.

We reach the edge of a cliff that towers above a sea stretching endless and gray. Wind lashes up from below, carrying the sting of salt and spray. The cliff face is harsh and broken, sheer walls of jagged stone plunging into the waves. Rocks jut out like teeth, sharp and unforgiving. There's no path, no slope, no rope, or bridge to guide us down. Only the impossible drop.

Far below, the waves crash against the base of the cliff, white foam breaking and pulling with each strike.

I gasp. I can't look away. The sea stretches out forever, alive and endless. For a moment all I feel is awe, a weight in my chest as though the sight itself is too big for me to hold.

Then, I see it.

Far out beyond the water, tearing into the horizon, a black void that splits the sky. A hole. A gaping wound in the world itself, wide as the sea and stretching upward until it swallows the clouds. Its edges churn like smoke and shadow, folding into themselves, never still.

It moves. Not with wind or storm but with something deeper, something alive. It beats like a heart, each pulse pushing through the air and into my chest. The ground beneath me seems to hum with it, a low vibration that rattles in my bones.

I glance down at the compass in my hand. The needle spins, clattering against the glass like it's screaming for me to turn back. I grip it tighter and push forward against its will.

Faeya presses her hand to her stomach. Her face is pale. "I don't feel well."

Kahra doesn't look away from the void. Her voice is low, steady, but there's a strain in it I have never heard before. "It's the bridge."

Faeya's eyes widen. Fear glints there, raw and sharp, and when I look at Kahra I see it in her too, though she hides it better.

But for me, the vibrations aren't just fear. They're familiar. The rhythm, the pull, the weight in my chest. I know it, somehow. Like the beat of something I've always carried inside me.

Between the bridge and the sea, I see them.

A row of long metal ships, dark and gleaming, lined along the shore. Their shapes cut sharp against the horizon, massive and cold. *The Foremen's ships.*

Faeya steadies herself on my arm, her voice faint but clear. "How are we going to get down?"

I have no answer. The cliff stretches on in both directions, jagged and unbroken, as if the land itself is daring us to try.

The slope looms before us, a scar down the cliffside. From a distance it looked like a path. Up close it feels like a trap. The sea pounds against the rocks below, every crash a reminder of what waits if we fall.

None of us speak. The danger hangs heavy in the air, as real as the portal behind us, as sharp as every moment that's brought us here.

I force myself forward.

My boot touches the slope, gravel crunching under the weight. I shift my balance, easing down. The ground gives. My foot slips.

The world tilts.

I throw myself down, grabbing at the ground with both hands. My chest hits the rock hard; the breath knocked from me. Jagged stone rips against my parka as I slide on my stomach, fabric tearing, the burn biting through to my skin.

My fingers catch a piece of rock. I hold, clinging, heart pounding, the roar of the sea below filling my ears.

My boot finds a ledge, just wide enough to press my weight onto. My hands grip the stone, rough and sharp, and I ease myself down. My body hugs the rock, shuffling inch by inch, my foot searching for the next ledge.

I reach back up to Kahra. "Your turn."

She hesitates, then follows. Her legs are shorter, and she struggles to reach the top hold. She stretches, fingertips scraping stone, her boots slipping against loose gravel.

"Got you," I say, keeping my gaze steady until her hands find a place. She lowers herself slowly, jaw tight with the effort. Then she holds.

Next is Faeya. She sets her hands against the stone but falters, wincing. Her palms are raw, burned, barely able to hold her own weight. I climb back up over Kahra to reach her, brushing past her back as I squeeze by. She flinches, and I glance at her, guilt tugging at me.

"Sorry," I whisper. She doesn't answer, but the look on her face is enough.

I help Faeya lower herself onto the ledge, guiding her fingers into the grooves. She shakes her head. "I can't—"

"You can," I tell her. "Go in front. Lead."

Her eyes widen. "Me?"

"You've always been the one to take the lead back on the compound," I say. "You've got this."

Something steadies in her eyes, fear turning to resolve.

She hesitates, then nods. With the scarf now wrapped snug around her neck, she shuffles along, feet searching for rock, hands sliding to each new hold. Kahra follows in the middle, and I take the back.

The ships shrink behind us, smaller with every step as we curve away from them down the slope. *At least this way we won't be seen.*

Kahra slips. Her boot loses its grip and her body jerks back. I grab her wrist fast, yanking her toward me. She jumps at my touch, the movement almost taking me down with her.

"Wait," I call to Faeya.

She freezes; her hands braced on the rock.

I lean in close to Kahra, probably closer than she'd like. "I need you safe," I say.

She doesn't look at me, but I know she hears.

Faeya glances back, her eyes on us. I raise my voice just enough for them both. "If you slip, I'll grab you to make sure you don't fall. When you're secure, I'll let you go again. Is that okay?"

Kahra doesn't move at first, then gives a small nod.

We continue.

More than once, she slips again, her fingers missing the higher stones, her boots scraping over loose rock. Each time I catch her, holding her steady until she finds her grip again. Each time she nods, and we move on.

We keep moving, slow and deliberate.

Faeya's hands give her trouble, every hold pulling at the burns until her face twists and she has to stop. She presses her palms against her clothes, trying to ease the sting before forcing herself to grip again. Each pause drags out the climb, the rock biting deeper into my arms as I wait for her to steady.

Kahra struggles too, her shorter reach making every choice of where she places her hands matter. Some rocks she can't use at all, forcing us to shift lower or edge sideways, finding new grips that take twice the effort. I stay close, guiding her where I can, lending a hand when she needs.

The descent stretches on like this, one piece at a time, every slip or misstep threatening to send us over the edge. The ships in the distance shrink smaller and smaller as we work our way down the slope in the opposite direction.

More ships depart while we climb. Long dark hulls glide away from the shore, disappearing across the horizon. Tiny specks of Foremen climbing onto the decks and vanishing into the top of the ships. I can see them, even from here, moving like ants around the metal giants.

I wonder if they know. If word has already spread about Helmsman Iman, or if Kerr is working to keep it all quiet. How long before someone notices? How long before the silence breaks?

Still, each ship that leaves gives me hope. If Kahra and Faeya can hold on, if I can get them to the bottom, they'll be on one of the next ones. They'll have their chance.

The questions linger in my mind longer than I'd like. Still, I move. Still, we descend.

From the ground, the cliff curves above us in jagged walls. The rocks bend in such a way that the ships are gone from sight. To reach them we'll have to walk the length of the shore, back in the direction we came from.

Kahra studies the horizon, her eyes narrowed. "The next ones will be leaving in thirty minutes. It's best we wait here. We're hidden, and if we start walking closer to the next departure, we'll blend with the timing."

Faeya frowns. "How do you know?"

"I noticed before," Kahra says, her voice low. "There's about a fifteen-minute gap between when they close the top hatch and when the ships leave the shore. If we move too soon, we'll be exposed. If we time it right, we can make it."

We all agree, settling against the rocks to take what little rest we can. The sand shifts under us, refusing to hold, but it's better than the cliff.

Then the sound comes again. A deep grinding, the churn of heavy wheels.

From the opposite direction, two trucks barrel toward us along the shore.

30
I AM AKASHA

"Are you kidding me?" Faeya's voice cracks through the air, high and ragged. She presses her fists against her face, her body folding as the tears come again. "I can't do this anymore, Akasha."

Her words land hard—because I know she means them.

The roar of the engine swells. Two trucks grind to a stop in the sand, side by side, throwing up grit and exhaust. The one from earlier, Joll's. And another beside it.

I step forward, pulling the pike pole from my back. This time, it won't be the blunt end against Joll's skull. It'll be the sharp one.

Kahra plants herself at my side, shoulders squared, her hands already steady as she draws from the air and sea.

Faeya hesitates, trembling, then wipes her tears with the back of her hand. The skin is raw, burned red. The sight cuts deep, but when she lifts her chin, there's fire in her eyes.

She tears the scarf from her neck knotting both ends in her fists, holding it like a lifeline. Then she steps forward, finding her strength, and joins us.

The door of the second truck swings wide. My chest tightens. It has to be Kerr. Chief Elder, master of everything on the compound. The one who invited me to join the Junior Elders because he sensed something different. Burned hands like Fire Elementalists who can't contain their gift. A weapon at his hip like Helmsman Iman's. If Joll is already on the ground, then Kerr is the one sending the attack.

It makes sense he'd come himself now, to finish what had been started.

But the boot that steps out isn't his. It's white. Unmistakably white. The only boot of its kind on the compound.

My stomach twists. *It can't be.* Batkins.

"You three have caused us a lot of trouble." Her voice is flat and sharp as she pulls off her fur-lined gloves and tosses them into the sand. Each word spits venom. She steps closer, eyes fixed, face hard as stone.

"Do you think you could leave this planet? Under my watch?"

The sand itself seems to hold its breath.

The words strike cold. She's not just here. She's in charge. I feel it in her tone, the weight behind it.

I glance at Faeya, who stares wide-eyed, as if she's seeing something she never believed possible. My gaze shifts to Kahra. She doesn't flinch, but the water rises to her call, rolling in waves toward her feet.

I grip the pike pole tighter, shifting its weight, ready for whatever might come.

The sand moves beneath me without warning, like the bottom dropping out. My foot slides, and for a heartbeat I'm weightless, off balance, arms flailing. I slam into Kahra, her shoulder solid against mine, but even she staggers as the ground keeps sliding away.

Faeya cries out. The three of us pitch sideways together, boots sinking as the sand pours downhill like water. It pulls us toward the sea, dragging our steps faster no matter how hard we fight to stand.

Kahra raises one arm high above her head, fingers pinched tight, the other stretched toward Batkins and Joll. Her movements are sharp and deliberate. Then, with a sudden shift, she flips them, arms mirroring each other in perfect reverse.

The sea obeys. Water surges upward, slamming against their legs and coiling around them. Joll curses, Batkins digs her heels into the sand, but it doesn't matter. Kahra drags her arms back to her sides, palms flat against her coat, and the pull is instant. Both of them topple, sliding helplessly toward the water.

Joll fights to plant his feet again, swaying as the water drags him, but Batkins twists to her side. Half her body sinks into the sea before she claws her way free. Both arms reach toward the cliff, fingers spread wide as if she could touch stone more than twenty feet away. Then she clenches her fists and yanks them down.

The rocks answer. She pulls against them, anchoring herself, and her body drags across the wet sand. She rolls to her back and drives one hand deep into the ground. When she whips it at us, the world explodes.

Sand slams into us like a storm. It fills my eyes, my nose, my mouth, my ears. I can't see. I can't breathe. We cough and choke, lost in the blinding whirl.

Batkins is an Earth Elementalist.

I reach out, trying to feel Kahra and Faeya but find nothing. I move backward, but the storm follows. It thickens, wind tearing through the sand and driving it harder against me, burying me in grit. I choke and stumble forward until I hit something solid, a bump.

I tighten my grip on the pole, sliding my hand closer to the head so it won't stab out blindly. I hold it tight against me, guarding Kahra and Faeya, wherever they are, from being struck by mistake.

The grains cut at my skin, sharp as glass, slicing my face and hands. I stumble, panic flooding me. The storm becomes a living thing, gnawing at every inch of me.

The same crushing weight from the Isolation Box surges back, intense, and almost uncontrollable. My chest tightens. I blink through the blur. Colors seep into the storm, and through the haze, I see them—two shadows of color, black and red. Both move with the storm, shifting sand and air, weaving the earth itself.

Sand lashes my eyes again and I squeeze them shut. My pole slides in my hands. I bring the head closer, gripping until the cold metal touches my fist. The sensation drains from my body and floods into the pole.

I wrap my other hand just below the first and hold it out in front of me. Pressing forward, I feel the sand tear apart, the path opening at my command.

I force my eyes open, red and burning, tears spilling as the storm parts.

The path widens as I go, the sand splitting in front of me. Shapes emerge through the chaos, and then Kahra and Faeya break through, stumbling into the cleared space behind me. They fall into step at my back, following the line I've carved. Together we force our way out, the storm thinning until the air clears.

But as we step free, the ground hardens under our boots, and I see them. Joll and Batkins stand only a few feet away, waiting. They each drop their guard. Batkins steps forward, eyes locked on me.

"So, you're the new Space Elementalist," she says, glaring. "Seven hundred years, and now you?" She tilts her head, the words more accusation than question.

Joll crouches, ready to spring, but he holds himself back. He won't move until Batkins tells him to. I can see it in the way his eyes flick to her, waiting. She's the power here. The real power. And who would have ever known?

Kahra and Faeya can barely stand, drained and staggering, their strength gone. My eyes burn raw, the sand slicing them so deep I can hardly force them open. Joll and Batkins close in, certain we have nothing left.

"What was your plan?" Batkins asks, her glare pinning me in place. "To leave here? To escape Adjórde on my watch? To close the bridge?"

Joll snickers behind her, already savoring our defeat.

"We're leaving here. Today." My voice cuts through the tension, steady and sure. The words are not just mine—they belong to all of us. I will not let them die here.

The conviction surprises even me, steel in the voice of a body that was shaking just moments ago.

I try to glance back, searching for Kahra and Faeya, but all I see are faint shadows, outlines barely holding. The pike pole is locked in my grip, thrumming with a power that feels like the bridge itself. I adjust my hold, pulling my hand back so I no longer touch the metal, and the feeling rushes back into me. The colors flare, bleeding through the haze, sharpening the world.

Joll and Batkins blaze before me, their twisted shadows of red and black burning bright. I see them now, clearly. And I know I won't back down.

I slide the pole over my shoulder. My arms drop to my sides, guard lowered. The storm inside me steadies, and I find my voice.

"Why?" I ask, my throat raw. "Why have you lied to us our whole lives?"

Batkins's eyes narrow, her lips curling as she glares down at me. "You will not be leaving here today, or any day," she spits, each word sharp as a blade. Then her tone hardens, colder still. "And I do not have to explain anything to you."

She reaches toward the cliff again, her hands clawing at the stone. Shards rip free, jagged edges tearing through the air. I step forward, closer to her, pulling myself away from Kahra and Faeya as I move. The wall explodes. Splinters of rock slice into my arm, punching through my parka and into flesh. White-hot pain flares and I scream, reaching out for her, but she is just beyond my grasp.

Joll steps forward in her place. He raises a hand to his face, thumb and finger forming a circle. He presses it to his

mouth, blows sharp, and then inhales. My chest caves in. Air vanishes. I drop to the ground, choking, unable to move, the breath ripped straight out of me.

His shadow looms as he closes in. But before he can reach me, a wave of water crashes into us, dragging me sideways. Fire cracks across the dark, whipping from a scarf, heat scorching the sand. Rocks rain down in a jagged assault. Wind whips in, seizing the storm and throwing it all into frenzy.

Earth, water, fire, and air collide. The sand mixes with the water, thickening into sludge that drags at my boots and pins my hands as I fight to rise. The wind lashes it all together, shoving fire and stone through the storm. The elements crash into one another, raging and devouring all around me.

I'm trapped inside, smothered in the chaos, every direction closing in. Joll's shadow claws for me, Faeya and Kahra lost in the whirlwind. I choke, my lungs screaming for air, my body sinking deeper into the sand. I'm at the center of it all, but powerless, caught in a storm I can't escape.

I claw at my chest, desperate to pull the air back in. Each breath comes sharp and shallow, stabbing at my lungs. Joll did something to me, something that ripped the breath straight out and left me hollow. I don't know how to undo it. My body won't listen. My chest won't rise.

I clutch tighter, nails digging through the fabric, fighting for air that will not come. My eyes roll back, the world tilting, colors bleeding across the storm. Shadows of red and black, blue and yellow, twist around me, moving in violent arcs. They step over me, kicking, crushing, raging.

Screams echo through the storm. I can't tell if they're mine or someone else's.

The world begins to slip away—fingers, light, sound—until only the pounding in my skull remains.

The moment I think it's all over is the moment everything crashes back in on me. A surge of energy rips up my spine, into my neck, then down my arms toward my fingertips. It pushes outward instead of drawing in like before. The sensation is different, jarring, and it drives me to my knees.

A dark cloud bursts around me faster than I can make sense of it. Sand kicks up at my face as feet stammer back. The bigger the darkness grows, the stronger its pull becomes. I stagger upright, unsteady, but the cloud follows, swelling with every breath.

Bodies scatter. I can't make out faces, only shadowed shapes fleeing into the storm. I find Kahra and Faeya, two smaller figures standing close to each other, and beyond them Joll and Batkins. No one dares move. The darkness stretches outward, trying to swallow us whole.

I don't resist. If I pull it back, I feel like it'll collapse into me, and I don't know what that will do. So, I force it outward. The cloud thickens, wrapping tighter around me, and I sense the figures ahead losing sight of me altogether.

I step forward, cloaked and shrouded in darkness. Joll and Batkins stumble backward, tripping over each other. When I get close enough to see their faces, their eyes are wide black holes, breathless, frozen in terror. Batkins jerks her hand toward the stone again, but I slam my boot on her wrist. She jolts and lets out a scream that stirs Joll, who thrashes blindly, searching for the source of her pain.

The darkness twists inside me, shaping me, pressing me to act, to drive it forward. I don't know what to do, only that I can't let it turn back. So, I give in and push harder.

I lift my boot from Batkins and glance over. Kahra and Faeya stand together, looking up at the massive cloud that's risen around me, their eyes wide, their bodies lost inside its shifting shape. The cloud moves as if alive.

I kneel between them, and the darkness follows, folding down around all three of us, swallowing us whole. Joll and Batkins's glowing outlines vanish into the void as the cloud closes over. The weight drops heavy on my back, settling just before where Kahra and Faeya are standing, and presses flat onto me, Joll, and Batkins.

Then I let go. I exhale, and the pressure releases. Slowly, I stand. My vision is blurred, but I can still see their eyes—Kahra's and Faeya's—shining wide in the dark. I turn toward where Joll and Batkins should be, but there's nothing.

They're gone.

Only emptiness remains. The same void I slip into when I fold space around me. A place of silence, a hollow with no walls, no light. Like the Isolation Box without a lantern.

Only, you never come out.

31
INTO THE VOID

Kahra walks to the trucks, her steps heavy but certain. She digs through the gear and comes back with three metal containers, round in the middle with narrow necks, capped tight. I don't know the word for them, only that I've seen Elders carry them before.

"Clean water," she says, handing one to me.

She twists hers open first and tips it back, pouring the water straight into her eyes, letting it stream down her cheeks. The grit slides away, leaving red lines cut across her skin like burns. I copy her, the cold stinging as it washes the sand out. Then she passes what's left of hers to Faeya, who does the same.

"Drink," she adds.

I take a sip, the taste sharp and clear, then pass it to Faeya. She drinks and holds it out to Kahra, who hesitates at first but finally lifts it to her mouth and swallows.

Faeya looks at me. "How did you do that?" she asks.

"I don't know," I say. The words feel thin, like even my voice doesn't believe them. I just knew that whatever was happening to me, I had to let it. If I tried to fight it, it'd hurt me.

My vision starts to clear, the blur softening into shapes again. Kahra suddenly bolts, running hard toward the cliff's edge that's kept us hidden.

"We're not going to make it," she says.

"Yes, we are," I tell her, pulling the boots from my feet. With the little strength I have left, I take the journal out, look at it one last time, then hurl it far into the Adjórdean Sea. The splash is swallowed by waves before it can echo back.

"Take them off," I say to Faeya. She tugs her boots free and kicks them aside. Kahra hesitates, but finally does the same.

Again, we run.

The sand doesn't shift beneath my feet now. By the water's edge it's firm, wet, and packed tight, giving us traction. Each stride picks up speed, faster and faster as we race along the shore.

Everything hurts. The rocks still sting deep in my arm, every stride tearing them deeper into my skin. My eyes burn raw, the salt from the sea cutting through them each time I blink. Every step feels like it should be the one that brings me down, but I keep running.

Faeya's hands are wrapped against her chest, red and blistered from flame. Her hair, singed with fire's touch, whips in the wind behind her as she pushes forward, faster than I thought she could.

Kahra trails just behind us. Her pace is slow but steady, each step deliberate, refusing to give in.

We're almost there, I tell myself. I'm getting them to safety.

Then I hear it, an engine roar. Louder than the trucks, so deep I feel the rumble through the sand beneath my feet. The sound shakes through my ribs, rattling my teeth. *It's a ship.*

"Let's go!" I shout, forcing everything I have left into my legs. The shape grows larger with every step, the ship looming in my view.

The water around it churns, rushing to the shore and back again, over and over, as if trying to lift it free and carry it out to sea. It must be the Foremen, moving the water from inside. But as we close the distance, I see no windows, no doors. Only a ladder fixed to the side.

It's massive, tilting and rocking as it rises, dragged little by little back into the ocean. Waves slam against our legs as we run. Kahra stumbles and goes down, the current pulling her under.

"Akasha!" Faeya screams, looking back at her.

I sprint, seize Kahra's arms, and with Faeya's help we drag her free of the water's pull. Her coughs scrape at my ears, raw and desperate, but she's okay. We run again, the ship climbing higher, its shadow stretching over us. The waves reach for us, dragging at our steps.

The metal wall towers above, smooth and cold, the ladder the only way up. My chest heaves, every muscle screaming, but I don't slow. We crash through the last of the waves.

Faeya's in front of me and reaches it first. She leaps through the water, arms flailing, and slams into the ladder. Her hands lock on the rungs, and she begins to climb, pulling herself up fast.

"Go!" I yell, as she takes hold, climbing with everything she has. Kahra follows, slower, but steady. The ladder rattles against the side of the ship as it rocks, each rise and fall threatening to rip them free.

I latch on, my arms burning. Blood seeps from the wounds where the rocks tore me, stinging with every pull. Higher, higher, the ground falling away beneath us. The sea slams against the walls, spraying salt in my eyes. I blink through it, refusing to let go.

They have to get to the top. They have to think I'm coming. So, I follow, slowly, keeping an eye on the waves crashing beneath me, so I can let go when the time comes.

I cling to the ladder as the ship rocks forward and back, the force so strong it sends my legs swinging beneath me, suspended in midair. Kahra and Faeya jerk side to side above me, struggling to hold on.

Faeya looks down, eyes wide when she sees I'm not climbing. "Akasha, come on!" she yells. Kahra looks down too.

"Akasha!" Faeya shouts again.

I meet her eyes, past Kahra, and shake my head. The motion feels heavier than my body, like I'm dropping something I can never pick up again. She knows what I mean. They both do. The ship slams forward again and I almost slip but manage to hold on. *This is it*. They need to go. They need

to get to safety. I can't risk what might happen if I return with them. I've done what I needed to do.

"Akasha, please!" Faeya screams.

Again, I shake my head, gentler this time. As I ready myself to let go, I yell, "Go!"

Faeya cries, her scream tearing through the waves. She slams against the ladder as the massive ship finally frees itself from the shore, floating.

"Go!" I shout again, tears stinging my eyes.

"Not without you," Kahra says, her voice firm as she looks down at me. She reaches out a hand. My body freezes. Her eyes lock onto mine.

"Akasha," she says. "Let's go."

Her voice cuts through the roar like a rope, pulling me back. I tighten my grip, then wrap my other arm around the next rung. My chest heaves as I begin to climb. Together, we rise, the ship rocking beneath us, until we drag ourselves over the edge and onto the empty deck.

Our legs give out. We collapse onto our backs, gasping as it carries us into the deep waters of the Adjórdean Sea.

We lie on our backs, heaving to the sound of waves slamming against the metal beneath us. After a moment I push myself up a bit and look around. The deck is bare, nothing but flat gray stretching out around us, slick and wet under the spray. No people. No Foremen. No one at all.

Just the opening where the ladder ends, and a round metal door built into the floor a few steps away. A thick wheel sits at its center, meant to twist and turn, like the lock to something hidden below.

I crawl across the wet metal toward the round door. My fingers grip the wheel in its center, and I glance back at Faeya and Kahra before twisting. It doesn't move. I shake my head at them.

They drag themselves to me and try together, hands slipping against the slick surface, but the handle won't spin. Locked. Sealed.

I back away, pulling myself toward the edge of the ship and lean against the raised side, my chest rising and falling with each ragged breath. Faeya and Kahra huddle together, pressing close for warmth, for strength. The sight of them, fragile against the storm of sea and sky, makes my chest tighten until it hurts.

The ship groans as it rocks forward, inching closer to the massive black hole. It swallows the horizon, a wound in the sea and sky. Water bends toward it, waves curling unnaturally before collapsing into the void. The air itself seems to pull, the sound hollow, endless, like a constant breath dragging everything closer. My stomach lurches as I watch it, as if the hole is already tugging at me from the inside.

I throw my head back and let the sea take me. Let it take us.

The vibration of the portal hums through the air and through me. It isn't just pulling, it's alive. It thrums in my chest, the same way I feel when I am in my element, when I let my Potential loose and stop fighting what I am. I lean into it, trembling, and for a moment it feels like the portal and I are the same.

I look to Kahra and Faeya. They're still huddled together, but it isn't rest. Their chests heave shallowly, eyes rolling back, like they can't breathe. Like they're slipping away.

I glance at the portal. It looms over us now, black and endless, and I know they can't get near it. They can't go through. Not from out here.

I crawl back to the round door and grip the wheel again, twisting with everything I have. My arms shake, muscles screaming, but it won't move. I look over my shoulder at them, at the way Faeya's head droops and Kahra trembles, and then I let go. My bare feet skid on the wet metal as I scramble back to them.

I press a hand to Faeya's shoulder. She turns her face to me, eyes blank, wide, turning white like they did when Joll had her by the neck. Kahra slips lower, slumping into her lap.

"No, no, no." I shake her, but nothing.

I reach for my pike pole, desperate, but it's not there. It's gone. Left behind on the shore with Joll and Batkins.

The loss hits like another wound, heavier than the rocks in my arm. Panic claws at me. I don't know what to do. I look at the bridge again. It's right on us now, dark and gaping, the front of the ship already breaking into it.

I look back at them. I think of Shosk, of the compound, of everything in between. Then I place a hand on each of them and release, letting the space around me fold in, instead of out. On the beach, out meant shadow and darkness. In means hidden. Protection.

I lean forward, wrap one arm around Faeya's back and the other beneath Kahra's shoulder, pulling them both close. Their weight presses into me, heavy, real, as if holding on

could keep them here. I focus on bringing them into the void with me.

Then I squeeze with everything I have and just as the darkness takes hold of the ship... I feel a squeeze back.

NEW-EARTH

The Book of Adjórde

A.J. ALFORD

Unlock your Potential. Release your Greatness.

PROLOGUE

<u>Present Day: New-Earth</u>

"I can't breathe." Shera coughed violently, her chest rattling.

If there had been enough moisture in the air, she might have drawn phlegm. Instead, blood spotted her lips.

"Put your mask back on, Shera."

"For what?" Her voice cracked. "Bag's empty."

She reached for the plastic pouch on the bedside table, lifting it weakly toward her husband. The tubing sagged from her grasp. "See? No water."

She let it fall, the pouch dropping against the side of the bed, stopped short by the cord.

He caught the mask hanging loose around her neck and pulled it up over her mouth and nose. His hand fumbled with the strap, securing it around the back of her head.

His fingers shook as though the thin elastic weighed more than steel.

Shera weakly raised a hand, pushing against his wrist as though to stop him. Her touch had no strength behind it, only protest.

Her nails barely grazed his skin; a ghost of resistance that broke him more than a shove could have.

Shera shook her head, but she was too weak to resist. He held it in place anyway. It was all he could do for her now.

The room around them groaned with age. Paint flaked from the walls in curling strips. A single table leaned against one side, two chairs with uneven legs pushed close together, their wood splintering. The bed they shared filled most of the space, its frame bent, the mattress thin. A window on the far wall was covered by ragged curtains, patched with holes that let the pale glow of the town outside bleed through.

Somewhere beneath the floor, the faint hum of waterlines stirred. Pipes that once carried life now carried nothing but air, a hollow echo of what no longer flowed. Above them, vents that once pumped rented moisture into the air were dried, cracked, and broken.

The silence between those dead machines pressed in louder than any sound could.

"Marv," she coughed, her voice thin.

He stood and walked to the window. The curtains tore as he dragged them aside, the fabric fraying in his hand. He peered through the holes to the street below. Nobody in sight.

Those who could afford it, or who knew the right people, relocated across the country, getting as close to Directorate City as they could. That was where the water was. Where the

shipments from the planet on the other side of the bridge went.

Here they lived, far too close to it, and thankfully far from the rift that sucked the life from the face of the earth. Trapped between them, caught in an imbalance that was never meant to exist.

As a younger man, Marv had once seen the bridge. Vast and dark, it loomed toward the sky, and the sight had never left him.

But the rift was worse. That hole had not been meant to exist. It was the accident, the monstrous tear said to drink the world dry. People claimed it could strip the air itself, that even the bridge paled beside its darkness. Marv had only ever heard the stories, and he prayed he would never see it for himself.

Here, they could watch the ice arrive through the bridge. There, at the rift, was where the last of the water was pulled, vanishing into emptiness.

From their windows they sometimes saw the Foremen, silent figures moving through the abandoned town, carrying what was now more precious than gold.

Ships came first by sea, dark silhouettes crawling over the horizon. At the bridge they shifted onto iron tracks, becoming trains that carved through barren lands, past abandoned towns and dying cities.

The ships pressed on toward Directorate City, where the promise of survival grew stronger. But it was a promise bound to a price Marv and Shera could never pay. And so they, like so many others, were left to wither in the shadow of passing water.

Marv's jaw tightened.

His teeth ground together until his gums ached.

His wife would die here simply because they could not afford to get closer to the city, where water flowed through the pipes and vents pushed moisture into the air. An elitist system, built to save some while the rest were left to rot.

He turned from the window and returned to his wife, lowering himself onto the edge of the bed. He sat at her side, the weight of it pressing down on him—the truth that he had failed her, that he could not provide the life she needed or the chances that might have saved her from this.

The mattress sagged beneath them both, as if the bed itself knew it could no longer hold them up.

Shera coughed again, harder this time, and could not stop. Each breath scraped like glass down her throat, the air too thin, too dry to cling to. It burned all the way in, and nothing ever seemed to fill her lungs.

Marv pushed up from the bed and staggered to the cabinets. His own chest wheezed from the effort, his breaths ragged. He rifled through what little they had left, finding nothing. No water. No vapor packs.

The hollow clatter of empty drawers answered him back.

The exertion forced him to stop. He gripped the counter, then slid down into the chair by the table to collect himself, helpless. He could only watch as she struggled, unable to do anything. The neighbors had long gone, and even if they had stayed, they would have had nothing to spare.

People like him and Shera were what the Elementalists called *Laics*, those with no Elemental Potential to wield. Far

less than special. To the Board of Directors, that made them useless. And useless people were disposable.

They had been abandoned by the leaders who promised to do everything they could to ensure fair and equal distribution of water from the ice collected. But none had come here in weeks. Sometimes months. Nothing grew. Nothing could be cultivated.

Surviving off prepacked food that needed water but was forced down dry, throats cracked, and stomachs twisted. Faces hollowed. Skin pulled tight. Every breath a labor so intense it felt like it could be the last, and at any moment, it might be.

Shera heaved, her body jolting forward as another violent cough tore out of her chest. She choked on the dryness, gasping for air that would not come.

The sound of her struggle filled the room like a storm no wall could keep out.

Marv rushed back to her side, catching her shoulders, holding her upright as she convulsed.

Her hands clawed weakly at his shirt, not to push him away but to cling.

"Breathe, Shera," he whispered, voice breaking, though he knew there was nothing left to give her. Blood flecked her lips, her eyes wide and unfocused.

Her pupils fluttered as if even sight was slipping away from her.

He pulled her against him, rocking like the movement itself could force breath back into her failing lungs. His tears streaked down, wetting the mask he had tried to keep over her face.

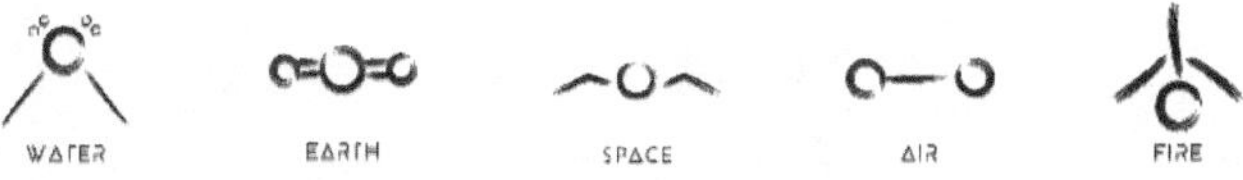

Shera's gaze shifted. She turned her head toward the nightstand and reached out, fingers trembling. Her hand brushed against the frame of a photo. Two children. A cat. Everyone Marv had once loved was gone. Shera was all he had left, and she was leaving him now.

His throat locked so tightly around his sobs it felt like he might suffocate beside her.

Her body shuddered once more, a ragged sound scraping her throat, then stilled in his arms.

Marv clutched her, his sobs filling the silence that followed.

The city lights beyond the curtain blinked faintly, indifferent to the death inside the room.

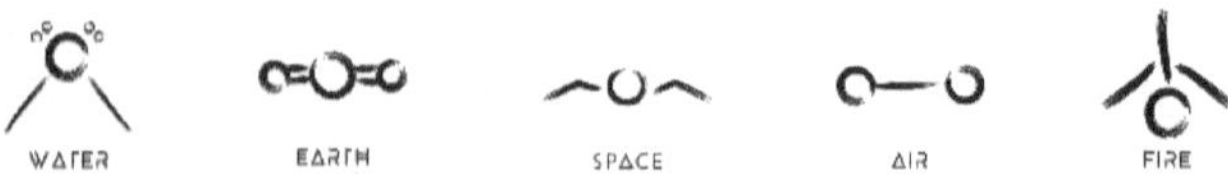

A Letter from the Author

Dear Reader,

Thank you for joining me on this journey into The Book of Adjórde: Akasha. Writing this story has been both a challenge and a joy and knowing it has reached your hands means more than I can put into words.

This book began as a spark of an idea about survival, connection, and the courage to ask difficult questions and make difficult decisions. It grew into something far more than I could have imagined.

Along the way, I poured pieces of myself into these pages: my hopes, my fears, and my belief in the power of stories that bring people together.

I am grateful for the friends, family, and early readers who encouraged me when the path felt uncertain. I am equally grateful to you, the reader, for choosing to step into Akasha's world, and a bit of mine. Your time and attention are a gift.

If this story spoke to you, I'd love for you to share your thoughts with others whether through a review, a recommendation, or simply a conversation. Every voice helps stories like this find its way to more readers.

Thank you again for walking beside me, Akasha, and my characters on this journey. This is only the beginning, and I cannot wait to share what comes next.

With gratitude,
A.J. Alford

www.ingramcontent.com/pod-product-compliance
Lightning Source LLC
Chambersburg PA
CBHW032344310726
48973CB00007B/1845